THE PERSONIFID PROJECT

THE PERSONIFID PROJECT

R. E. BARTLETT

REALMS
A STRANG COMPANY

Most STRANG COMMUNICATIONS/CHARISMA HOUSE/SILOAM/REALMS products are available at special quantity discounts for bulk purchase for sales promotions, premiums, fund-raising, and educational needs. For details, write Strang Communications/Charisma House/Siloam/Realms, 600 Rinehart Road, Lake Mary, Florida 32746, or telephone (407) 333-0600.

THE PERSONIFID PROJECT by R. E. Bartlett
Published by Realms
A Strang Company
600 Rinehart Road
Lake Mary, Florida 32746
www.realmsfiction.com

This is a work of fiction. Names, characters, places, and incidents are products of the author's imagination or are used fictitiously. Any similarity to actual people, organizations, and/or events is purely coincidental.

Cover design by studiogearbox.com
Cover photo of pods by Infinity2
Coverphoto of man in room by Bruce Ando/Indexstock

Quotation from *Out of the Silent Planet* by C. S. Lewis is used by permission of the C. S. Lewis Company, Ltd.

Library of Congress Cataloging-in-Publication Data:

Bartlett, R. E.
 The Personifid Project / R.E. Bartlett.
   p. cm.
  ISBN 1-59185-806-2 (pbk.)
  I. Title.
  PS3602.A8397P47 2005
  813'.6--dc22

                                                2005015802

First Edition

05 06 07 08 09 — 987654321
Printed in the United States of America

To my father—from whom I learned
to love the Way

and

To my mother—from whom I learned
to follow the Way

Acknowledgments

T HANKS TO SUSIE for all your help (I couldn't have done it without you). Also to Jeff Gerke (for getting me to make this story more complete).

Prologue

"I T'S NO GOOD," Lev muttered, and buried her face in her hands, her long black hair spilling down around her neck. "It can't be done."

"Lavinia, we're just about ready, I think," Ryan said, stepping into the small laboratory. He touched her shoulder as she sat there at her desk, ignoring the red lines of code that spun slowly in the air before her. "Lavinia? *Lev,* look at me. Are you all right?"

Lev sat upright and forced a smile. "I'm fine."

"Good. This is no time to be nervous." Ryan glanced over at the personifid body that lay on a table against the wall. It had been designated as a fem, its limbs slim and supple, the pale facial features delicately formed. To the untrained eye, it appeared perfectly human, more so than a mere android. "She made the right choice," he said as he looked critically at it. "I'm glad she didn't choose this one. It's not as pretty."

Lev looked up at him. "Are you absolutely sure she wants to do this?" She flicked her dark brown hands at the lines of code. "Omega, close this file. We'll work on it later."

The code disappeared.

"We've been over this a thousand times," Ryan said. "Her mind is made up." He went to his desk and picked up a pocket-sized Life Enhancer. "Tranquility," he said into it, and pressed it lightly against his forehead.

"You use that too much," Lev said, frowning.

"You don't use it enough," he answered. "Now come on, Imogen is waiting for you. She is not going to go through this without you."

Lev slowly got up. "I'm afraid."

"Nonsense. We've done this many times before. What are you afraid of?"

"Yes, but it's Imogen! I've never seen it happen to anyone I know!"

"It makes no difference."

"Then why did you just take some Tranquility? Admit it, you're nervous, too."

He turned his back to her. "I admit nothing. Let's go."

Lev followed him out of the room and into the main Personifid Project Transference Laboratory. It was a large area that contained half a dozen small, round, windowless transference chambers. These were made of a special material—the only known substance that souls could not seep through, the same material as the cores of the personifid bodies were made from. The formulation of this material was a highly guarded secret, preventing other amateur personifid labs from successfully making infusions. Lev had designed the chambers herself and, together with Ryan, had made the Personifid Project possible.

It was true, she had seen the transferences happen hundreds of times, but to watch her close friend discontinued so that her soul could then be transferred into a personifid body would be different. She did not want to stand inside one of those chambers and watch it happen. The best she could hope for was a painless cessation of life for Imogen's body, but there was no telling how Imogen would react when it actually happened to her.

Some people found it hard to handle having their souls reassigned to artificial bodies—becoming a personifid was not always as easy as the commercials made it seem. It would take time to learn how to control the new body, and some people were quicker to learn than others. Lev had seen those who found it harder to maintain control, and she silently prayed that Imogen would not be one of them.

Transference chamber eight had been readied for Imogen, and as Lev walked across to it she drew in a sharp breath—Sevig was standing there, talking to Imogen.

Sevig stood beside the slight figure of Imogen, his thick golden brown hair glinting under the laboratory lights. He was a tall, good-looking man in his late forties, with eyes that were calculating and capable of masking his thoughts easily. He glanced at Ryan and Lev as they approached, a slight smile on his firm lips. Imogen looked up at him, her large brown eyes earnest beneath their thick lashes. Long chestnut hair curved down around her slim body. To Lev she seemed frailer than ever, and she hated to see Sevig standing there acting as though he cared.

"What's he doing here?" she hissed to Ryan.

"Why do you think? And I couldn't stop him, now could I? He's already threatened me once before, and you know I can't tell him what to do. You should have stopped him yourself."

She bit her lip. "We're not speaking to each other right now."

"Great. So he's speaking to my wife instead."

Lev said nothing more as they approached Sevig and

Imogen. Imogen turned and smiled nervously, her pretty face paler than usual. "I'm ready," she said bravely.

Lev smiled back. "We are, too."

"We will come into the chamber with you, Imogen," Sevig said authoritatively. "No need to be in there all by yourself. We'll keep you company throughout the process."

Imogen gave him a shaky smile.

Lev glared at Sevig, but he ignored her and put his arm supportively around Imogen's shoulders. "Nothing to worry about," he continued. "You know that, don't you?"

Imogen shrugged his arm off, looking quickly at Ryan.

"Wait outside, Sevig," Lev snapped. "You shouldn't even be here."

"This is my laboratory. I'll do as I please."

"You know what I mean. We don't want you here."

"You don't speak for Ryan and Imogen, do you? What do you say about this, Haldane? Do you want me to leave?"

Ryan shifted uncomfortably on his feet. "We're just not used to having observers, that's all."

"You know I like to watch you work," Sevig said. "It's such an interesting process."

"You don't usually come all the way down here to watch people become discontinued," Lev said sharply, "and there's no need for you to be here now. Leave us to do our job."

"Nor is there a need for your attitude, Lavinia," he said coolly without looking at her. "I think your personal feelings are affecting you at this moment. Imogen knows I'm here only to offer support."

"Liar," Lev seethed.

"Don't burst a blood vessel," Sevig replied pleasantly. "We need that brain of yours in working order, although I must say it has not proven itself very well lately."

"Sevig, don't," Imogen protested.

He smiled at her, his eyes cold. "Very well, to please Lavinia—and Lavinia knows I always try to please her—I will wait outside the chamber."

Imogen took Lev's hand, and they entered the chamber together. Ryan followed. The door closed behind them and was fused shut so they were inside a seamless cocoon. In that small space there was a low couch for a person to lie on while the transference took place, and in the center of the room in a steel chair sat the empty personifid body, ready for possession. It gazed blankly, sightlessly at them, and in appearance was very much like Imogen. She was naturally beautiful and had decided not to enhance her new body's appearance very much.

Imogen turned and held Lev's hands in her own, while look-ing her in the eye. "Lev, dear friend, don't worry about Sevig. Don't let him get to you."

"He just makes me so crazy," spat Lev, clenching her fists. "After everything he has done to me—I—," she strode across the small space and almost kicked the console beside the per-sonifid's chair. "Give me Tranquility!"

"Tranquility given," came the pleasant voice of the cham-ber's computer.

Lev sucked in a deep breath as the Tranquility took effect and turned to look at Imogen and Ryan standing together. "I'm sorry. I'm ready now. I should be thinking of you, not him. Are you sure you're ready for this?"

"Yes, a thousand times, yes," said Imogen, and reached up to kiss Ryan. "I want it done now before I become incapacitated from this stupid disease. Now, while I feel strong enough to face it."

"We'll do all we can to make the transference easier for you," said Ryan, stroking Imogen's hair as he held her close.

Lev said nothing. She knew Ryan was only trying to say something reassuring. There was nothing that could be done to cause a transference to go more smoothly—it was all up to the computer's programming. Death, then the capture of the soul, and then placement into the new, completely artificial body. Neither Lev nor Ryan could do anything to help that process.

Imogen looked past Ryan's shoulder at the personifid body. "I had thought I was used to the sight of it, but now that I see it sitting there, I feel strange."

"Don't call your new self 'it,'" Lev said. "This body is top of the line, the very best." She and Ryan had worked on it personally, not leaving this one to be programmed and personalized by anyone else.

"You'll find it much better than your natural body," Ryan said. "Now, tell me when you're ready, and we'll start."

Imogen got onto the low couch and lay there with her eyes closed and her hands clasped together. "Ready."

"Brain scan now in progress," came the voice of the computer. "Sedation beginning."

"Just remember," Lev said, "you are God's child, Imogen. He'll take care of you."

Imogen did not open her eyes.

"I love you, Imogen," Ryan said softly. "Everything will be OK. We're right here with you."

"Subject sedated," the computer said. "Commencing separation of the soul from the body."

The lights in the chamber flickered.

"What was that?" Lev asked.

"A slight power surge," the computer answered.

"Another one? We've been having too many of those lately,"

Ryan said. "We're going to have to work on that next. Continue reporting Imogen's progress."

"Chamber prepared and ready for personifid placement," the computer answered.

"What?" Ryan snapped. "No, tell me what is happening to the transference."

"No transference currently occurring. Please assign subject information."

"Something's wrong!" Lev rushed over to Imogen's side and bent over the still body of her friend. "Computer, check the soul life signs of Imogen, now!"

"No soul life signs found," said the computer.

"*What?*" Ryan shouted.

"Search the chamber again!" Lev screamed. "She has to be in here!"

The computer's voice was perfectly calm. "No soul life signs found."

Four Years Later

"OH, YOU'RE CRAZY!" Aphra laughed and dodged as the chair came flying at her blonde head.

Michael caught it easily and threw it aside. He took her by the hand, and they dashed along the narrow street flanked by towering steel-gray buildings. They ran unhindered through the crowds of people thronging the street, as everyone stepped out of their path to let them by. Aphra saw a blur of shocked faces as she pulled Michael through, but they managed not to collide into anybody.

"Ryan! Where are you?" Michael shouted, his eyes wide as he scanned the street. His dark brown hair was windswept as they ran, and it streamed back away from his rugged cheekbones and strong jawline. He could easily have outpaced Aphra, being taller and stronger, but he let her take the lead.

"Quiet," Aphra urged. "Don't let him know where we are now." She ducked into a doorway and looked out over the crowd for any sign of their pursuer. A scruffy little dog weaved in and around the legs of people, almost causing some to trip as they exclaimed in surprise. Aphra crouched down to it and took hold of its collar. "Where is he, girl? Where's Ryan? Are you going to lead me to him?"

The dog wagged her tail, woofed, then turned to look back at the street. Aphra patted her and was about to straighten up when the dog suddenly turned and seized her, its teeth clamping down on her forearm.

"Deactivate!" she shrieked. The dog's jaw released and its head bowed. "Ryan! That's not funny!" Aphra pushed the dog over in one swift movement. It toppled stiffly and fell with a soft *thunk*. Then she got up and carefully felt her arm, looking for any sign of blood showing through her sleeve. "Why did Ryan do that?"

"It's a fear game," Michael said. "You like those."

"Not when it hurts!"

He turned to her then, took hold of her arm and caressed it gently. "I'm sorry. I didn't realize the dog had bitten you that hard. We can stop the game if you want."

"I—I don't know. It's funny when Ryan does unpredictable things, but I like that in a fun game, not a fear game. He shouldn't have tampered with my dog." She looked down at the rigid animal that lay at their feet, the eyes fixed and glazed as it stared straight ahead.

Carmel came running to them, panting and puffing, two pink spots of color high in her white cheeks. She was a fem in her mid-teens with an eager smile and an urchin-like face framed by short black hair. She bent over, hands to her knees, and looked up at Aphra, her eyes sparkling. "I know where he is. I think I have a plan."

"You tell me where he is, and *I'll* make a plan," Aphra said.

"OK. He is two segments away from here, and I'm pretty sure he's disguised himself."

"He didn't follow you?"

"I don't think so."

Aphra frowned. "He's not playing fair. I don't like it."

"He never does," Michael said. "I don't know why you asked him to join our game."

"I didn't ask him to," Aphra said. "He's the one who invited us this time. He said I'm the best fear game player he knows."

Michael smiled down at her. "Yes, you are the best. Now, tell us what to do."

"Well, if he's going to cheat, then so am I. Maybe we can start this game all over again and play it properly. Deactivate the crowd," she ordered.

The people in the street disappeared, and all was instantly silent. Aphra, Michael, and Carmel stood in the city alone. The bases of the buildings and the wide, paved footway seemed to brighten in color as the shadow emulations that had come from the people were also removed.

Ryan was alone out in the virtual street. He threw his hands up as he looked around. "What are you doing? The game isn't over yet!"

He was some distance from them and began walking in their direction, the brisk steps from his short legs heightening the impression of frustration that Aphra thought she could sense from him. He was so different from most men: he did not care about his appearance and made no attempt to obtain a muscular-looking build. Small and neat, with short, straight, dull brown hair—that might even be natural for all she knew—and intense hazel eyes in a face that often scowled at her. In a strange way she liked that about him. It made for a pleasant change of pace.

"You're not playing fairly," Aphra said as he neared. "Throwing chairs at my head and changing my dog, you can't do that. You can't change the program; the computer should run the game, not you." Aphra watched him nervously. "That dog hurt me," she added.

"I don't like dogs," Ryan said. "You shouldn't have brought it into the game."

Carmel crouched down beside the dog and waved her hand in front of its eyes. Michael touched her lightly on the shoulder and slowly shook his head.

"Besides," Ryan said to Aphra, "how is it that you're worried about a chair when you've been dodging lasers? What's the matter with you?"

"OK, the chair *was* funny," she said, "but I wasn't expecting it. It's not realistic to have something like that happen."

"If you know everything that's going to happen in a fear game, then it won't work, will it?"

She said nothing in reply, but looked at his face trying in vain to read his expression.

He walked over to her. His hazel eyes, which sometimes seemed warm and friendly toward her, were empty, and he looked at her as though she were not really there. "You and I alone."

She stared back at him, wondering what he could mean. "I tried that in a fun game with you the day before yesterday. I don't remember it being much fun," she retorted. She still did not know where she stood with him; he confused her with friendliness one day and coolness the next. "Why do you always have to pit yourself against me? We should work together."

"Go away, all of you," Ryan said, waving his hand at Michael, Carmel, and the inactive dog.

"You can't tell them to go," Aphra said, clutching Michael by the wrist. "They're my friends."

"That's right," Carmel said. "Only Aphra can tell me what to do."

"Precisely my point," said Ryan. "You need to learn what it's like to not be in control, Aphra. What if something really did happen to you that you couldn't control? How would you react to that?"

Carmel looked with concern at Aphra's face. "You're upsetting her. Stop it."

"Shut her up, can't you?" Ryan said to Aphra.

"You shut up," said Michael, taking a step forward and looking down at Ryan, his fist clenched.

"You don't know what real life is," Ryan continued to Aphra, as though he had not noticed. "Things happen. You can't control life. You sit in your apartment and you don't know anything about real life. You sit behind that reception desk, all comfortable with the other fems, but you know nothing. Nothing!"

Aphra stared at him, aghast at the change in his voice.

"You might as well be an android," he snapped at her.

She could think of nothing to say to defend herself. It was not true—too much had happened in her childhood that had been beyond her control. Life had only become manageable now that she was on her own. Ryan had no right to accuse her. She could choose to live her life any way she wanted. "It's not any of your business," she finally said.

"Hey, you're the one who befriended me. You're the one who thinks I'm so terrific. You're the one who thinks I'm so in control. I'm going now, that's how in control I am." He turned away from her. "Computer, I'm leaving."

Instantly he disappeared, his virtual link to the games room severed. Once, the other day, he had joined her physically for a gaming session, but such things were rare.

"Ryan!" Aphra shouted, tears starting in her eyes. "Get back here! I'll show you!" No response came, and he did not reappear. She collapsed into tears, and Michael wrapped his arms around her.

"He doesn't mean any of that," he said gently. "He's just angry."

"But why? What did I ever do to him?" she sobbed as she buried her head against Michael's broad chest.

"I've never seen you do anything to him," Carmel said. "He's angry for no reason. It's not your fault."

"You can go now, Carmel," Aphra said in a muffled voice.

Carmel sat down and deactivated. The light in her eyes dimmed as her body stiffened, but the smile on her face remained fixed.

"I wish I could do that to Ryan sometimes," Aphra said.

Michael grinned. "Me, too. Maybe you and I should play games together without any other real people. We'll just have androids join us."

She smiled up at him through her tears. "I'd like that." Inwardly, she wondered if she could go back to that. Since meeting Ryan, there was no avoiding the fact that her life had become more interesting. "Tranquility."

"Tranquility given," the games room computer's mild fem voice said.

"Are you OK now?" Michael asked, smoothing her hair gently and kissing her forehead.

She nodded and wiped the tears from her face. "I think so." She studied his handsome face a moment, feeling reassured by his stillness as he looked back at her.

"Aphra Vessey," the voice of the games room computer

said. "Your free time has almost expired."

"Back to work, I guess," Aphra said, reluctantly drawing back from Michael's embrace.

"I guess so," he answered. "We'll play another game soon, huh? Next time a fun game."

"Yeah. Put Carmel and the dog away in the games room storage for me? Then go home, Michael; I'll see you later."

He smiled fondly at her. "OK."

She reached up, wrapped her arms around his neck, and kissed him. "You're the best."

His eyes dimmed subtly as she spoke.

"Oh," Aphra said, looking intently at him, "it looked like you almost shut down. You'd better run your maintenance program when you get home. "

With that, the games room door slid open, and she went out into the foyer, blinking a little in the brighter light. She quickly made her way back toward her desk at Sevig Empire receptions.

Aphra's footfalls were muffled in the carpet as she walked through the wide, lemon-colored corridors that linked the staff leisure rooms. A few other people went by, but she said nothing to them, nor they to her. She passed games room doors, some open, silently revealing ever-changing scenes inside— beaches, parks, racetracks—ready for someone to go in and choose a game. Other doors were closed, occupied.

She came around a corner and ran up against a tour group coming along the corridor. A Sevig robot led a cluster of people and hovering screens, life-sized faces looking eagerly through them. Annoying things, these tourists, going through

Sevig Empire on an almost daily basis. The link-ins she could understand, but why some people had to actually come here in person instead of taking the virtual tour she did not know. She supposed it had something to do with a fad for realism.

There was no avoiding them now. The robot leading the group had detected her presence and read her imprint. "Aphra!" it called in a clear ringing voice.

This was a top-of-the-line model: gleaming white body shell, limbs highlighted in blue and green, almost no sound of servos or hydraulics when it moved. It was a showpiece in modular style.

"Everybody," it said to the people and screens, "this is Aphra Vessey. She is one of our receptionists. She is one of the persons who will greet you if you call Sevig Empire for any reason. Aphra, perhaps you could say a few words about what it is like working for Sevig. For instance, is he as benevolent and generous as they say?"

It was too much. The company did not pay anything for these little speeches, but all employees were expected to do them—if trapped by a group like this. If she did not do well, she knew the recording would be scrutinized by the unfriendly eyes of the personnel staff.

Aphra smiled reluctantly and put her voice into what she hoped sounded like gentle bafflement. "Well, I'm sure he is. However, I've never met him myself. Perhaps your tour will take you by his offices."

The robot's head tilted. "Excellent transition, Aphra! In fact, the next item on our tour is to speak with Sevig himself." It swiveled its head back around to face the group. "Let's do that now, shall we?"

A virtual screen appeared amongst the group, twice the size of the ones already there. Sevig's face was on this screen, his golden brown hair perfectly groomed. He stood with the confident posture of one of the world's richest men. "Hello, everyone," he said, smiling. "Welcome to Sevig Empire, the largest producer of robots on Earth and inventors of what I'm sure you've all come to see, the personifids." He paused and smiled again.

Aphra had heard this recording a thousand times before. She began working her way around the group.

"Are you a personifid?" a man asked Sevig's image on the screen. His voice sounded vaguely hostile. "Tell us."

Aphra looked back. This question had come many times before in the media, but she had never heard Sevig answer it. The artificial intelligence running the recording of Sevig had answers queued for all the most frequently asked questions. She waited to hear what response would be activated by such a question.

Sevig smiled again, his eyes cold. "Here at Sevig Empire we have achieved the only successful soul transferences. Many competitors have tried but failed. Sevig Empire stands alone."

"Monopolizes, you mean," said the man. "And you didn't answer my question. Are you a personifid?"

"You're not going to get an answer to that," a fem in the crowd said scornfully. "Just look at him. Anyone can tell he's a personifid. He's so handsome and perfect."

"I say he's still a person," someone from a link-in screen said. "His silence on the matter confirms it."

"He's only silent because there's no recording of an answer for the program to use."

"Not here, I mean in the news."

The group fell to debating, and Aphra left them to it.

❭   ❭   ❭

"You say you cannot find it?"

Sevig got up from his comfortable chaise and strode across the pale marble floor to his desk. He was in his penthouse office, a light airy space with windows looking out over the city. And indeed it did look out *over* the city, for this building was the highest in Min City. Situated in the center of a tight hub in Min City's business district, Sevig Empire was surrounded closely by other skyscrapers. Sky cars threaded through and around these buildings, a myriad of colors flying swiftly.

"Yes, sir," came the cool voice of Jamon, Sevig's personal computer. "It is not in his offices or at his home."

"I don't believe he would destroy it. We will simply have to increase the pressure."

"Perhaps he does not have it. Perhaps he gave it to—"

Sevig raised his hand. "Do not speak her name."

"Ryan believes she is alive, sir. We cannot ignore that possibility. Perhaps he has passed the information to her."

"Their parting was acrimonious, and look at him now. What makes you think he would speak to her?"

"She became a Follower. Therefore, she believes in forgiveness."

Sevig's brow furrowed. "But he doesn't. And don't be so naïve to think that she could really change."

"As you say, sir, perhaps I am mistaken. However, this seems to be our strongest lead, given their history."

"He talks to no one else?"

"He does have two other contacts, only one of whom I have been able to track."

❯   ❯   ❯

Aphra looked blankly at the personifid who stood in front of her desk.

A hum of voices filled the large, dome-ceiling space of Sevig Empire receptions. It reminded Aphra of a university rotunda of centuries gone by—but done in an ultramodern style. All fifteen receptionists were seated comfortably behind the long arc of the gleaming black desk that stretched across the center of the receptions area, a shining deft stroke against the dark marble floors. Aphra was at the far right end of the desk.

"I'm sorry, that is not allowed," she said firmly, reaching to take the package from the personifid's smooth white hands.

His small, curved lips moved awkwardly in his narrow face. Pale blue eyes watched her intently from beneath the shock of blue-black hair. "My employer wishes it." He stepped back, hugging the package to his chest, his slim frame swaying uncertainly as he moved. "Call it an ec-eccentricity-ty, but she-she does not want it to go through your lumin-luminire."

"Our luminire is absolutely safe and faultless," Aphra answered, wondering which part of him was going to twitch next. "In all the time I've worked here, I've never seen a problem with it. Please give the package to me so I can deliver it."

"I cannot go against my employer's wishes-ishes," he said, with an erratic twitch of his perfectly formed eyebrows. "Perhaps you would hand de-deliver it yourself?"

"I suppose I could, but it is highly irregular. I've never done such a thing before, and I assure you our luminire can deliver it with no security breach or change in molecular structure. Your employer has nothing to fear."

"Please hand deliver it-it. I will ac-accompany-pany you to make sure that you do not use a luminire."

"There is no need to do that," she said as she took the

package from him. "Besides, unauthorized personnel cannot go through the doors—the alarm will go off, and our security fields will prevent you from moving any farther."

He looked keenly into her eyes, and for a moment she wondered what thoughts were going through his mind. She never could tell what personifids were thinking. That was part of their charm.

"Well then," he said, "it is a matter of trust. But be-be assured that my em-employer can most certainly check to see if her wishes were fulfilled-illed, and penalties against you and I-I will be put in place if they are not."

She smiled. "Of course. In the meantime, can I make an appointment for you to visit one of our clinics and talk about having an upgrade? You're a C-series model, aren't you? The new E-58 is simply amazing."

"I am still paying for this model and cannot-ot afford-ord another." He might have been trying to scowl at her, but he managed only to wiggle his eyebrows.

"Well, perhaps you will gain greater control in time."

Aphra stood and walked to the large doors behind her desk. None of the other fems turned their perfectly groomed heads to watch her go; they were busy with their own clients—either on screen or there at the desk.

She walked across the dark marble floor, conscious that the personifid's eyes were on her, and went through the opaque glass doors, the zip reading the imprint in her wrist as she passed through. Once through the doors and into the quiet corridor, she went to one of the many lifts in a long row and stepped inside.

The door slid shut, and she was enclosed in a light sandalwood scent. The smell indicated that the lift had cleansed her as she had walked through the door. It irritated her only a little now. She would prefer to not be automatically cleaned as though she were a robot—but she had grown so used to the random doorway cleansings at Sevig Empire that she no longer took offense.

"Where is Sevig?" she asked. "Can I take this package to him?"

"Sevig is presently on the top floor in his offices," came the voice of the computer. "Go straight to the end of the corridor there and in through the door. You are not permitted access to Sevig, but his aide will be standing before his door."

"Take me to the top floor," Aphra said, and the door to the lift slid shut.

The lift moved at a tremendous velocity, but shields held her body in check and kept her mind from feeling the pressure. In fact, she sort of liked the warm, stable feeling it gave her.

A moment later the door of the lift opened. "Here you are," the computer said.

Aphra stepped out and walked along the corridor. She had been up to the higher levels only once before, and this time felt strange doing so while Sevig himself was there. But the lift had assured her it was all right, so she kept walking briskly.

The sound of voices echoed down the empty corridor. She paid no attention to them. Instead she glanced at the black Chinese script artwork that hung at intervals along the charcoal-gray walls, interested in the sharp simplicity of it. The air was cool, and she walked silently along the black carpet, intrigued by the classy atmosphere of the level.

She wondered if she would get a glimpse of Sevig in person. Lately, he had been coming to Min City more often, and his presence in the building had led to a heightened air of stress. Everyone was trying to do their jobs even more perfectly than usual. Aphra was no exception, for this job was important to her—working for Sevig Empire meant she was one of the first to get the latest androids, and any maintenance done to them was free.

When Aphra came to the door leading into the room where she was expecting to find Sevig's aide, she hesitated. One of the voices she had heard before became louder and seemed to be right on the other side of the partially open door. The door slid open a little more, and she stepped back, unsure of what to do, whether she should wait for the person on the other side of the door to come through or whether she should make her presence known.

She was about to speak, but as she opened her mouth the conversation came to her more clearly. The words horrified her, and she was suddenly struck dumb with fear and confusion. The package she held almost slipped from her trembling hands, and she gripped it tighter, hugging it to herself so as not to drop it. Fighting down panic, she made herself turn and calmly go back to the lift, trying not to convey any urgency in her stride. She recognized one of the voices as it began shouting; then the lift door closed and cut the sound out.

"How silly of me," she said, trying to make her voice sound casual as her heart pounded rapidly. "I forgot something; take me back down."

With every look and mannerism, she tried her best to express calmness and indifference, but inside she was a raging turmoil as the words she had heard repeated over and over in her mind. The door opened, and she walked briskly out of the lift and back down the corridor to the doors leading to the large reception area.

An android walked past. "Hello, Aphra. Have a pleasant day. Would you like me to carry that for you?"

She smiled shakily. "No."

The android entered a lift, and the door slid shut.

She stood there a moment, realizing she had to do something with the package before she went back into the reception area where the client was probably still waiting for her. She wished she had said yes to the android, but she had been too flustered to think of that before it had gone into the lift. So she put the package down on the floor against the wall just before she went through the doors. The client was indeed still there, and she smiled and made a gesture with her hands to show she no longer had the parcel. He returned her smile and nodded, then turned and left.

Aphra took a deep breath and went back to her seat behind the desk. "Tranquility please," she said in a small voice.

"Tranquility given," answered the voice of the computer she worked with.

Feeling the calmative take effect, Aphra turned to Giulia on her left. Giulia's sleek white blonde head nodded slowly in time to the music her computer invariably played inside her ears. This had gotten her into trouble more than once. Her pretty ivory face was vacant while she watched informercials and waited for her next client.

"Giulia, would you deliver a package for me please?" Aphra asked. "It's just inside the door back there." She jerked her thumb backwards. "Just put it through the luminire. It needs to be delivered to Sevig's aide with instructions to deliver it to Sevig himself. I would do it, but I have to make an appointment to see a doctor. I seem to be having some hearing problems and also trouble with carrying things. I don't understand it, it came on suddenly."

"Sounds serious," said Giulia loudly, so that Aphra would hear her. She got up and went to do as Aphra had asked.

"George," Aphra said to her computer, "I need you to make

an appointment with Dr. Abbot concerning hearing loss. And please magnify my calls the rest of today."

"Certainly," answered her computer. "You're sure you don't want me to check you?"

"No, I'd rather see a real doctor."

Aphra looked down at her empty desk and tried to still her trembling hands. She knew it would eventually be discovered that she had heard some of what was said, if they did not already know by now. It was at a time like this that she thought of the cameras that were everywhere and that she could do nothing without being observed.

"Do you want to leave now to see the doctor?" George asked.

"Can I?"

"Yes, Dr. Abbot has a time slot free if you leave now."

"OK, good."

"Appointment made, and I have requested a sky cab. It is now making its way to the Silver Entrance."

Aphra left the reception area—choosing to walk rather than take one of the sliding strips that would carry her through and stop at an advertising display when she would not want it to. She walked through the large, almost empty foyer where a few people sat sipping drinks in comfortable chairs shadowed by enormous artificial plants that had an iridescent glow as they gently swayed.

Then on she went into the outer foyer filled with robots giving demonstrations of their abilities to people and androids and to those who had called and now spoke to them through hovering or fixed screens. A few of the latest models of personifids stood on display, ready for possession, each guarded by a large android who showed interested clients how the face and body of a personifid could be tailored to an individual's wishes.

"Now, you, sir, for instance," one sandy-haired android with an amiable face said as it took hold of a man from the group. "Come and stand alongside our latest fem model personifid. Look closely, everybody. If you had never seen this man or this fem before, would you be able to tell me who has the personifid body and who does not?"

The android did not wait for any answer, but continued its patter, the inflexions of its voice musical and pleasing to the ear. "Granted, you would think this beautiful personifid fem standing before you a great deal healthier in appearance than this man. Also, you might think that she is more appealing to the eye—and I mean no insult to you, sir; you have obviously styled your hair and eye color to suit your own preferences. But here we have no need to fear that your customized looks might disappear if you passed through an electrical surge. I'm sure you will all admit to hearing what happens to people who try to change their hair and eye color by using their computers to crudely mask their faulty genetic matter.

"Now silent in operation and even more agile in mobility, the personifid body does not move or sound like a robot or android—we like to keep our differences between our mechanical helpmates, do we not? Yes, there is nothing more distinguishable than the mere fact that you will not only be stronger, better looking, and more healthy in appearance than those who keep their weak, defective human forms…"

Except for the eyes, Aphra thought as she walked past. She had looked into more than her fair share of personifid eyes and believed she was becoming adept at seeing the difference between theirs and that of a person's. When a real person looked at her, there was a stronger sense that they actually saw her, were actually directing their mind at her, unlike the emptiness behind a personifid's or android's gaze.

"…but you can be guaranteed the security of knowing your soul will remain with your chosen body forever," the android said. "No more threat of discontinuation! No more disease or illness! Genetic engineering? A troublesome thing of the past, creating more flaws than it erased. Here at Sevig Empire we have found the answer to the problems of the imperfect human body!"

The group clapped appreciatively.

Aphra went on, ignoring the robots and androids who called her name, as she almost always did unless she was thinking of buying, and went over to one of the grand entrances there on the fourth floor of the Sevig Empire building.

She had only just walked outside and onto the wide light-gray access ledge when the cab, a one-seater jade bubble, dropped down out of the streams of traffic and landed in front of her.

She stepped in, and the moment the door slid shut a flurry of advertising screens the size of her palm appeared, hovering hopefully in front of her face. She shut her eyes. "No! Advert-free. I'll pay!"

"Thank you," said the sky cab computer as it read her imprint again and deducted from her credit account. The screens disappeared, leaving only a black square set in the small, curved purple panel in front of her.

Aphra sat, gripping her knees, watching Min City pass beneath her as the cab rose up and whizzed along amongst other sky cars. The world outside her window was a whirl of color and movement that she could hardly focus on. Her mind was churning and seething with anxiety—the Tranquility she had taken was starting to wear off much too soon.

The cab stopped at one of the portals to the doctors' offices. She stepped from the hovering vehicle, the zip in its door reading her wrist as she went, and entered the building.

She was now in the quiet reception area, the sounds of the city effectively blocked. The walls around her showed scenes of crystal blue water streaming down over green moss, along with the accompanying sounds of a distant waterfall.

The door to Dr. Abbot's office opened at her approach, so she went straight through.

"Hello, Aphra, how nice to see you again," Dr. Abbot said, looking up with a pleasant smile. Dr. Joan Abbot was in her fifties and had light brown hair in a bun. She got up from her desk and smoothed the creases from her flowery dress, then held out her hand to shake Aphra's. "How are your mother and father?"

"I'm sure they're fine," Aphra replied as she briefly shook the outstretched hand, then stood still, looking out the window. The last time she had seen her adoptive parents, which had been some time ago, they had been fine. They were always fine. She could probably announce to them that she was about to give birth to an alien, and they would smile at her and be fine about that, too.

"That's strange, I'm not finding any hearing problems in you," said Dr. Abbot, as she walked in a circle around Aphra, one finger on her chin as if in thought.

"I feel OK now," Aphra answered quickly, "but earlier today I went into a lift, and when I came out, I felt a strange sensation in my ears that quickly turned into a ringing sound. I couldn't hear anything else, and I felt disorientated, so I went back into the lift."

Dr. Abbot stopped pacing and looked at Aphra. "Your heart is beating rapidly. If I didn't know you better, I'd think you were lying."

"I don't need you to check if I'm lying. I'm worried about

what could be wrong with me," Aphra said, turning to look earnestly at the doctor.

"I am sorry. You know it is standard procedure to check your heart rate. It helps me diagnose your problem—I will turn it off now. Do you want some Tranquility?"

"*Yes.*"

"Tranquility given," said Dr. Abbot.

Aphra breathed in deeply and sighed.

"A scan of your ears and brain shows no sign of hearing loss. I suggest you call me directly if you have any problems again. And I do recommend you consider taking a personifid body, as yours will not last forever."

Aphra left the room, and the zip in the clinic door read the imprint on her wrist. After she left, Dr. Abbot deactivated to await her next patient.

"Aphra, do you need a cab?" came the hushed voice of the reception's computer.

She nodded as she walked through the waterfall reception area and toward the exit. A sky cab soon approached as she stood waiting outside on the breezy platform, and she got in quickly.

She hoped her visit to the clinic would serve its intended purpose. Anyone tracking her movements through the city's computers would find that she had been to Dr. Abbot complaining about hearing problems. Maybe it would be enough to make them think she had not overheard anything on her trip to Sevig's offices.

Aphra took the cab straight home. The Tranquility hardly seemed to have lasted long at all, and she began to feel deeply agitated again. She considered asking the cab for some, but decided not to in case it looked suspicious for her to take a third dose in such a short timeframe. If she was investigated, there might be a slight chance that the cab's data would be checked, so it would be best to wait until she was safely home. She chose instead to watch one of her favorite shopping channels as she traveled through the busy traffic routes and hugged herself to try to keep herself steady.

The routes were crowded, and she barely noticed her near collision with another sky cab as her automaton driver weaved in and out of traffic like a maniac. The words she had heard still repeated over in her mind, and she tried to think what she should be doing about it.

The cab finally came to a large apartment block on the west side of the city. The clean lines of the green, rectangular, static buildings contrasted against the backdrop of the colorful, slowly rotating and altering knot of dodecahedron shapes of another apartment block. Aphra had tried living in one of those apartments, but she had found them irritating. It seemed each time she looked out of the window in the morning, she had to orient herself as to where she was again.

The sky cab dropped Aphra off at one of the fourteenth floor's entrances of her apartment building. It waited until the zip in the building's door had recognized Aphra and allowed her to enter, then it left. Aphra walked briskly to her apartment door. Her computer let her in, then closed the door behind her. She breathed a sigh of relief that she was finally in the safety of her own home.

"How are you?" asked Marlena, her household computer.

Aphra sat heavily on the couch and rested her head in her hands. "Awful. I have had such a shock, and I don't know what to do. Give me some Tranquility."

"OK. What happened?"

"I overheard something terrible. And I think if it becomes known that I heard it, I'll be in trouble."

"Tell me all about it," said Marlena, materializing. Not only was she Aphra's computer, but she was also her best friend. Her settings were that of a white fem around Aphra's age and height. She had brown hair that was short and sleek and tapered down the back of her neck, and her eyes were large and green and programmed to be full of concern. She sat next to Aphra and put her slender arm about Aphra's shoulders.

"Where's Michael?" Aphra asked.

"He's out," Marlena said. "He said to tell you he'll be back soon and will bring you something special."

Aphra smiled faintly.

"So what happened today? Why are you home so early?"

Aphra leaned back against the couch cushions and slipped her shoes off. "I was taking a package up to Sevig's offices, and I heard talking, and then I heard what was said. I recognized one voice after a bit—I'm pretty sure it was Ryan."

"What was he saying?"

Aphra thought through the conversation for what seemed like the hundredth time.

"You are discontinuing innocents and setting others up for a life of entombment. That is not what the Personifid Project is for! I will no longer be a part of this. I've changed the way I see things!"

"You cannot disassociate yourself from this, Haldane. It was your idea as well. Remember that. Do you see this chain? This is your wife, and I will not hesitate to break this capsule and let her leak out to nothingness if you do not continue to give me your work."

"No! She is lost. I was told she was lost! Give her to me! Give her back to me!"

"Step back. If you remove this chain by force, she will be gone. You will do what I say, or I will discontinue her."

"No!"

Aphra shuddered. "Ryan's wife isn't dead," she said to Marlena. "Her soul is held in a capsule."

"That is terrible!" exclaimed Marlena, assessing Aphra's tone of voice and facial expression and choosing her response accordingly. She pressed her cheek against Aphra's and rubbed her shoulder gently. "Would you like to eat some ice cream?"

"And I'm not sure, but I think it sounded like Sevig is the one who has her," continued Aphra. "I must be wrong, though; he would never say something like that. But that's not all— it sounds like there's something strange going on with the Personifid Project."

"What?"

"I don't know. I'm definitely not going to get it done for myself now. Not until I know it's safe." Aphra stood, went over to her window, and looked out at the traffic speeding past, then turned back to her friend. "Poor Ryan. Marlena, let me talk to him."

"Do you think that is a good idea? You are upset and will not appear at your best."

"I just want to see how he is."

"OK, connecting now." Marlena caused a screen to appear before Aphra.

"Yes, Aphra," said Ryan, looking at her through the screen as he sat at his desk. His face was drawn, and he did not smile. "What do you want?"

She could see little of his surroundings, but from the glimpse she had of his desk and the outline of a door she thought she could make out some distance in the aubergine wall behind him, she gathered he was at his apartment.

"I just wanted to see if you are all right," she said.

"I'm fine. How are you?"

Aphra gazed at him, uncertain how to frame her thoughts. "I-I heard it."

"Heard what?"

"I heard it," she repeated, thinking he should know what she was talking about and that she should not have to broach the awkward subject.

He stared back at her warily.

"Your wife," she said.

Ryan scowled and ran a hand through his tousled brown hair.

"I overheard you talking with someone about it. Is there anything I—"

"I don't want to talk about this—certainly not here and not now. Why do you think it's any of your business?"

"You've talked to me about her before. I'm just trying to be a friend!"

"Go away, fem. I don't want to talk about it." Through the screen, Aphra heard someone else say his name, and he looked around with a start. "What do you want? I told Sevig I would support him!" Ryan exclaimed.

Aphra then saw two men entering the room behind Ryan, and he got up from his chair and moved away from them. The screen tilted and followed him so that she was still able to watch his face. She did not recognize the men—the brief view she had of them did not even reveal whether they were people or androids. She watched Ryan's face as the color drained from it and his eyes widened.

"No," he said, looking past Aphra. "I've done nothing. I will support the project. I don't have what he wants!"

Aphra stood transfixed, staring at Ryan, wondering what was happening. A white light suddenly flashed and laser fire surged across the screen, striking him. She watched in horror as his body convulsed and he fell to the ground. Ryan turned his face toward the screen and gave her a pleading look.

"Go. Get out of there," he whispered, and closed his eyes.

A face with dark emotionless eyes thrust itself in front of the screen and looked at Aphra. She screamed and jumped back, covering her face with her hands, and cried, "Disconnect!"

Marlena did so, and the screen disappeared, but the image of the strange man's face remained in Aphra's mind. She could still see the dark brown eyes as they stared at her, looking right into her.

"I shouldn't have talked to Ryan! Change my appearance and clothes!" Aphra shouted to Marlena.

"To what?"

"Anything!"

Marlena paused a moment until she had decided upon a certain look, then redid Aphra's hair and eye color and changed her clothes. In the blink of an eye, the long blonde hair was gone, changed to shoulder-length red. The naturally blue eyes were covered with green. Her uniform was changed to casual trousers and sweater, and shoes reappeared on Aphra's feet.

"Done." Marlena tilted her head to one side as she smiled and admired Aphra. "You look so pretty. Why are you so upset? Do you want to talk about it? We could watch a movie together. Wouldn't that be fun?"

"I need you to erase everything we said when I came home and the call made to Ryan," Aphra said, hurrying to the door.

"Done."

"And erase your memory of how I look once I leave," added Aphra.

"Where are you going?" asked Marlena.

"I don't know, but I know I have to get away from here."

The door opened, and Aphra almost screamed. But it was

only Michael. He stood before her, looking at her as though she was the only one in the world. He reached to embrace her. "Hello, darling."

She pushed him aside. "Get in there," she ordered.

He obediently stepped through the doorway as she left the room. She paused for a moment, looked uncertainly up and down the corridor, and then caught a sky cab at the same entrance portal she had used moments ago. She knew she would be easy to trace if she stayed inside the cab, so she got the driver to set her down in the street below.

The street was busy, and she forced her way through the crowds of people, robots, androids, and personifids. Nobody paid any attention to her or let her by easily; she was jostled up against them all as she held her arms up in front of her chest to shield herself. "I can do this," she told herself, trying to pretend she was simply in a fear game. But her heart beat too loud and her breath caught in her throat as she pushed her way through the sea of unfriendly faces. She found she could not look directly at them, although she tried her best to keep an eye open for the face she had seen in her call to Ryan. Surely that man would come after her. He was probably already through the luminire to her building and was at that moment trying the door to her apartment.

Aphra looked behind her, but she did not see him. She was swept along with the crowd as she looked around desperately, wondering where she could go to be safe. She found herself next to a bar, and its door opened for her. She slipped inside and looked around at those there. Jazz music played above the murmur of voices and clack of billiard balls. Clusters of people sat at round tables while others leaned against their pool cues watching the billiard tables. She could see no sign of a luminire anywhere.

The robot bartender rolled along the top of the bar toward her. It had a humanoid upper body and was connected to the bar itself, able to swivel around and reach for the drinks behind or below it.

"Hello, Aphra," it said, giving her a friendly smile as it read her imprint. "What would you like to drink? Your favorite?"

"Nothing. Help me!"

Those in the bar who heard her looked up in surprise and curiosity. One man got out of his chair, clearly touched by her plea for help. "What's wrong?" He stood tall at six foot three, strongly built with dark blond hair.

"Would you like me to contact the police?" the bartender asked politely.

Aphra involuntarily looked back as the door behind her opened again and a personifid entered the bar along with an android. She recognized the personifid as being the dark-eyed man she had seen with Ryan, and he stared at her with the same impassive expression, chilling her.

"Come here," he said as he walked toward her.

"No!" she screamed, and stumbled back into the blond man.

He gripped her by the arm and pulled her behind him. "Hello, Mari," he said.

"You," said the personifid with some surprise in his voice. "This doesn't concern you. Let her go."

"He's going to discontinue me!" cried Aphra. "Don't let them take me! I saw what he did!"

The bar door slid open again, and a unit of four police came inside. They were tall robots, with no prosthetic skin on their bodies or clothing as had their android counterparts, but were gleaming metal. The shallow, polished contours of their faces were set in stern masks, a transparent section of metal below their foreheads revealing the glow of their eyes.

The robots marched together in tight formation, heading straight for Aphra.

"What's going on here?" asked one in a loud masculine voice, turning its face to Mari. It then looked toward Aphra, the dull green glow of its mechanical eyes flickering in a steel, skull-shaped head. "You screamed. Explain why."

"He is threatening me," Aphra said nervously, pointing to Mari.

The robot nodded its head. "View grid thirty-four, time-frame point five to twenty," it said. In a moment it spoke. "You may leave, Aphra Vessey. You two will remain here for questioning," it said, pointing to Mari and the android. As the robot pointed, it sent a deactivation code to the android so that it went slack, arms by its sides, eyes fixed straight ahead, no longer seeing.

Aphra pushed past to get through the door, while Mari watched her leave. The bar door slid shut behind her, and she looked out over the busy street, no clear idea of where to go next. She began to run down the street, knowing that at any moment the robot police would finish their investigations, not find anything conclusive, and allow the personifid and android to leave.

"Wait!" she heard a voice call from behind her.

The voice spurred her ahead. She weaved in and out of the general public, trying to lose herself in the crowd and put as much distance as she could between herself and the bar. She tried to think of her fear game strategies, hoping for some way of escape. Her breath had never come as fast as this, though, and she felt panicked and dizzy.

Somebody caught hold of her arm. "I said wait!"

She tried to struggle free, lashing out blindly with her free arm. "Let go! Let go! I didn't do anything!"

"I'm not going to hurt you. I'm trying to help you!" It was the blond-haired man from the bar. "If Mari is after you, you're in real trouble. I can help you."

Something in his voice stayed her, and she wavered between suspicion and the desire for help. "Let go of me."

He released his grip. "You asked for help back there, and I'm offering it."

Aphra stepped back and looked up at his face, wondering if she could trust him. He stood looking earnestly down at her, concern in his blue eyes. He had a kind, strong face, but she told herself he may have been altered to look that way. Yet something about his eyes made her feel she could trust him.

He cast a brief look over his shoulder. "Look, it's obvious that you're in trouble with the wrong people. Whether you've done something or not, I'm not going to judge you, but I will help you. I have a safe place where you can stay until you sort yourself out."

The crowds of citizens streamed around the two, paying no attention to them. He stood still in the midst of chaos, an air of Tranquility about him. Aphra knew the police would soon be finished with their inquiries and that the personifid would resume looking for her. She tentatively took the outstretched hand offered to her and drew a deep breath. This would either be out of the matter recycler and into the atomizer, or this man could really be the help she desperately needed.

She looked up and met his gaze. "OK."

"Good," the man said, and he began to lead her quickly through the streets. "My name's Birn. What's yours?"

"I'm Aphra."

"Listen, Aphra, I have a friend who can help you. You'll be safe with her."

They came to a row of white luminires. These particular

transportation booths were just large enough for two people to stand inside. Min City's Tunin district logo was branded across their plastic doors in swirled fluorescent orange letters.

Birn led her to the nearest luminire, and they stepped inside it together. The door slid behind them, shutting out the rest of the world and enclosing them in the white-walled booth. It felt strange to be in there with him. Aphra's senses were alert as Birn's scent closed in around her, and she heard him breathing. She wanted to look at his eyes again to try to see if he was a personifid, but she was too self-conscious to look his way.

"Destination," came the voice of the computer.

"Blaketown Promenade, and I'll pay," Birn said.

After a moment the door opened. "Thank you," the computer said.

They stepped out of a gleaming blue Blaketown Promenade luminire and into an entirely different scene. Blaketown Promenade was a parking complex near the east gate of the city. The buildings here were not very high, seven floors being the highest allowed this close to the city boundaries. A few had slowly revolving floors that stayed securely within the building's frame. Aphra could see glimpses of the desert waste beyond the edge of the city, rocks blushed with yellow and orange in the late afternoon sun.

She and Birn stood in the ground floor lobby area next to a dozen luminires and as many lifts, the difference indicated by the letters of their logos. It was busy in this part of the city, as multitudes who were coming and going left their sky cars there to avoid the traffic congestion in Min City. Any fumes from older sky cars were quickly filtered and cleansed by the city's computers, keeping the air safe to breathe. Many visitors chose to use the plentiful sky cabs available once inside the city, or they used the hover-riders and luminires. All the same, Min City was usually clogged and overpopulated.

Birn led Aphra quickly to a lift. Once inside, he said, "Third floor."

"Thank you," the computer said, and opened the door after a moment. They were in a multilevel landing garage for sky cars. Cars were landing or taking off with the precision and buzz of bees at a hive.

They got out, and Birn ushered Aphra toward a steel blue sky car. It was not a very impressive-looking vehicle, and she looked at it in some distaste and began to have feelings of distrust. The door opened out and up as the car's computer recognized Birn, and Aphra thought that seemed rather clunky instead of having a simple sliding door.

She backed away at the sight of it. "I don't know."

"I'm not going to hurt you," Birn said. "I want to help you."

She looked up at his face, and they locked eyes for a moment. His were clear and without menace, and there was a friendliness in them that drew her.

"You have to get out of the city fast," Birn said. "I know Mari, and I know he works for people who have access to all the information they need to locate you. If he is after you, you're in serious trouble. Am I right?"

She nodded, tears coming to her eyes as she allowed herself to think of Ryan. In that moment, she threw caution aside and got into Birn's vehicle. He got in after her, and the door shut behind him. Aphra was surprised at the interior of the sky car; the outward appearance had truly been misleading. She had not been able to see through the windows, and as she got in, she was relieved to find comfortable, deep-cushioned brown, leather-feeling seats—two in the front that were separated and self-adjusting, the fixed rear seat curved so that it was along the inner sides of the car as well.

She sat in one of the front seats next to Birn and looked at the dark blue dashboard in front of them both. She knew she had misjudged the sky car then. This dash showed no evidence of inner workings across its smooth surface, but as Birn put his hand over it, the section beneath his hand glowed, and Aphra could then see a small display of colorful lines appear. He moved his finger along one of the lines, and freshness instantly came into the interior of the sky car. This was manual control, something she had not seen very often. She looked with interest at the dash, but the display disappeared as soon as Birn removed his hand.

"Gina," Birn said, "we're going home. Is Gun about anywhere?"

"He called in not long ago," answered the fem voice of the computer. "He said he had business to take care of and would stay longer."

"OK."

The car hummed as it rose up in the air and made its way slowly to the edge of the third floor.

"Mask as soon as we leave the city," Birn said.

"Of course," Gina replied.

"Just relax," Birn said, turning to Aphra. "Once we're out of Min City, you'll be safe."

The car picked up speed once they left the building, and they flew along to the east gate of the city, joining the streams of traffic.

Min City's East Gateway had twenty lanes, ten incoming and ten outgoing. The lanes were unbreakable transparent tunnels, creating the only openings through the city's shields, and were heavily monitored. The circular stations at the entrance of the tunnels had high-powered zips that read the imprints of all the occupants of the vehicles that passed through, penetrating all known car shields. Any anomaly was noted, and the station's computers would temporarily disable vehicles that might be in breach of regulations.

Aphra was nervous as it came their turn to enter the round steel station at the start of a tunnel, and she fidgeted with her right wrist, which bore the faint marks of her imprint. But they got through with no problems, and she sighed with relief as they flew swiftly through the transparent tunnel.

Once outside the city and the protective shielding that surrounded it, she looked back through the vehicle windows that were steadily growing darker to stop the glare of the harsh sun. They flew along quickly, and she watched the immense city diminish very slowly behind them. The blue haze of the dome-like shields surrounded Min City, protecting it from the sun, allowing life to go on in comfort. She looked at the dome with interest; sometimes it was easy to forget it was there—it was never visible to those inside the city.

The terrain Aphra now flew over was sun-beaten rock. All greenery had withered and died long ago. She had not been outside Min City very many times before, but having left there now gave her a sense of safety, albeit mixed with uncertainty about where she was now headed and what she should do about what had happened. She grew tense and nervous the more she thought about Ryan, feeling that it was a problem too big for her to know how to cope with.

"I hope you have the shields on," Birn said to the computer.

"Of course," came the pleasant reply of Gina's voice.

Birn sat back in his seat and looked to his left at Aphra sitting huddled in her seat beside him. She looked back at him, hoping she would be safe with him and that, while away from Min City, she could think things through and decide what she had to do to make things right again so she could return home.

〉　　　　〉　　　　〉

"What went wrong?" Sevig demanded. "Why didn't the police take hold of her?"

"I'm sorry, sir," answered Jamon, Sevig's computer. "It was too late for me to access the police banks and enter a request. You know I didn't have the time to do that, and I cannot easily manipulate the police."

Sevig slammed his hand down on his desk in frustration. "That fool Mari—he's made a mess of things." He went over to a window and looked down on the city from his high viewpoint.

"He's requesting to speak with you," Jamon said.

Sevig turned. "Display," he said curtly.

A communications pane appeared before him with Mari's expressionless face in it.

"We've lost her," Mari said.

"Jamon, find her. Now," Sevig ordered. "Also, give Mari a listing of her family members and known friends. Mari, don't fail this time. I want her."

Mari nodded.

"Disconnect," Sevig said. He stood by the window, a brooding look in his blue eyes as he gazed into the distance. "This is getting out of hand."

2

ONCE THEY WERE out of Min City there was no restriction on their speed, and Aphra was astonished at the velocity they appeared to be traveling. She knew now that this was the most advanced sky car she had ever traveled in, and she wondered at its mediocre outward appearance.

She felt nervous as she looked at Birn, but he sat easily, watching the landscape through the windscreen.

"Where are we going?" she finally said.

"I told you, I'm taking you to a place where you'll be safe." Birn closed a large warm hand over her small one.

She quickly drew her hand away.

"Distrustful, aren't we?" He smiled, seemingly not offended, and placed his hand back on his knee. His sleeve had fallen back a little, and Aphra could see his wrist clearly. It was bare of the familiar markings.

"You don't have an imprint!" she exclaimed.

Birn showed her his right hand. "This is my imprint," he said, fingering the chain bracelet on his wrist. "That is to say, John Raymond's imprint."

Aphra looked at it, puzzled. "A bracelet? How could it possibly work since it's not part of you? Why do you have something like that? Are you an offender?"

He pushed his sleeve down and leaned back in the seat. "Maybe to this world I am."

She looked sideways at him. "You haven't discontinued anyone, have you?"

"No."

"Then why don't you have an imprint?"

He smiled cryptically. "Haven't you ever wanted privacy?"

"I'm sorry. I won't question you any more."

He grinned. "No. I mean, haven't you ever wished you didn't have your imprint? That no one knew anything about you? That you were anonymous?"

"No. Besides, I don't know how I'd manage without an imprint. I could never live like those who don't have one."

"Why do you say that?"

She looked directly at him, wondering if he was serious. Perhaps he did not realize the benefit of having a real imprint. "Being without one is too hard. Having personal ID that can't be stolen or duplicated ensures that I can continue my life relatively free of hassle, and my identity can be verified without any problems."

He looked at her and raised one eyebrow.

Aphra reddened, feeling stupid. Ironically, her problem now was that she had an imprint and could easily be traced.

"They're troublesome things," he said. "I had mine removed." He clasped his hands together and stretched his arms out in front of him briefly. "Gina, give me a link with Lev."

The front windscreen of the vehicle became opaque, then gradually grew clear again, revealing a different picture. Aphra saw a very dark-skinned fem reclining on a sofa, her eyes shut.

"Lavinia," Birn crooned. "Wake up!" He whistled a short, sharp blast.

Lev opened her eyes and looked up at the screen hovering above her. She sat up quickly, rubbed her eyes, and yawned. The screen shifted its position, following her as she sat up, and came around in front of her. "What are you whistling at me for? I'm not a dog," she said sleepily.

Birn laughed. "What are you doing, sleeping at this time of day?"

"I just shut my eyes for a few moments," Lev returned, smiling and flicking a few stray wisps of her shoulder-length black hair out of her face.

"Listen, sweetie," Birn said, "I have someone with me. This is Aphra. She needs somewhere to stay, so I'm bringing her over to our place."

Lev shifted her gaze from Birn and smiled at Aphra in welcome. "Hello, Aphra. There's plenty of room here for you, and you can stay as long as you like."

"Thank you," Aphra said uneasily. At least this man was not acting like some kind of molester. What kind of hardened criminal calls home to check with his wife?

Lev looked back at Birn. "Where's Gun?"

"Still in Min City. Not sure what he's doing."

"I need him here, but you can help me instead."

"How's Tubby?"

Lev put a hand to her mouth as she giggled. "He's just chewed up one of your shoes."

"Brat! Tell him I'm coming and I expect him to be on his best behavior."

Lev giggled again. "All right."

Birn blew a kiss at her. "See you soon."

Lev smiled.

"Disconnect," he said.

"Disconnected," Gina said. The screen dimmed and cleared to reveal the outside landscape again.

"That was my wife," Birn said with a hint of pride in his voice.

"Marriage is fashionable again, isn't it," Aphra said, then bit her lip, wondering if she had said the wrong thing.

Birn looked at her, an amused expression on his face. "Is it?"

She nodded and wrung her hands. "Computer, Tranquility please."

"I'm sorry, I am not equipped with any," Gina answered.

"I don't carry the stuff," Birn said. "While we have some time to spend, why don't you talk to me about who you are and what your problem is. Maybe I can help you with it somehow."

"My name is Aphra Vessey, I'm twenty-three years old, and I work for Sevig Empire," she answered, knowing that this information could easily be discovered by reading her imprint, so volunteering it would do no harm. She was reluctant to say anything else, wondering how she should go about telling him what she had seen. She had never seen anyone being discontinued before, except in a game, but then it had not been real. This *felt* unreal, but she could not tell herself it had been a game.

"Uh-huh." He nodded his head and shifted his gaze to the horizon. He waited for her to say more, but she was silent. "Why were you running from Mari?"

"Because I'm in trouble. Now I'll ask you a question. Why are you helping me?"

"You looked so lost and alone," he answered. "And then when I saw Mari, I knew I should help you—he's not someone you want to get mixed up with."

"How do you know him?"

"He was a friend of mine once," Birn answered grimly. "So, he was after you...why?"

She sat fidgeting with her hands.

"Tell you what," he said, "since you won't tell me why you're running, how about I tell you? You've gotten yourself in trouble with Sevig, am I right?"

"What? How could you know that Sevig has anything to do with this?" She shrugged. "Anyway, I don't even know for sure that he is interested in me. I just know that the one you call 'Mari' is."

"Mari does not act on his own—he works for Sevig."

"How do you know?"

"Because I used to work for Sevig, too."

Aphra felt her eyebrows rise. This man knew Mari, used to work for Sevig, and had no imprint. What kind of man had she gotten into the car with?

He was watching her. "How well do you know him?"

"Sevig? I don't," she said anxiously. "I just work for him. I've never even met him personally. I've just seen him like everyone else, on screen."

"What happened, then?"

She did not answer.

"Gina, stop," Birn said.

The sky car slowed and came to a halt, hovering above the sun-baked rock floor. Heat shimmered up like the edges of a dream.

"What are you doing?" Aphra asked, her eyes widening.

"I want you to tell me why Sevig is interested in you," he said firmly. "I don't want to be mixed up in something this big without knowing what it is."

Aphra sighed and covered her eyes.

"It's OK. Just tell me what it is."

There was nothing for it but to trust him. She had come too far already to act as though nothing very serious had happened. The thought of Ryan choked up inside her, a tight feeling pressing in her chest as she began to speak of him. "My friend," she whispered. "They discontinued my friend." Tears slid slowly down her cheeks. She wiped at them with embarrassment.

"Why?"

She sniffed and tried to hold back the sobs that threatened to come, but she found that she could not.

"I'm sorry," he said gently. He began to reach out his hand toward her shoulder but withdrew it again.

"I heard Sevig say he holds my friend's wife prisoner!" she wailed. "And Mari and someone else discontinued him!" The tightness in her lungs and throat rose. "*Agh!* I need some Tranquility! Give me some!"

"I don't have any," Birn said. "Look, you're not making any sense to me. Why don't you tell me what happened to you—from the start."

She wiped her eyes and choked down her sobs, trying to master herself. After a few moments she was calm enough to continue. She stared dully through the window. "I was delivering a package to Sevig's office, and I heard voices arguing. Then I heard what they were saying, so I left quickly. No one saw me," she said rapidly. "Ryan—that's my friend—was one of the voices I heard. Later I talked to him. I called him. That's when I saw Mari and another one discontinue him—in the middle of our call. Then I ran. He told me to go. Ryan did, I mean. He looked at me and told me to run."

"So how does this involve Sevig?"

"I don't know. Maybe it doesn't. I thought I heard Ryan

saying that Sevig had taken his wife and that the Personifid Project is a fraud and that Sevig is using it somehow."

As each part of that statement came out of her mouth, Birn's expression of surprise expanded. Now he looked stunned, as if someone had just shot him with a taze pistol. Then he blinked and shook his head. "What else can you tell me about this, Aphra? What *exactly* did you overhear?"

The words were easy for Aphra to recall, and she blurted them all out to Birn. Then she looked at him to see his reaction.

He was gazing at her with a worried expression. "This is big. You're in danger, all right. Don't worry; you'll be safe with Lev, and she will understand this better than anyone. Continue, Gina," he said, and the sky car began to move again.

The sky car descended into a jagged basin of rock. A long time ago, this area had been covered by the Pacific Ocean. Aphra looked at the wind-blasted stone around them, then back at the blue shield covering Min City. It appeared like a small arc slipping slowly down on the horizon. As they moved lower into the maze of stone valleys, her home was no longer visible.

They traveled along for a while without talking, as Aphra did not know what else to say or how to converse further with Birn. She was used to her friends who were programmed to make conversation. To have someone sitting silently beside her, looking out at the scenery with a calm, thoughtful expression, was difficult for her. She wished real people were easier to talk to. Yet, she was relieved at having been able to share her problem. She wondered what he thought of her, whether he really believed her. She hoped he did not think she was a crazy loon who had made up such a strange, unbelievable story about Sevig.

"Sky car approaching from five thirty-three," Gina's voice said suddenly.

Birn sat up straighter and scanned their surroundings. "Make us look as though we have four occupants."

"Done," said Gina.

After a few minutes, they saw the vehicle as it appeared above the cliff up ahead on their right and came down into the winding valley. Burgundy, with the image of blue and white flames adorning its roof, it was a low, sleek racing model. The sky car headed toward them, and Aphra watched uncertainly.

"Gina, give us a look at who's inside," Birn said.

The car flashed past them in an instant and kept going. Gina displayed a picture on the windscreen.

The picture revealed a lean man with long and wavy light brown hair, sitting slouched in his seat inside the sky car, dressed in black trousers and a dark gray shirt. His eyes were a pale color and looked disinterested.

Birn looked over at Aphra. "Do you know him?"

"No," she answered, as she studied him. Yet something about his face looked familiar. She supposed she had met him while working at Sevig Empire—she saw many faces come and go each day.

Their sky car cruised low to the ground, and Aphra looked about at the rock formations with interest. The sky was a pale yellow orange as usual, hard on the eyes. She missed the cool blue of the shields around Min City. The dimmed windows on the sky car did much to dull the ferocity of the sun, and the temperature inside was kept constant. Heat rose in ripples from fissures in the rock beneath them, vents that would have warmed the ocean bed years ago but now just added to the general scorching temperature of day. Aphra had never set foot outside of a protected city; she had only traveled inside either the loop jets or sky cars. People did hike in special personal shieldings, but she had always thought of that as a high-risk thing to do. What if the power units failed and left them exposed? It had been known to happen on occasion, and rescue had not always occurred in time.

"Where are we going?" she asked. "Which city are you from?"

"I don't live in a city. I live out here in the rocks."

Her eyes widened. "I've heard of people like you."

"People like me?"

"Rock-dwellers."

He grinned. "I think you'll be surprised. We don't go around wearing rags and crawling about in dark holes."

"Is it safe?"

"Yes, if you have the right equipment. Which we do, so no worries."

She chewed the inside of her cheek for a minute, debating with herself. Finally she spoke. "Birn?"

"Yes?"

"Thank you for helping me."

His smile was quick. "That's all right."

❯   ❯   ❯

"I cannot locate her," Jamon said, his modulated voice the perfect volume in the executive office. "I am unable to track her imprint."

Sevig looked up in surprise. "Recount to me her last movements."

"Last appeared in number four building in Blaketown Promenade," the computer said. "Took a lift to level three, entered a sky car."

"And? Was she with anyone, or was she alone?"

"She was with one John Raymond," Jamon said.

"Track the vehicle?"

"Unable to."

"Who's John Raymond? A lover?"

"Thirty-one-year-old male, residential address Saja City, apartment block Talma, level five, apartment five-two-five, currently unemployed. Searching… No records of them having been together before."

"I want to see them entering the vehicle and departing."

A flat screen appeared in the air before him, and he saw and heard the grainy recording of Aphra and Birn as they stood by the sky car talking. Sevig watched with narrowed eyes, studying everything carefully. He watched them get into the car and leave the building, then the picture changed to the viewpoint from outside of the parking building, and the sky car flew along and joined the streams of traffic on the East Gateway.

"So?" Sevig said.

"The vehicle disappeared," said Jamon. "None of the exiting sky cars match. The imprints for John Raymond and Aphra Vessey are no longer able to be tracked."

Sevig frowned and stared thoughtfully at the last image frozen in front of him. "It must be a mask."

"I could not detect a mask."

"It must be one, there is no other logical explanation. I suggest you analyze this properly because you have been deceived." He stood up. "A very clever mask," Sevig said quietly. "This person, whoever he is, complicates matters."

"Sky car approaching from two zero five," said Gina.

"Use the same superimpose as you did just before," Birn said to the sky car computer, "and show us who's inside."

Aphra looked for the vehicle. It came from their left this time and crossed overhead.

Gina displayed a picture on the windscreen, and this time it revealed a fem with short black hair, blue eyes, dressed in a navy slink suit.

"Know her?" Birn asked.

"No," Aphra answered decisively.

Other sky cars crossed paths with them, and Gina kept displaying pictures of the occupants, but Aphra recognized no one. She began to feel safer.

The sun became a dark red ball of fire and sank slowly on the horizon until it slipped from their sight as they flew through the canyons. Aphra idly wondered how far they had traveled and tried to resist the sleepiness stealing over her. It had been a frightening day, but the warmth of the sky car and the comfort of the seat she sat in had helped her to feel at ease. She missed Marlena and her own Michael, and she wished she had been able to bring them with her.

She thought also of Ryan, who had been her only human friend. She had met him in one of the staff leisure halls—he had bumped into her, she had spilled a drink on him, and they had struck up a conversation. The robot on cleaning duty had whisked over to them, and Ryan had told her a funny story of how a robot of the same model that he had worked on had mistaken him for a piece of dirt in its first cleaning trials and had chased him all around the laboratory trying to clean him. Then she found that they shared the same taste in movies and holo-games. From then on, they met often in the leisure halls and played many games together. She thought of how he had complimented her on her game-playing abilities and told her that she made a great partner in action games.

Aphra had liked Ryan right away, and a certain fondness had

grown between them. Ryan had made it clear he did not want her as anything more than a friend; he had said that he was still in love with his late wife. Aphra had not minded so much; she had Michael to love. He was always reliable and safe. Ryan had stirred up some fluttery, confusing emotions in Aphra, but she had thought it was only from the uncertainty of having a real person for a friend. Real people were so unpredictable.

Aphra had once asked Ryan cautiously about his wife, and she discovered she had been discontinued in an accident. He did not elaborate on the subject, and she did not prod further although she was curious. Having him confide in her, even in small ways, made her feel like she mattered to him. It was not something she had often experienced. It reminded her of when she had been a young child and had lived with two siblings. Vague memories of them had come up since meeting Ryan. She had never done anything about finding her brother and sister, but she told herself she would do something one day, just not yet.

〉　　　　　〉　　　　　〉

The voice in his head spoke again, and he found himself obeying it—not because he wanted to, but because it seemed to be the only action he could perform. There were niggling thoughts in the back of his mind, but it was too difficult to hear them.

He sat up, trying to get more comfortable. His body felt heavy and unresponsive at first. He shook the dullness from his mind by repeating to himself the words he had heard. Nothing mattered but those words. He stood slowly, flexing his hands experimentally. He was ready. Ready and willing to follow.

The instant the voice continued speaking, his sense of it

became more alert, more in tune. He could feel it inside his mind searing into the depths of his being and drawing him close.

Obeying the voice was the only way. The right way.

›   ›   ›

The moon and stars were glowing in the black sky when the sky car finally began to make its approach to Lev and Birn's home. Aphra sat up and shook off her drowsiness. She could see nothing but a rock face illuminated in the pale blue lights of the sky car. Then a section of rock slid smoothly across, and they entered the cave that was revealed. The rock door closed behind them and lighting came on.

The irregular cave seemed big enough for at least three sky cars. The walls were dark and rough, and Aphra looked with fascination at them—it looked like something out of a rock-climbing simulation game. It sparked her interest to know that this was real rock.

The doors of the sky car opened, and Birn got out quickly. The fem from the video call—Lev—came through a doorway in the far wall of the cave to greet them. He enveloped her in a bear hug and kissed her several times. Aphra got out of the vehicle slowly, uncertain of what she should say or do. She reached over and lightly touched the wall next to her, but was disappointed to find that the rock felt no different from simulated rock.

She turned to look, but she could see no trace of the door that had opened to allow them to enter.

A scrabbling, yelping sound behind her made her jump, and she turned back to see a brown medium-sized, smooth-haired dog come bounding into the cave through the open doorway beyond Birn and Lev. It seemed to Aphra that it was running evenly, almost clumsily. It barked and yelped, wagging its tail furiously as it threw itself at Birn.

"Tubby!" Birn cried, letting go of Lev and turning to the dog. "Tubby, tubby, tubby! You beast! Ramius, you big tub, you're a beast!"

Lev went over to Aphra, a friendly smile on her face. She was shorter than Aphra, and her brown skin looked even darker than it had on screen. Her hair was sleek and black and hung down just past her shoulders. Lev was of a slim build, and Aphra felt large and awkward beside her.

"Hello, Aphra," she said. "Come inside."

The dog saw Aphra and ran over to her, growling and barking. Aphra waited for it to stop, but it did not, and she wondered at its programming—she had never seen one as noisy and berserk as this.

"Stop it, Ramius!" Lev called, trying to catch hold of it. "Be quiet!"

But the dog evaded her grasp and continued barking. Aphra stared at it, hoping it would not blow a fuse while near her. As Lev chased Ramius around the sky car, Aphra followed Birn into the room adjoining the garage.

It was a living room with a seating arrangement of three couches around a long, low table. A few large plants in pots were against the flat, smooth, smoky-blue walls. A large painting dominated one wall—it was an incredible, dramatic scene divided into two halves—the left side looked like the desert waste of Earth, and on the right were lush grass, trees, and flowers. In the center of the picture, straddling the dividing line between the ruined landscape and the lush land, was a tree. The left half of it was burned and stunted. The other half of the tree was blooming with life.

The air in the living room felt warm and cozy and had

a distinctive aroma. The smell of spiced bread? Aphra was unsure, but it made her feel suddenly hungry. If it had not been for the jagged rock ceiling in this room, she would have thought she was in a windowless apartment. A large, spacious apartment, but a regular apartment nonetheless, not a hole inside a rock formation out in the middle of nowhere.

Lev came in behind Aphra, Ramius bursting past her. "He's being a silly twit. Don't mind him, though; he's all noise." The door to the garage slid shut behind them. "Sit down," Lev said to Aphra. "Make yourself comfy."

Aphra went over to one of the couches.

"Have you eaten anything this evening?" Lev asked.

"No."

"Birn!" Lev exclaimed, giving him a playful slap on the arm. "Why haven't you fed this poor fem?"

He shrugged. "I didn't think of it. Sorry about that, Aphra."

"You just sit right there, Aphra," Lev said, tugging at Birn. "I'll get you something to eat."

Aphra sat silently, watching Birn and Lev as they went over to the far part of the room to the right of the door she had entered through.

Ramius slunk around the corner of the couch, drawing her attention, and stared at Aphra. She was pleased to see that he was quieter now. She held out her hand to him, but he flinched back. Puzzled, she withdrew her hand. Ramius edged up to her once more, looking at her with big innocent eyes, and again she put her hand out to pat him, but he jumped back. She sighed and looked back at Birn and Lev.

They were talking quietly to each other behind a waist-high barrier that partially divided that space from the seating area. The barrier was a countertop that formed a U shape with two of its sides set against the walls. Above it on the far wall were cupboards, and underneath the counters there were drawers. Birn was leaning against the counter watching Lev as she busily got things out from the cupboards and drawers. Aphra watched with curiosity as she saw that Lev was getting plates, utensils, and food. It all seemed to have been sitting in the cupboards; she did not see things appear through a food delivery system or hear Lev ordering anything. Lev took a green container and ladled its contents onto two plates, gave one to Birn, then brought the other over to Aphra.

Aphra suddenly realized that the area of counters and cupboards was a *kitchen* and that Lev prepared food the old way.

"It's just leftovers," Lev said. "I haven't had time to cook today." She handed the plateful to Aphra.

Aphra thought about how Lev would have touched the food as she had made it, so she ate slowly, chewing carefully and hoping it would be all right. She was very hungry, and it did taste nice.

"You were too busy sleeping," Birn teased, as he walked over to the couch opposite Aphra.

"Brat," Lev said sharply, and poked her tongue out at Birn.

Aphra noticed that Ramius was to the left of her, next to a plant by the wall. He lifted one of his hind legs and began to water the plant. "Your dog is malfunctioning," Aphra said in surprise, pointing with her fork.

"Ramius!" Lev shouted and hastily made her way over to the floppy-eared dog. "I told you, don't go in here. Bad dog! You come with me, now!" She led the dog out by the scruff of its neck, past the couches and down the corridor behind Aphra.

Birn laughed. "Aphra, the dog is real."

"*What?*" she spluttered.

"It's a real, live dog. Haven't you ever seen one before?"

She pulled her feet up on the couch. "No. They're dirty and carry disease."

"Well, maybe, if you don't look after them and keep them clean," he replied, and continued eating from the plate on his knee. "But Ramius is all right. He's only five months old and is still learning. He's a pretty funny dog once you get to know him. Still got a lot of growing to do. We're not sure how big he's going to get, but his mother was huge."

"Where did you get him from?"

"One of our neighbors. I think there's still two puppies left from the litter, if you're interested," he said with a grin.

Aphra shook her head and allowed her legs to uncurl slowly. "I wouldn't know what to do with it. I prefer having something I can turn off."

"Oh, that's no fun."

Aphra began to eat again, and presently Lev and Ramius returned. Ramius bore a sheepish expression, and Aphra stared at him with great interest. Lev sat next to Birn, and Ramius clambered up onto her knee.

"You get your face away from my food," Birn said to the puppy, who was straining to sniff at Birn's plate. "Go on, get off!"

"He's really real?" Aphra asked.

"Yes, he is." Lev smiled, hugging Ramius closer so that he would not reach Birn's plate. "Omega, please clean up the mess Ramius made."

A thin pencil of light appeared over the puddle and erased it.

"Lazy!" Birn said with his mouth full.

Lev elbowed him, causing him to scoop too much food off his plate and slop it onto the couch.

"There, now look what you've done," Birn said. "You'll have to clean that one up because it was your fault."

"Ramius can lick it up," Lev answered.

"And cover the couch with slobber? I don't think so."

"Then maybe you should—it's your food, after all, and we don't want to waste it."

"And cover the couch with slobber? I don't think so."

Lev broke into a peal of laughter.

Aphra stared at them—they seemed to be arguing, but there had been a sparkle in their eyes and the curve of a smile on their lips. Now Lev was laughing and Birn was grinning. It confused her.

"Can I touch the dog?" she asked when the laughter had subsided.

"Sure!"

Aphra put her plate onto the low table in front of her and walked slowly over to the dog on Lev's knee. She gently touched him: he felt warm. The dog turned his head to look up at Aphra, and as she stroked his side, he swiped her with a big pink tongue. The main difference she found was that his skin was a lot looser and more elastic-feeling than that of a simulated dog. He also had a strange odor. She backed away, retrieved her plate, and sat on the couch again.

"What do you think of him?" Birn asked.

She shrugged and began to eat again. Tiredness began to slip into her as she relaxed in the warmth of the room, and she found herself barely able to keep hold of her fork.

"Where are you from, Aphra?" Lev asked.

Aphra looked up in mid-mouthful and looked at Lev. She was smiling an encouraging smile, similar to what an android was programmed to do when it began to converse. Aphra almost started to roll her eyes and tell it to shut up, but she caught herself. Lev was not an it, and this smile was real. "I don't want to talk," she said instead.

"She's worn out, Lev," Birn said. "She's had a lot to cope with."

"Poor thing," Lev said, looking sympathetically at Aphra. "As soon as you're ready, I'll show you where you can sleep."

Aphra nodded and continued chewing slowly. She watched Birn and Lev out the corner of her eye as they talked, grateful that they no longer spoke to her. Some real people when talking did not seem to notice whether or not she actually wanted to talk to them. She always avoided people like that when in the staff leisure halls. In fact, she generally avoided people of all kinds.

Once Aphra had finished eating, Lev led her through the open doorway into the corridor behind the couch Aphra had sat on. The long dark corridor became lit, albeit dimly, once they stepped through the doorway. The walls were of the same smooth texture as the living room walls, and the ceiling was slightly rounded. Its shape was emphasized by thin pipe archways set into the ceiling at regular intervals. The flooring was smooth stone, and lights from either side of it illuminated the corridor in a cool blue wash of light. There were a few tiny lights spread wide apart in the middle of the ceiling, and they emitted a dull glow. So far, their home was not at all like Aphra had been expecting. She felt disappointed that it was not rockier in appearance.

They passed two pipe archways, and then Lev turned to the right. An unseen door slid open silently, and they entered a small bedroom.

"I hope you'll be comfortable here," Lev said. "Your cleanroom is through that door." She indicated the door set in the left wall of the room.

"It is very kind of you to give me a place to stay for the night," Aphra said awkwardly.

"You're welcome," Lev answered, startling her with a friendly squeeze of Aphra's arm. "Good night," she said as she left the room. The door shut quietly behind her.

In the cleanroom Aphra was surprised when she looked into the mirror. Who was that person in the reflection? Then she remembered she had changed her appearance back at her apartment. She fingered her shoulder-length red hair and looked at her green eyes. She sighed and leaned against the cleanroom's countertop, still looking at herself in the mirror, thinking through the events of the day.

She was about to ask the computer for Tranquility, her usual routine before going to bed, but then realized she did not need any. As she thought about it, she realized she had felt calmer once being inside Birn and Lev's home, as though she had entered a deep stillness of the depth of the rock. She could feel tangibly that Tranquility was present in the atmosphere, yet it was a different Tranquility than what she was used to. She opened her hand and looked at her fingers as though she expected she could grasp the solidity of quietness in her hand. Perhaps being far from the madness of the city was the only place she could have this sensation.

"Computer," she said, running her fingers through the air. "What is this?"

"Please indicate what you are referring to," answered Omega's deep male voice.

"There is Tranquility of a sort in this room. What is it?"

"I sense no chemical tracings in this room of the kind you indicate. There are no Life Enhancers here."

"But I feel it."

"It is tracings of the Tri-une Soul's life signs that you feel. Birn and Lev speak regularly with Him."

"What?" Aphra whispered. "You mean to tell me they're Grovelers?"

"No, Followers," said Omega. "The term you use is an

incorrect assessment of their practices and not at all humorous to most who follow the Way."

Aphra looked at herself in the mirror, half-expecting some ghostly face to join her, but then dismissed the thought immediately. It unsettled her to be told that Birn and Lev were Followers; she had not thought of them in that manner. Oh, she knew such people existed, but she had never spoken to any of them. Or if she had, they had not let her know of their beliefs.

Ever since it had become possible to detect soul life signs, the disturbing truth had been discovered—there were other, unseen entities in the world. The beliefs of older societies in the history of mankind had been right, after all. Some people thought of these entities, commonly known as interterrestrials, as merely shadows, traces of older souls that had departed their human bodies. Other people insisted that these traces were nothing more than glitches in the relatively new technology used for soul detection. Still others gave avid attention to these so-called glitches, worshiping them even. Followers were one of these groups.

Followers of the Way, as they called themselves, claimed that these interterrestrial soul life signs had always been detectable. They said this was especially true of the one they called the Tri-une Soul—the God who had supposedly been knowable from the beginning of time. This God's soul life signs were purported to be different, more enigmatic than any other.

Aphra was not sure what she believed about such things. She rarely gave it much thought, and she had certainly never seen or met any interterrestrials before. And now, in this home out among the rocks, being told that what she felt as Tranquility was possibly traces of the Tri-une Soul…it made her feel oddly small inside as the ambience encircled her.

Once Aphra was in bed and the lights were off, her mind remained wide-awake. She was not used to being alone. It was too quiet. The strange Tranquility had almost become too overpowering now that she knew what it was, and she did not know what to think of its presence there. There was nothing stifling about it; she did not feel suppressed by it, but rather more curious and alert as it touched her senses.

"Computer," she said, "I don't want to be alone. Will you talk to me until I fall asleep?"

"Certainly," answered Omega. "What do you wish me to talk about?"

"Anything."

"I will read you a story. What kind of story do you like?"

"I don't know, just anything. But first, am I safe here? Who are Lev and Birn? Why do they live out here? Can I trust them? Why are they helping me like this?"

"Yes, you are safe here. And I am sorry, but I do not give out private information. I can only tell you that Birn and Lev have chosen to live out here. As for whether you can trust them, I do not know how trusting you are, so I cannot answer your part of that responsibility. On their part, I observe that they are usually people of their word and do their best to hold to certain standards of behavior in all their connections with others. They are helping you because caring for someone in need is one requirement of those standards."

Aphra's brow furrowed. "Can I call my home from here?"

"One moment while I ask—"

"No, don't."

"In that case I cannot give permission. Are you sure you don't want me to ask Lev and Birn if you can call home?"

"I don't know."

"Tell me when you do know. In the meantime, would you

like me to begin telling you a story?"

"Yes."

"*Out of the Silent Planet* by C. S. Lewis," began Omega, and his voice altered to a softer tone. "The last drops of the thundershower had hardly ceased falling when the Pedestrian stuffed his map into his pocket—"

Aphra closed her eyes and settled back. Omega's words drifted over her until she was finally lulled to sleep.

❭ ❭ ❭

"Where is she now?" Sevig asked aloud.

"Is she that important?" Craf asked.

Sevig looked disdainfully at him. Craf was an angular-bodied metallic robot six feet tall. His sharp, burnished edges were clearly defined in the light of the office. He was human-oid in proportion but as like to a person as a wooden-carved Pinocchio to a boy.

"Don't ask idiotic questions," Sevig said. "I'll have you reset if you don't stop interrupting my thoughts."

"Sorry."

"Ryan had very few friends, and Aphra Vessey was one of them. Now she has run, and we can't find it. What do you think?"

"I think we should find her," Craf admitted. "She may have it in her possession."

"Exactly."

"Sorry," said Craf, bowing his metallic head in simulated shame.

WHEN APHRA AWOKE the next morning, she looked at the unfamiliar surroundings and wondered where she was. Then it all came rushing back.

She sat up in bed and hugged her knees, feeling sick as she remembered Ryan. Had that been only yesterday? It was hard to believe that his life had been discontinued so quickly. It did not seem real, yet here she was in a strange place after having had a strange day. The image of Ryan as he fell, his body tossed limply to the floor, kept playing over in her mind. He had fallen so differently from an android in a fear game. Ryan had seemed to crumple, and she could not forget his face as he looked his last at her.

She got up and refreshed herself, dressed, and then sat on the edge of her bed and fidgeted, wondering what to do. The sense of Tranquility was still there in the room, but it was no longer as strong as she had felt it the night before. She would have to go out of the room and speak again to Birn and Lev, but she did not know what she would say to them. No clear decision about what she should do now had come to her.

Was it possible she had overestimated the danger she was in and that she could simply return home and straighten things out there? Perhaps it did not matter what she had seen and overheard—she was nobody important and could do nothing anyway.

"Computer," she said tentatively.

"Call me Omega," came its deep voice.

"All right. Omega, I'd like some Tranquility and some Confidence."

"Sorry, you won't get any of that here."

"Why not?"

"I'm not equipped to give any."

"Why not?" Aphra said with exasperation. "Everyone has it; why not you?"

"Lev's specifications," said Omega. "She prefers not to be chemically altered."

"But why?" Aphra said, clenching her fist.

"She says it is healthier."

"I need some!"

"You will have to talk to Lev about that."

Aphra stood slowly and looked at the door. She chewed her fingernails and paced around the room, looking at the floor, the walls, the bed, then into the cleanroom and looking at things there. She touched the small sensorpad for cold water and watched it slosh into the crystalline basin. Her emotions were so disordered that she did not know how to deal with them, and in fact, she did not even recognize what half of them were. So she busied herself with touching the sensorpads in the cleanroom and watching what happened, just needing to occupy herself with doing something, anything.

After awhile, Omega said, "Birn asks if you want to come and have breakfast."

His words came as a jolt, and Aphra blinked. She had been in the middle of placing little fish ornaments at evenly spaced intervals along the narrow shelf below the mirror—although why it seemed so important for her to place them so exactly she had no idea. She looked at herself in the mirror and ran her fingers through her red hair.

"Breakfast," she said, feeling a sense of relief at knowing what to do next.

"Yes," answered Omega.

"Can't I have it here?"

"No."

"I don't like how I look—it's all wrong. Change my appearance."

"I'm not equipped to do that."

She groaned. "You need upgrading." She left the cleanroom and went out of the bedroom into the corridor.

"So," Birn called as she entered the kitchen, "do you want some breakfast?"

She was struck again by his muscular build and the warm friendliness of his features. "Yes," she said.

He turned to the cupboards. "I think there's some stuff around somewhere." He opened one cupboard after another by touching the small circle on each one.

Aphra went over to the countertop that divided the kitchen from the living room and watched him. "Why don't you have your food delivered?"

"Lev likes the old way of life," Birn explained. "More effort on our parts and less laziness. And I think she's planning to do away with these cupboards and drawers and make ones we have to open by pulling manually." He paused, then muttered, "Where is that food I had for breakfast?"

"It is in the top right cupboard," came Omega's voice.

"That's it," Birn said, and opened the appropriate cupboard.

Aphra watched as he pulled out a clear container filled with something unfamiliar looking. Then he stood still for a moment, a puzzled expression on his face.

"Left drawer," said Omega.

Birn nodded, and removed a plate from the left drawer.

"How did Omega know you were looking for a plate?" Aphra asked.

"Oh, he's a smart old thing," Birn said with a grin, and then turned to another drawer. He opened and shut it without taking anything.

"Utensils are in the next drawer," said Omega. "Why do you never remember this?"

"Go bother someone else, will you?" Birn said as the drawer slid open. "How am I supposed to remember when Lev keeps moving things around?" He tipped some of the food out onto the plate. "How much of this do you want?"

"What is it?" she asked.

"Muesli. It's just oats, grains, dried fruit . . . anything Lev can find to put in it."

"That's enough," she said, holding her hand out to stop him.

"Here you go then." He handed her the plate and spoon.

She took it and went over and stood in front of the painting on the wall. The colors in the right half of the picture seemed even richer than they had the night before.

"Earth, before and after?" she asked, pointing with her spoon.

"Kind of," Birn said, looking at her. "More like life, before and after."

"Oh, right." She tilted her head. "But if it was Earth before, the green part should be on the left, shouldn't it?"

"Maybe."

"I love it," Aphra said. "It's an amazing painting. Where did you get it? I've been wanting some artwork for my apartment but haven't really found anything. So far everything Marlena does for me isn't really what I'm wanting. I have downloaded more art programs for her to increase her creativity, but I still haven't got anything I love enough to have on my walls."

Birn smiled. "I painted it myself."

"You did? Not your computer?"

He shook his head. "Just me."

Aphra stared at him, amazed. She had never met an artist who was human before. He grinned back at her. "It's fantastic," she said. "You're really talented."

"Thanks," he said, leaving the kitchen area and coming to stand beside her. He looked critically at the painting. "Yes, it's not bad."

"Have you done any more?"

"Hundreds," he said. "I'm freelancing now. We actually traded one of my paintings for Ramius. I used to work in conceptual designs for robots, games room visuals, that sort of thing. I'll paint you something if you want."

"I'd like that."

He reached down and flicked a hair off the lower edge of the painting. "I'll show you some of my stuff later on, and you can tell me what sort of thing you're interested in."

"OK."

Aphra sat on one of the couches and began to eat. The food tasted odd to her but was not unpleasant, so she ate it without complaining. Ramius came trotting into the room on his gangly legs. Aphra understood now that his clumsy gait was not some malfunction but rather the delightfully random motion of a living puppy. Ramius stopped when he saw Aphra. He sat quickly, a small distance away, and eyed her.

"It's all right, Tubby," Birn said. "It's only Aphra, remember?" He pulled gently on the dog's brown ears. Then he straightened up and turned to Aphra. "I'm going to the lab. You can join us when you've finished. It's straight down to the end of the hall."

Ramius stayed, watching Aphra with a mixture of timidity and curiosity. She made a face at him, then smiled, and he came closer. When she had eaten enough, she took a spoonful of the leftover food and dropped it onto the floor. Ramius's eyes lit up with interest, and he forgot his bashfulness. He scrambled toward the food and noisily slurped it up while Aphra reached over and patted his ears lightly. The scrap of food disappeared in a second, and then he tried to get onto her knee to reach her plate.

She was holding her plate high in the air with one hand and trying to push the dog off with the other when the door to the garage opened silently. A tall man with long black hair came through into the living room. He was lean and graceful and looked as if he had American Indian genetic material in him. He stopped in surprise as he saw her sitting there, and Ramius shifted his attention from Aphra's plate to him and leaped away, yelping and whining with pleasure as he rushed over to the man. His strong, tanned, noble-looking face changed from stern and serious to warm and animated as he bent down and held the squirming puppy in his arms.

He looked up at Aphra with dark, penetrating eyes, and his face became stern again. "Who are you?"

"Aphra. I'm staying with Lev and Birn for a while. Just for today, I think." She found it difficult to meet his eyes, he gazed at her so steadily. She heard herself babbling nervously. "I came here yesterday. They invited me. I don't know them, but I needed to get away from the city. I've never been out in a home in the rocks like this. I live in Min City, in an apartment."

He stared at her skeptically. "Are Lev and Birn in the lab?"

"Yes."

He let go of Ramius, then stood up and walked over to the corridor. "Are you coming?"

She put her plate down on the low table and stood. He continued on up the hallway without waiting for her. She followed, unsure of herself. Should she say anything more to this stranger? He had seemed to have invited her to follow, yet he walked on ahead without saying any more to her.

The hallway was more brightly lit now that it was day, and she walked a few paces behind the man. Ramius romped alongside him, jumping up and mouthing his hand. Aphra could not help but smile as she watched the puppy's behavior and the ungainly way he leaped about.

The man stopped at the end of the hall, and an unseen door dissolved before him. He turned and looked at Aphra, then went through. The section of wall instantly reappeared. She was uncertain for a moment; then she walked right up to it, and the door dissolved again.

"You must do this," said the voice in his head. He stared at the things in front of him for a moment, as though suddenly remembering where he was. What had he just been doing? He felt as though he had been sleeping. Nothing in front of him seemed to make sense, shapes of color, textures of steel and plastic.

"Yes," he said, and as he did, he saw that he was in the sky car. Everything became clear.

Aphra walked through the doorway and through a three-meter-deep rock entranceway to the laboratory.

The lab was softly lit with a warm glow, individual spotlights spreading fans of light across the artwork on the dusky green walls. She recognized the paintings as Birn's handiwork—the style seemed unmistakably similar to the painting she had admired in the living room. No potted plants stood in this room, making it seem almost severe.

A large permanent screen was affixed to the wall to the left of her, and beneath it on a long shelf lay two black panels, a few millimeters thick, sixty centimeters square. Aphra knew enough to know that these squares were very expensive pieces of equipment, being the housing units for computer and power applicators. There was one, half the size, in her apartment building that served everyone in the building. She was surprised at the sight of them, as she had been thinking that Omega was stripped of some basic functions and supposed that it was because of a lack of power out in these isolated surroundings. Now she saw it was not so; the computer and power applicators were huge.

She followed the man across the gray stone floor to the center of the room, where two black couches faced each other on a large, jade-and-charcoal patterned rug. Birn was sitting on one couch, leaning forward as he watched a handheld screen. Lev was at a desk by the far wall to Aphra's right, studying images that appeared before her, shifting, changing shapes of light. She spoke quietly now and then, causing the shapes to change.

"Hey, Gun," Birn said, glancing up from his screen. "Didn't expect to see you so soon."

Gun sat on the couch opposite Birn. "I finished what I had to do."

"You've met Aphra, then?" Birn said, smiling up at Aphra.

Gun nodded, his face expressionless.

Aphra sat next to Birn, feeling like she was imposing upon them. But then she noticed that what he was watching so intently on his screen was a baseball game.

"Where's Zellie?" Birn asked. He tapped the screen off and set it beside him.

Gun shrugged as he put his feet up on the low table between the couches. Ramius scrambled onto his lap.

Birn turned again to Aphra. "You feeling OK?"

She nodded.

He looked back to Gun. "What did you discover?"

"Talk about it later," Gun answered, looking pointedly at Aphra.

"Did you see Sanchia?" Birn asked.

"Yep."

"Well? How is she?"

Gun did not answer, but just stared at Birn, his dark eyes betraying no emotion.

Birn grinned and looked at Aphra. "You can see that Gun is the talker in our family."

She barely raised her eyes to look at Gun, though she did wonder how he was related. His facial features were too different from Lev's, his skin too light. Possibly he was her brother, genetically tailored to account for those differences. Then again, if that was the case, he might well be related to Birn. She was curious to know if he too was a Follower. She could feel the strange Tranquility in this room as well, but it began to make her more agitated. This was surely no time to be relaxing! She had to work out what she should do about Ryan. She looked hopefully at Birn.

"What am I going to do?" she said abruptly. "I don't know what to do."

"The first thing you're going to do is stop worrying," Birn said. He reached over and laid his hand on hers. "Nobody can find you here. You're safe."

"You're not going to hurt me, are you?" she said slowly, looking down at his hand and then back into his eyes. She could see a depth behind the twinkling blue that was reassuring.

"Of course not!" Lev exclaimed.

Aphra looked over to where she sat, but Lev's attention was still on the images before her.

"Of course not," echoed Birn.

"But why are you helping me? You don't even know me."

He smiled. "I'm impulsive. Now calm down and relax. We really need to talk about what happened to you yesterday and try to figure it out."

"I can't," she said, picking at her sleeve. "I need some *proper* Tranquility, but Omega doesn't have any."

Birn turned and looked over his shoulder. "Lev!"

"What?" she snapped, not looking up.

Birn grinned. "Perhaps some music would be helpful?"

Lev looked up a moment and met his eyes. "Yes," she said thoughtfully. "Omega, dc Talk's *Supernatural*, please."

Instantly, music filled the room.

"There you go, that should help," Birn said, turning back to Aphra. "Just try to relax, and we'll talk when you feel like it."

Aphra listened to the drumbeats and soaring voices accompanied by musical instruments. "This is unusual music."

"It's from the late twentieth, early twenty-first centuries," Birn said. "The old sound takes a bit of getting used to, but it's really good once you do."

"I like their singing," she said, and settled back into her seat as some of her tension began to ease.

They spent the next hour or two listening to music, talking

idly now and then. Gun hardly said a word, but sat with his long legs stretched out before him and his head resting back, eyes closed. Aphra looked at his tanned stern face often, finding that for all his reticence there was something warm and intriguing about him. She wondered how he could be so expressive while doing or saying nothing—it was not what she was used to. Androids were not like that; they were either on or off. Here, Gun's eyes were closed, and the only movements he made were when he breathed, when he slowly moved his hand to pat Ramius, or when his foot twitched in time to the music. Yet he resonated life.

She looked at Ramius and found he was the same—grunting and snuffling as he licked himself, chewing his paws and staring at her with wide innocent eyes, yawning and leaning right back so that his head was against Gun's chest as he looked up at Gun. There was the constant movement, the constant sense of life emanating from the puppy—so different from robotic dogs, no matter how elaborately the dog had been programmed to move or behave.

And Birn, when he talked to her, sometimes did not listen or wait for her to respond. He did not treat her as though she was the center of attention, though when he looked at her he made her feel like she was important. Again she could see that something in his eyes that made her think of kindness, friendliness.

As Aphra sat in that room with three people and a dog, she experienced a real feeling of companionship, almost to the point of being overwhelmed by the nearness of others.

Late in the morning Lev stood, stretched, and came over to sit next to Gun. He opened his eyes and gave her a brief smile.

"Aphra," Lev said, her dark brown eyes fixed on Aphra's face, "I need you to tell me everything that happened to you yesterday. Can you talk about it now?"

Aphra looked down at the low table between the couches. "I told Birn," she said awkwardly.

"I'd like to hear what happened from you."

"Why do you want to know?"

"Because it's important."

Aphra chewed on her fingernail and glanced sideways at Gun. "All that happened was that I saw a friend of mine being discontinued. And then I was chased."

"Before that," Lev probed. "What you overheard about the Personifid Project. I need to know everything you remember."

"Why?"

"You can't trust us, yet we've taken you into our home?" Gun said, looking at her intensely.

Lev put her hand on Gun's. "I understand, Aphra, but honestly, this is the only place you are safe right now. Mari was looking for you, so there's obviously something wrong somewhere. Are you sure you heard Sevig say he has a soul in a capsule?"

"I think it sounded like him, but I'm not sure."

"This is unbelievable," Lev said to Birn. "If this is true, we *have* to get that capsule." She turned to Aphra once more. "And the other speaker was Ryan Haldane?"

"Yes," Aphra said in a low voice.

"You're absolutely sure?" Lev said persistently.

"I think so."

"And you say you saw him being discontinued?"

Aphra nodded. "Over the video call."

Lev sat staring at Birn. Aphra tried to read the expression in her face, but she could not. Gun got up and left the room, and she watched him go, wondering if she had offended him somehow. She knew it was not pleasant conversation, but Lev did seem so insistent on knowing what had happened.

"Is Mari going to try to discontinue me because of what I saw?"

"That's what's puzzling me," Lev said. "Why would *Mari* be after you if all you did was that? I wouldn't have thought Sevig would care."

"Then is it maybe because of what I overheard?"

Lev's forehead creased. "He probably wouldn't care about that either—it's your word against his. And if you obtained any security camera footage, I'm sure he would find a way to establish that it was False Artificial Representation. There's no knowing why Sevig is so interested in you, but he's not some-one you want to be on the wrong side of." Lev looked at Birn. "Why would Mari be the one doing this for Sevig?"

"You've got me," he said with a shrug. "You'd think Sevig would just use a regular metal-head."

Lev turned back to Aphra. "Is there anything else you can tell me? Anything that Ryan said to you?"

"All Ryan told me to do was go, and so I—"

Omega interrupted. "We have someone, unidentified, out-side the front entrance."

"Visual," Birn said.

They all looked at the large screen on the wall and saw the dry barren landscape under the late morning sun. A sky car hovered into view.

"Give us a look at who is inside," Lev said.

The screen focused in on the sky car and then through its darkened windows.

Birn's eyes narrowed in recognition. "That's the guy we passed yesterday."

The man with long, wavy light brown hair sat stiffly upright, his pale eyes scanning the surroundings. For a moment his eyes looked right at them, and Aphra stared back, feeling a strange sensation as she looked at him. They saw his lips move in speech, and then he paused, his brow creasing with determination.

"I can detect no imprint on him," said Omega.

"He's staying around in this area too long," Birn said. "I don't like it."

"Omega, tag him," Lev said.

"Tagged," answered Omega.

Birn looked at Lev. "Why'd you do that?"

"Just a feeling I have," Lev said thoughtfully.

"He's going," Birn said, looking back at the screen.

They watched the sky car swivel and speed away. As it left the limit of Omega's visual range, the screen began to dim.

Lev waved her hand. "Omega, wait. Did he leave anything?"

"Searching," came the deep voice of the computer.

They waited in silence while Omega's sensors searched the area outside the cave.

"I have a beacon," said Omega presently.

"Movable?" Lev asked, her brow furrowed.

"Yes, if its movement sensors are bypassed."

"OK, work on that," Lev said, standing. "I'll have to go out there and move it myself."

"I can do that for you," Birn said.

She shook her head. "This will be delicate. I'd rather do it myself—this is not a job for your banana fingers."

"Hey!" he protested, grinning.

"I'll get Gun to help me—I'm sure he'd like to have a look at it as well." Lev rumpled Birn's hair playfully and left the room, with Ramius trotting after her.

Birn leaned back into the couch and smiled at Aphra. "Well, it's just you and me, kid."

"Do you think that man was looking for me?"

"It's possible. We don't usually have people around here unless they're looking for a place to settle."

"I'm scared," Aphra admitted, clasping her hands tightly together.

"You don't need to be," he said warmly. "Lev is the best when it comes to the computer stuff. We've been here for a few years now, and nobody has found her. You're safe."

Aphra looked at her hands. "Why live here?"

"It's good place to be. You're independent of any city, solitude and privacy being the main perks. I've never liked the craziness of the city, especially Min City. We have only one neighbor close by. A few others further out. And that suits us."

"I've always thought it must be a hard way to live. Don't you find it too quiet and isolated?"

"Well, we visit our neighbors to trade and socialize, so we're not totally isolated." He stood up. "Come with me; I want to show you something."

She followed him out of the room and turned to watch the stone wall materialize behind her.

"Fancy door, isn't it," Birn said with a grin. "Lev likes gimmicks like that."

She and Birn walked a few meters along the corridor that branched to the right, following it as it curved around. The illumination in the corridor grew strong and brilliant, and as they rounded the curve, Aphra could see a doorway of bright light. As they moved closer, her eyes adjusted to the light, and she realized she was looking at the sky. She followed Birn up a couple of steps and gasped as she stood in the doorway.

"I had no idea we were so close," she said, gazing out over the sparkling gray sea in the distance. "Is it safe?" She stepped closer to the large jagged hole in the rock. She had only ever seen views like this in a game—knowing it was real gave her a thrill of excitement.

"We're protected," answered Birn, smiling down at the look of astonishment on her face. "You'd feel the sun if we weren't."

"Oh, of course." She walked right to the edge of the room and looked down at the rocks below. "We're so high up!" The cliff cut away below them, reaching a greater depth than the garage-side entrance. Rough forms of rock were starkly outlined in the light, and she looked at them, feeling a different sense of perception from their reality. She involuntarily caught hold of Birn's arm.

"There are trenches and gullies everywhere around here," Birn said as he steadied her. "The rock formations are pretty wild. There are old wrecks of seagoing ships out there, too. When I first moved here, the sea came a lot closer to the edge of the cliff. It slowly recedes, little by little, day by day. It's sad to think that one day the Pacific Sea will be gone."

She let go of his arm and looked up at his face, surprised to see him looking so serious. "We don't need it," she said, trying to reassure him. "It's just nice to look at, that's all."

"No, it's a lot more than that," he answered grimly. "Our world used to be so green and full of water, with animals and fish everywhere. Now look at us. We're clinging to life on a dry, burnt piece of rock, self-contained in our little cities, ignoring the fact that this has happened, thinking everything's OK as long as we're in our bubbles."

Aphra shrugged. "The probes are still looking for other planets to inhabit."

"They've been looking for years," he said. "Centuries. In the meantime, we have more of our fishbowl cities up there on the moon. Why? Just because we can."

It interested her that he spoke with such passion on such an ordinary subject. "Why does it bother you? It's good that we have everything we need to build cities—even on the moon. It shows that we aren't reliant on nature."

"Remove nature, and you remove humanity."

What a strange person. No wonder he lived out in a place like this. "I don't understand," she said. "Our life is good, and we have made so many advances and have attained great knowledge."

He smiled. "You watch too much TV. Great knowledge doesn't mean great wisdom." He walked to the edge of the rock and looked into the sky. "Don't you find it incredible that a couple of centuries ago the sea would have been over our heads here?"

"Was it really?"

"Water covered about 70 percent of the earth. Don't tell me you didn't know that."

She looked out at the sea, trying to imagine what it must have been like. "No, I didn't. I knew it was a lot, but I had no idea it was that much. There mustn't have been many cities then."

"There were more than there are now," he answered, looking down at her. "You don't know much history, do you?"

"I never thought it was important. The present is the only thing that matters."

He nodded. "In a way. But history is important because it shows us how we got here."

The moment Birn finished speaking, Aphra felt herself falling. The stone floor rose up to meet her, then everything became black.

❯   ❯   ❯

"Nothing," said Jamon.

Sevig frowned. He looked up at Craf, who stood motionless by the window, the daylight reflecting off his metal body. "This is definitely his work. I knew it. It was very crude of him to do this."

"Yet he fooled you, sir," said Craf.

"Yes, he did," Sevig agreed, not offended. "He is a clever one. He has made things a little more difficult, but not impossible. First priority is to find the fem—" he paused mid-sentence and his eyes narrowed.

"You have an idea?" Craf asked, interested.

Sevig looked appraisingly at Craf. "I do, my friend. A sudden flash of inspiration, you might say."

"Another sense of yours," Craf said. "I want that kind of intuition. Give me that faculty."

"We're still working on that one. It is not easily manufactured."

"Incoming call from Antha," said Jamon.

"Display," Sevig answered.

A face appeared in the screen before him.

"Have you thought about my deal?" came a drawling voice.

Sevig's composed expression did not alter. "Do you have something to show me?"

"I will have, if you agree."

Sevig looked away from the screen in disgust. "That's not good enough. I've told you my conditions. Disconnect."

"Disconnected," said Jamon. The screen disappeared.

"Amateur," breathed Sevig.

❯   ❯   ❯

"She's coming out of it."

"Aphra, can you hear me?"

Aphra opened her eyes wearily and looked up into Lev's face. She said nothing, but looked into Lev's dark eyes with confusion. Every detail of Lev's face stood out clearly to her—the long eyelashes, the sparkle in the depths of her eyes, the smooth chocolate skin, the sleek black hair.

"You're not Marlena," she muttered. "You're a person."

"It's me: Lev. You're here with me and Birn, remember?"

Aphra sat up from the couch she was lying on and looked around at the lab.

"Do you remember?" Birn asked. "Are you OK?"

"I don't know," Aphra said. She was silent for a few moments while she tried to think. "Everything seemed fine. You were talking, then I just blacked out."

"Do you want Omega to give you a medical scan?" Lev asked.

"No. No, I don't need anything. I just want to go home."

"I'm not sure that's a good idea," Lev said, gi   quizzical look.

"Aphra," began Birn, "we are able to mask you   that you can't be traced, but once you get inside   ment, or even inside the building, the chances a   will know you are there. And once we leave you   nothing you can do to hide."

She had difficulty returning his gaze. It felt very   ing, blacking out like that. She wished she were   from their scrutiny. "Didn't you say he wouldn't   knew anything about Ryan?"

"I'm pretty certain he would think nothing of it   "He probably would think nothing of it if you ha   discontinue Ryan himself. But the fact remains th

Mari after you, and I'm not sure why. There's no certainty you'll be safe if you go home now."

"And don't forget that guy outside the cave who seemed to be looking for something," Birn added.

"I want to go home," Aphra said simply. She had no clear idea of what she should do once back at her home, but the events of yesterday seemed so far removed from reality that she was beginning to think she had imagined everything.

"I'll take her," Gun said firmly.

His voice came from behind Aphra. She turned her head sharply to look at him, surprised that he was there.

"Then she can see for herself whether or not she is wanted," he continued.

"No," Lev said, "I don't think—"

"She'll be perfectly safe," Gun interrupted. "I'll ensure she is. You know that."

Birn folded his arms. "If you're going, I'll come, too."

"You don't need to," Gun said. "What could you do that Omega couldn't? We'll be shielded. I'll get Aphra out of there if there's any danger. You go on to Cantabria, and I'll meet you there if anything happens. We'll be all right," he said confidently. "Trust me."

"I know you will," Lev answered, but worry showed in her eyes. "Be careful, and stay in close contact with us in case there's trouble."

Gun looked down at Aphra. "Let's go."

"I—wait a minute—" she stuttered.

"You want to go home? I'm ready to take you."

Aphra stood meekly and followed him to the doorway of the lab.

"Aphra, you're welcome to come back here if you need to," Lev said. "We will monitor you and make sure that it's safe for you to be home again once you're there. Take care of her, Gun."

Aphra glanced back at Lev and Birn before she left the lab. Their concern for her had been touching and unexpected, yet she hoped she would not have to return. She wanted to resume her life as though nothing had ever happened. Things like this never happened to her. Her life was predictable. And, she suddenly realized, dull.

She walked along behind Gun down the corridor, looking at his long black hair and the straightness of his back. Now she would have to be alone with him in a sky car.

I need some Confidence and Tranquility, she thought, wishing that Omega could give her some. Confidence and Tranquility, she repeated over in her mind, willing it to come.

They came to the garage, and she looked at the two sky cars inside, one the steel blue vehicle she recognized from yesterday, and the other a dusky green. The door dematerialized on the green one, and Gun got in. Aphra got in nervously after him. She sat there quietly, trying not to fidget, and watched the garage door as it closed, causing the warm light of the sitting room to disappear behind it.

The interior lights of the sky car glowed softly in the darkness, illuminating Gun slightly. When he spoke, his voice seemed to reach closely around her in the small space. "Casey, we're going to Min City, and I need all safeguards in place. Give me warnings of any moving objects in your scanning range."

"Understood," came the pleasant fem voice of the computer. "I should probably tell you that there are signs of life at five zero sixty-four. It's just Julian, though."

"Continue," Gun said. He reached into a side compartment and took out a small chain. This he put on over his wrist. It was the same kind of chain Aphra had seen Birn wearing, and she wondered how it could possibly work as an imprint. Imprints were only supposed to work in living flesh and bone, and it was supposedly impossible to duplicate them by any means.

Daylight flooded into the cave as the outer door opened swiftly; they sped out and into the glare of the day. The cave door closed swiftly behind them, and the high rock formation seemed like any other once again. Aphra looked sidelong at Gun, who ignored her and gazed straight ahead.

"Music," he said.

Instantly, music blared into life, and Aphra breathed easier now that she did not have to think of making conversation with him.

"Computer," she whispered against the window, careful to not let Gun see her speak.

"Yes, Aphra?" came Casey's voice close to her ear.

"Can you give me some Tranquility and Confidence?"

"I'm sorry, I'm not equipped with that."

"Not you, too! I need it," Aphra replied, gritting her teeth.

"I will change the music to something more soothing," said Casey. "That should help."

"Stupid music," muttered Aphra.

4

N OW AND THEN as they sped along the rocky landscape Aphra saw Gun nod his head and his lips moving in speech. What he said was drowned out by the music, and she wondered what he and the computer were talking about. Once, as she was looking at him, he turned and looked steadily at her, an expression in his face that she could not decipher. The gaze from his dark eyes became too much for her and she felt herself blush, so she quickly turned her head and looked out through the side window. She made herself think of Michael and how he would look and smile at her and make her feel at ease with him. It would be good to be home and with him again.

Their journey to Min City was uneventful. When Aphra saw the familiar half-circle of blue bulging on the horizon, she began to relax and stopped gripping her knees so tightly. The sky car sped closer and closer, and the city loomed up before them. The music that had filled the sky car since they had left the cave abruptly stopped, and Aphra heard Gun talking.

"It is vital," he said.

"Understood," answered Casey.

Gun turned to Aphra. "Once inside the city you will not run from me. You will stay by my side."

"I'll do whatever I want to," Aphra retorted.

"No, you won't," he replied coolly. "Casey will make sure of that, so don't bother to struggle. You'll only look demented."

She began chewing what was left of her fingernails.

They drew nearer the city and joined the stream of sky cars making their way to the transparent access tubes.

"Lev," he said.

"Yes," came the sound of Lev's voice.

"We're on our way in now. Stay close."

"We have your position; go ahead," Lev said. "Cease communication until inside."

They entered one of the ingoing tubes and flew swiftly along its length. Thin circles of colored light flashed across the sky car, and the round steel station at the end of the tube loomed nearer, its base shining like a pool of water. The sky car flew across it and out into the clear warm sunshine of Min City. Aphra looked around with relief.

"Park in Greyston building, above ground," Gun said.

"OK," said Casey.

The traffic was thick, and they zoomed in and out of the criss-crossing streams of vehicles. The sky car slowed, and they entered the open side of a tall parking building and maneuvered into a space.

Gun glanced at Aphra, then looked beyond her through the window. "Everything in place?"

"Of course," Casey answered.

"We're with you," came Lev's voice.

The car doors opened, and Aphra got out eagerly. She was home now and did not need Gun anymore. She made to run—but could not. It was as Gun had said: a force field held her. The warm, stabilizing sensation enveloped her like a cocoon. She stood meekly by the car and turned back to look at Gun.

She was startled to see that he had undergone a significant change in appearance. He was now a white, middle-class citizen, with short, neatly combed brown hair and blue eyes. He even wore a suit. A thought occurred to Aphra, and she looked down at herself—

She saw black hair resting on her shoulder.

She looked back at Gun and he smiled, feigning familiarity with her. He came around the car and took her hand in his, and they began to walk away. She tried to speak, but found she could not. It scared her that his computer could do something like that to her.

She walked across the parking garage with him, wondering how it was that no sensors could see what he was doing to her. She longed to hear the blast of an alarm and to see him struck down, but they walked casually along, unmolested. They entered a luminire, and the door closed behind them.

"Destination?"

"Tunin district," Gun replied.

Aphra knew then that he had read her imprint and found out where she lived.

"Thank you," said the computer after a moment, and the door opened.

Aphra looked out at her neighborhood, glad to see it again.

Gun led her away from the luminire. "We have to be quick."

They walked swiftly through the busy crowd, hand in hand. His hand was warm in hers, and she looked up at him and caught herself enjoying the closeness she felt at that moment. Then she told herself to stop being ridiculous, that he did not care about her but was only escorting her home as a favor to Lev.

As they walked along she saw a familiar advertisement playing on one of the large screens high up on a building, extolling the greatness of the Personifid Project. She thought, as she always did when she saw it, that she must get the process done for herself when she had enough credits. Over the course of her extended life she would save a bundle on doctor's visits and medicine that were always necessary for a natural body. And of course she would live forever. How could you put a price tag on that?

Citizens, human and inhuman, walked along the streets, shadows of overhead sky cars and hover-riders flitting across their faces, hand-sized screens floating ahead of them as they held conversations or watched TV. Others passed by silently, considerate enough to receive audiocasting pinpointed to their ears only. The air smelled like rain—not that Tunin district was usually scheduled to receive a rainfall simulation, since most citizens there were against it, but the smell was often enjoyed.

It was not long before Aphra saw the green rectangular lines of her apartment block towering ahead of them. Glimpses of it were visible behind the knot of dodecahedron apartments that were bowing and raising slowly like mechanical dancers showing off their colors, winking in the sunlight as sky cars flew around and under them. Aphra glanced up at Gun. He seemed watchful but aloof.

They came to her apartment building too soon, and she reluctantly let go of Gun's hand. They walked in under the building—the ground floor was wide open to pedestrians, as a street continued right through. Sights and sounds assaulted them there—the building's dozen or more huge round support columns had advertisement screens wrapped around them, and the ceiling overhead was ablaze with moving light as still more advertisements played. Gun's brown hair was tinged orange, then blue, then red as they passed under different ads.

Four green luminires, solid and noticeable by their lack of advertising, were set in a square beneath the center of the building. These were usable only by the building's occupants. Some of Min City's apartment buildings did not have lifts, but simply had their own luminires as this one did. It increased the cost of living there, but since luminires had fewer mechanical moving parts to worry about, it reduced the possibility of breakdowns.

"Your apartment is 1437, correct?" Gun asked as they came to the luminires.

She nodded as they stepped inside one of them. The luminire door slid shut behind them, encasing them in silence.

"One-four-three-seven," Gun said before the computer had a chance to ask for the destination.

"Hello, Aphra," said the computer.

"Blast!" Gun said.

"Here you are," said the computer, and the door opened.

"We're uncovered," Gun said urgently. "How did that happen?"

"Unsure," came Lev's voice.

Gun ran with Aphra along the hall to her apartment door. It slid open. Like the building luminires, her apartment's door had been set to penetrate the mask in place around Aphra's wrist. Gun pushed her inside.

Aphra's apartment was as she had left it. She stood in the middle of the small living room and saw nothing out of the ordinary. Perhaps she really could go on with her life as before. Perhaps there was nothing to worry about anymore. She smiled as she saw her Michael sitting there in an easy chair.

"We're inside," Gun said as the door slid shut. "Place the shield."

"Marlena," Aphra called, relieved that the numbness in her throat had gone, allowing her to speak again. "Marlena, show yourself." No answer came from Marlena, and she did not materialize, but Michael got up and moved toward Aphra.

"Hello, darling," he said, holding his hands out to her.

"Casey, begin," Gun said.

Aphra heard his sky car computer's voice respond. "Searching," said Casey.

"I have set the door on a changing lock," Lev said. "We have detected Mari—he has just left the luminire and is in the hall now. I knew it! Gun, get her out of there right away."

"OK," Gun said. "Talk to you later. Casey, disconnect."

"Marlena!" Aphra called again, wondering where her friend could be.

Gun stood just inside the door, looking at Michael. "Your computer is probably not here."

"Darling," Michael said, hugging Aphra tightly. "I've missed you. Where have you been? I was worried."

She returned his hug, feeling a little embarrassed that Gun was there. She was sure he would know Michael was an android companion. She wondered if she could pass him off as a personifid instead. "Not so tight," she whispered, as Michael began to squeeze her.

He kept squeezing. "I missed you."

"Ow, let go!" she squealed, surprised that he would disregard her request.

"I missed you," he repeated, his arms around her like a vice.

Aphra struggled. "Michael, you're hurting me. Release!"

The arms tightened with the remorselessness of a machine.

There was a brief flash of red light and the staccato clacking sound of a laser weapon firing. Michael's grip released, and he staggered back from Aphra, holding his side.

"No!" Aphra cried.

Gun shot him repeatedly, and Michael fell to the floor.

"No!" She knelt beside Michael's body and cradled his head in her arms. "How could you do this to him! I love him!"

"Absurd," Gun said, holstering his weapon. "It's just an android."

"Marlena!" Aphra shouted. "Marlena, I need you! Save Michael!"

"I just told you, your computer is not here," Gun said.

"He's right, Aphra."

She froze at the sound of the familiar voice. Surely that was Sevig, but how had he transmitted audio into her apartment? Audiocasting by ultrasonic waves without invitation should have been blocked by Marlena, so as not to allow just any old person to transmit in. It was understandable that Gun could retain his personal link to his computer through his pseudo imprint, but to have unauthorized entry by this new voice?

He spoke again, and this time she became more certain that it was Sevig. "Your Marlena is currently in my possession."

"Big surprise," Gun said uninterestedly.

"Name yourself!" barked Sevig.

Gun went over to the window and looked down at the busy traffic routes. "No."

"Where is Lavinia?" Sevig said. "I know I heard her voice. Tell me where she is."

Gun ignored him.

"I don't know," Aphra answered.

"Casey, shut her mouth," Gun said.

Aphra felt the same paralysis of her vocal cords. It was a terrifying feeling.

"You, whoever you are," Sevig said, "answer me! Where is Lavinia? I don't know what she thinks she's doing, but she's meddling in something that does not concern her."

"Casey," Gun said, "anything you have to say must be coded and directly implanted into my brain."

"You'll find nothing in the apartment," Sevig said.

Gun stepped away from the window. "Well, you obviously found nothing."

Aphra stood motionless, staring down at Michael in disbelief. The android lay at her feet, thin curls of smoke coming from the damaged body as his vacant eyes gazed at the ceiling. The most disturbing thing was that she did not feel as devastated as she thought she should. In fact, she found herself already thinking of what kind of replacement she would buy.

There was a pounding on the front door.

Mari, Aphra tried to say.

"There's nowhere for you to go," Sevig said.

Gun's calm expression did not change. "That really would presume I haven't thought ahead."

"Lavinia!" Sevig snapped. "I know you're still alive! Now you listen to me—"

His voice was cut off in mid-sentence.

"That's better," Gun said. "Casey, anything?"

Mari shouted threats and continued to pound at the door. Aphra turned and saw that bumps were beginning to appear in the smooth surface. It was such a strange sight that for a moment she could do nothing but stand there and watch.

A sky car suddenly hovered outside the window, casting a shadow into the room.

"Casey, police," Gun said sharply.

It was indeed a police vehicle. Aphra could see four robots inside looking at her. She began to raise her right hand so they would be able to read her imprint more easily. She wanted them to see that she was doing nothing to cause any harm to anybody and that it was Mari they should be focusing on, not her. In a moment, they turned their heads and moved on.

"Clear," Gun said. He paused, listening to Casey's voice in his head. "Yes."

Aphra wondered what he was hearing. He looked her in the eye for a moment, as if sizing her up, calmly ignoring Mari's shouts and attempts to break down the door.

Another sky car paused outside of the window, its windows darkened so they could not see who was inside. Aphra drew back, trying to hide from view.

"Do you have them?" Gun asked.

The sky car abruptly dropped down.

"Yes," Gun said. "OK, we're ready to go."

Aphra suddenly thought of something and went into her bedroom, with Gun following her. Her hand moved to a small panel by the bed, but instead of opening for her, it remained closed, and she struck her fingers against it. She tried again, moving her hand to it then away, over and over, but the panel remained closed.

"We've finished here," Gun said. "Time to leave, and you're coming with me."

She nodded readily, the threats and pounding from outside her apartment door not doing anything to make her feel as though she would like to stay and face Mari when he broke through.

She pointed to the panel that she had been trying to open. She pointed emphatically, and finally Gun told Casey to allow her to speak again.

"I need to open this panel," she said. "Can you get Casey to do that?"

Gun drew his weapon again and adjusted it, then shot the panel, leaving a gaping hole in it. The acrid smell of burnt plastic drifted through the room.

Aphra quickly put her hand in and drew out an item, which she then pocketed. She turned and looked at Gun, feeling uncomfortable that she was in her bedroom with him watching her, so she began to walk past him.

He caught hold of her arm. "Stay in here."

"No," she said, and shook his grip from her.

"Yes." He clutched her tighter. "Stay close to me."

"Let go!"

"Stay close," he warned, releasing his grip.

"How are we going to get out?"

"We'll get out all right."

She turned her back to him and caught sight of herself in the mirror on the wall. When she saw her reflection, she was startled. She saw her now-black hair and bright blue eyes. It dismayed her a little that this was the appearance he had chosen for her. Black hair had never seemed to suit her. She told herself that it was merely for the purpose of disguise, and not to read any more into it.

"Aphra," Gun said, "come here." He sat on the edge of the bed and indicated the space beside him. "Sit next to me."

"I don't think so," she said, backing away.

"Don't be stupid. I'm not going to do anything to you," he snapped. "Hurry, we don't have much time."

She sat on the bed, but an arm's length away from him.

"Sit close to me and hold my hand," he said with frustration.

She shook her head.

"Aphra, do as he says immediately! The link is breaking, and

I need to bring both of you through at the same time," came the voice of Casey.

Understanding came to her then, and she hastily shifted over to Gun's side and took his hand.

"Don't let go," she heard him say, then the world around her became gray and indistinct.

For a moment she could not breathe, and she gripped tightly to Gun's hand, unable to see anything.

Then gradually her vision cleared, and daylight shone into her eyes. She found herself seated in a moving sky car, and she leaned back with relief into the padded seat. Gun let go of her hand.

"We're here," he said. "Continue."

The sky car surged forward.

Aphra looked out the windows and realized they were outside of Min City. She turned in her seat and looked at the city behind them. For a moment she was speechless, amazed at the power that had brought her here. She knew it was no easy thing to transfer through the shields of the city. It was not something the average citizen could do with an average personal computer. Only high-powered luminires could do that. She thought of the large power applicator units back at Lev and Birn's laboratory.

"Casey, return us to natural appearance," Gun said.

Aphra looked at him now. His tanned skin, long black hair, and dark eyes reappeared. He glanced at her. "So you're a blonde," he remarked impassively.

She looked down at her shoulder-length hair and saw the dark gold tints of her original color that had come back. "Mirror, Casey."

A small mirror materialized before her face, and she looked at herself and at her gray blue eyes, glad to see a familiar appearance again. She looked at Gun and the mirror disappeared. "What was all that about? What was going on back there?"

"Tricky business," he said, and leaned back into his seat. His expression was serious and brooding as he gazed out at the dry landscape.

She hesitantly touched his arm to try and draw his attention. "But why am I involved? What does it have to do with me?"

"You believe now that they are after you?"

"Yes, but why? Lev said Sevig probably wouldn't care about what I'd seen."

His dark eyes moved to her face, but she could not discern what meaning was in his steady gaze. "You have something they want."

"You were looking for it in my apartment?"

He nodded.

"What? What do I have?" she asked, confused.

He looked out again at the landscape. "Something Ryan gave you."

At the sound of his name she felt a pang of fear and sorrow. "But what? Ryan never gave me anything. When?"

"Information, and I don't know when he gave it to you."

She thought of the times they had met and tried to remember if Ryan had ever given her a gift. "I'm telling you, he never gave me anything."

"That's what you think."

"What's that supposed to mean?"

He turned back to watching the poisoned landscape as it sped beneath them.

Aphra sighed. "Why me?"

"I don't know." He shut his eyes. "Casey, music."

Instantly, pounding music filled the sky car, making it

impossible to talk to him. Aphra turned her face to the window. She could see many other sky cars traveling in the same direction, spread out above and below them, speeding across the sunbaked rock. Gun's words did not make sense to her, and the events back in her apartment were confusing.

If Sevig was so concerned about her witnessing Ryan's death, did it mean he really had been responsible in some way? The thought was inconceivable. The benevolent head of Sevig Empire, the genius responsible for the Personifid Project, the hope of mankind? He had always had detractors—what genius did not? But to think he could actually be associated with wrongdoing...it was impossible.

And now this talk of information from Ryan? What information? He had never said anything about his work in the personifid laboratories. He had hardly said anything personal at all. The only time he had, it was about his wife, and even then he had never said her name. As for something tangible that could be found in her apartment, she was sure Ryan had given her no such thing.

Yet the fact remained that her door had been pummeled out of shape and someone had modified her Michael to act bizarrely and had taken Marlena. She hoped Marlena was all right. A computer like that was worth a lot of credits. The upgrading alone would cost dearly, let alone any damage that might be done to her. As for Michael, well, she tried not to think about him.

"I can't see her," he said in answer to the voice, at a loss for what he should do now. His direction had seemed so clear before, but now he was motionless, as all action had been stripped from him. A heaviness in his limbs puzzled him, and he found himself looking for reasons why. Too many questions began to fill his mind. They were his own thoughts this time. He tried to hear them, for he felt they were important. But the voice spoke again, obliterating everything.

❭   ❭   ❭

After a while, Aphra realized they were not heading in the direction of Lev and Birn's home. She looked at Gun, who sat comfortably, head resting back and eyes closed.

"Casey, where are we going?" she asked quietly, under cover of the music.

"We are taking a detour," said Casey, "as Gun thinks it is best. We don't want to lead anyone to Lev and Birn's place."

"Are we being followed?" Aphra asked, turning and looking nervously out the back of the sky car.

"Uncertain," replied Casey.

Aphra shrank down in her seat.

"Don't fear," said Casey. "No one can see you. For those who attempt to see through our opacity, they will see only what I cause them to see."

Aphra relaxed a little. "I need some Tranquility. Give me some."

"I am not equipped with any," replied Casey. "You don't remember you asked me that before?"

"No," Aphra said, uninterested. "I'm hungry; are you at least able to get some food delivered?"

"Not at this time."

"Why not?"

"Because I would have to use an imprint to order the food, and we are currently secured with a mask. Using an imprint would be an indicator of where and who we are."

"Oh, whatever," Aphra said grumpily.

After some time, the music in the car ceased. The windscreen before her darkened and then became light again, revealing a man sitting at a desk. Gun sat up.

"Request authorization," the man said, looking at Gun.

"Sending," Gun replied.

The man looked slightly to the left on his screen, as he scanned the data scrolling down. "Accepted," he said. "Please prepare yourself; transportation will take place in five seconds. Cease all communications."

Gun nodded.

The screen darkened.

"What's happening?" Aphra asked, suddenly fearful.

Gun said nothing.

"We are entering Cantabria," answered Casey.

Cantabria was a huge underground city that had been built long ago before the dome-like shieldings of aboveground cities had been perfected. Populated mainly by those who did not trust the aboveground's safety, Cantabria was also home to many "Earthers"—people who shunned artificiality in their own appearances. Nowhere else were people as free to age with wrinkles and gray hair if they so chose, or to have an older model robot and have no fear of it being collected by scrappers.

Suddenly, they plunged downwards. Aphra's stomach seemed to hang in the air for an instant. She looked out her side window, but it was also darkened. The sky car sped down and down, and she gripped her seat with both hands.

"Don't fear, Aphra," said Casey, "your personal force field is in place."

Aphra did not lessen her grip. "Where are we going?" she

wailed, feeling as though they were descending into a bottomless pit.

Gun ignored her.

"You are safe," said Casey. "We will be stopping soon."

Aphra gritted her teeth and closed her eyes as she clutched tightly to the seat. Down and down they went. She wondered when they were ever going to stop.

Finally they began to slow, and Aphra opened her eyes cautiously. She could see a glow of light beneath them, growing brighter by the second until they ceased moving. She looked out the windows. They were in a large, brightly lit hangar. It had gray concrete walls and a concrete floor dusted with a smattering of sooty marks—some of which were busily being cleaned by small gray disc-shaped robots. Four other sky cars were stationary on the ground some distance away from them, while a dozen more moved slowly, low to the ground, through the hangar toward a gaping black opening in the far wall. She saw other robots and human figures moving around. One robot whizzed toward their sky car and circled them swiftly, analyzing every part of the vehicle. Then it stopped, and Gun's door opened.

"Wait here," Gun said to Aphra, as he stepped out.

She watched as he stood and waited for the two androids who were walking toward him. One was very tall and bulkily built—it towered above Gun and looked down at him with menace.

"It's just programmed to look that way; it's just programmed to look that way," Aphra whispered to herself as she leaned across the seats and looked up at the large android.

The other android was very short. The top of its head just reached Gun's belt. It looked almost like a child, a young girl, but the voice it spoke in was a deep, metallic, nonpersonalized tone. In its left hand was a small weapon, and Aphra saw that the android's finger was on the trigger. It came closer to the open door and stared in at Aphra, unblinkingly. "You have an imprint," it said matter-of-factly. "Remain where you are."

She sat back in her seat. "Casey, what is all this?" she whispered.

"Your computer is not permitted to respond at this time," said the small android.

After a moment, Gun bent down and looked in at Aphra. "It's OK now," he said. "Get out."

"That one told me to stay here," she replied, pointing at the android.

Aphra's door opened as she spoke, and she turned and saw that two robots stood looking in at her, so she cautiously stepped out of the sky car. The air was cool in the large hangar, and she looked up at the high steel ceiling and wondered how she and Gun had entered the hangar, as there were no signs of any opening above them.

Cantabrian security was unusual in that it relied heavily on robotic units to personally examine every visitor. There was no standard, generalized scan as in the entrances to other cities, but each robot or android intercepted any visitors and made their own judgments first. Then, and only then, were the visitors released from the hangars and permitted access into the city proper.

As Aphra looked around the hangar, she saw many models of androids and robots that she did not recognize. It made her feel as though she had come into a foreign land. One of the robots that stood near her was a low, chunky gray model with no noticeable head or limbs, although many panels hinted at the possibility of such inner workings. Another was balanced on one wheel, archaic as that was, with a humanoid-shaped upper body and chiseled head. The latter robot took hold of her right hand, and she drew back, startled, then realized that it had snapped a firm wrap around her wrist, covering her imprint. It was a thick, rubbery kind of plastic that fit snugly. She could still bend her wrist, but the wrap stayed firmly in place.

"You are free to continue," said the large android who stood over by Gun. "Enjoy your time here. Your sky car will be parked in Quadrant C." Having said that, it walked away to another sky car that had just come down through the roof of the large hangar.

Gun began to walk away, too, and Aphra moved quickly after him.

"Why are we here?" she asked, rubbing her wrist.

"It's best for now," he answered, not slowing. He looked down at her, and his face momentarily softened as he saw her anxious expression.

They came to one of the hangar's walls, and a door slid open before them. Instantly a hubbub of sound came to them, infused with rich and spicy scents. Aphra saw a busy street and buildings before her with an immense, high steel ceiling overhead. They walked through the door, and it slid shut behind them.

"There you are!" called a familiar voice.

Aphra felt relieved to see the welcoming face of Birn. He stood up from his seat at a table outside a small café and walked over to them.

"You got here all right then," he said warmly, smiling at her and Gun.

"No problems," Gun answered.

Birn laid his hand on Aphra's shoulder. "How are you doing?"

"I don't know," she said, looking up at him. "Confused."

"Well, that's life," he said mildly. "You look different."

She fingered her blonde hair self-consciously and said nothing.

"Lev made me promise I would remember to ask you if you have eaten anything lately," he said, his face creasing into a grin.

"No, I haven't." She eyed the large number of people, personifids, androids, and robots going about their business. She found herself staring at some of them. It was an eclectic mix of old and new, tarnished and gleaming. "Are we safe here?"

"We should be," Birn said with a smile. "This is Cantabria."

"I don't know this place. I've heard of it, but I kind of thought it didn't exist anymore."

They began to move along the main walkway.

"Really?" Birn asked, surprised. "Where've you been hiding yourself?"

She shrugged. "Nowhere."

They walked slowly along the street together, following behind Gun. Aphra saw pubs, game houses, personifid styling shops, cafés, and numerous other gathering places. Robots brushed past, some on wheels, some on metal feet, and she looked at them in amazement. Many of them were of an older design and should have been dumped or recycled eons ago.

The people were also intriguing. Most were dressed very casually and sat in small groups at tables outside the places of business, idly watching passersby while talking to each other. People in the streets did not seem to be rushed or have an air of busyness about them. That struck her as very strange, very different from Min City. Many of them seemed quite odd to her—something about their faces seemed rough and uneven. The fems' faces, especially, seemed to be lacking vibrance. Their craggy, lined faces unnerved her. She had never seen such people before. Death seemed to be written clearly in every line.

> ❯ ❯ ❯

"They've gone to Cantabria, sir," said the voice of Jamon.

"That hole in the ground?" Sevig asked, looking up from the screen on his desk. "You're certain?"

"Yes, sir," his computer replied. "Her imprint has appeared in the entry logs of Cantabria."

"Do we have anyone in place there?"

> ❯ ❯ ❯

"Aphra," Birn said.

She opened her eyes and looked blearily up at him. He was bending over her, his rough hand gently touching her cheek while he looked at her with concern in his eyes.

"What happened? Where am I?"

She found she was lying on the pavement of a crowded street. She tried to get up, and he helped her. He led her off the street and over to a nearby seat.

"You fainted again," he said. "You're scaring me. I think you should go to a doctor."

"No," she muttered. "I'll be fine. I just need something to drink. Go get me something. Get me a Blue Horse." She realized as soon as she finished speaking that she had ordered him to do something just as she would have ordered a nonperson. She covered her face with her hands and hoped he had not noticed.

"A Blue Horse," Birn said. "OK. I should get you something to eat as well. Wait here." He got up and weaved across the pedestrian traffic to enter a café. She looked around, wondering where Gun was. She could see no sign of him anywhere, and she felt a sense of disappointment that he had left her. Perhaps her fainting had disgusted him—displaying such weakness or illness was sure to be very unattractive.

A thought occurred to her, and she reached into her pocket. She drew out the thin rectangular item she had taken from her apartment. It was a portable Life Enhancer. She held it to her lips. "Tranquility." She pressed it against her temple and felt the calmative enter her body. She checked to see if Birn was coming back yet, but did not see him. "Strength," she said, then pressed the Life Enhancer against her temple again.

Aphra was sitting quietly when Birn came back.

"You look better," he said. "Sitting down did you some good, it seems." He handed her a tall blue drink and a burrito, and she took them both without meeting his eyes.

"Where's Gun?" she asked, sipping the drink.

Birn sat next to her. "Gone to his favorite watering hole, no doubt."

"Is Lev here?"

"No."

She sniffed the burrito, wondering if it had been prepared by a person. "Why are we here, Birn? Why didn't we just go back to your place?"

"We're here because we didn't want to lead anyone to Lev," he said. "This is a good place for us to be—no weapons can be used here. Everyone who comes to Cantabria gets their weapons disabled. It's a peaceful city," he said in answer to her incredulous expression. "So, it's down to brute force if anyone wants to harm us, and the last person who tried that on me didn't come off too well."

"I don't doubt it," she said, looking at his muscular build.

"But surely you'd be no match for a personifid? Mari's one, isn't he?"

"Yes, he is, but I do all right for myself," he said, and grinned suddenly.

"You're ... well ... what I mean is ... "

He guffawed. "Spit it out, Aphra. Go on."

"Well, you're ... *not* a personifid, are you?" Although she felt certain he was not, she just wanted to make sure.

He laughed. "Aren't I too scruffy-looking to be one? No, I'm not a personifid. They're not going to suck my soul out and put it in a synthetic body. I've never got into that idea, somehow. You?"

"No, I'm not one," she said, taking a bite of her burrito. "I want to get it done, though."

"Why?"

"So I can live forever, of course."

He looked at her appraisingly. "Are you afraid of death?"

She was surprised by his bluntness and took a moment to collect herself. "Naturally. Aren't you?"

"No."

She looked sideways at him, unsure whether he meant what he said. "Now that we know for sure we have souls that are distinct from our bodies, I really can't stand the thought of floating around who knows where once my body is discontinued."

He nodded slowly. "You know, though, ancient sages knew of the existence of the soul. It took a long time for science to catch up to that. It's nothing new, really."

She took a sip of Blue Horse. "But the sages couldn't prove it. They just had fanciful imaginations."

"Did they?" he said, raising his eyebrows.

"How could they have known?"

He looked at her and said nothing. She met his gaze, trying

to perceive from his expression what his thoughts were. She supposed they had something to do with him being a Follower. She had heard their approach to being discontinued was quite different from what was normal and accepted. They expected new, permanent bodies to be given to them by the Tri-une Soul. And not only that, but they then lived in another, unseen dimension with that divine being. Aphra did not know what to think of the idea at all. She preferred having the ability to stay in this life and control where she would live and whom she would be with.

She smiled at Birn, relieved he did not seem to be going to say anything more on the subject. "What are we going to do here? And how long do we have to stay until things are cleared up?"

"I need to wait to hear from Lev," Birn said. "We have to get Mari and Sevig off your back first by finding out what they want."

"Gun said that Ryan had given me something, but I don't remember him ever giving me anything."

"Really?" Birn said.

"Not a thing." She took a bite. "This is good," she said, waving the burrito.

He smiled, but she could see that he smiled with his lips and not his eyes and that his thoughts were elsewhere.

"I think we should find Gun and decide what to do from there," he said.

"How about a game first?" she said, looking appealingly at him. "I saw a games room back that way somewhere."

"You can think of playing a game at a time like this?"

"What can I say? I'm addicted to gameplaying."

He smiled, the concern on his face easing. "Well, maybe it would be a good idea to have a break before we move on again."

She polished off her meal, and they walked together down a side street and around a winding walkway. As they walked along between the low buildings, Aphra looked up at containers of flowers hung by the windows and saw the colorful heads drooped over the side as if they were looking down at her. She smiled at the sight of them. There were no sky cars humming through the air under the steel roof that sheltered Cantabria, and she could see no buildings over four stories high. They passed entry points to the lower levels of the city, and Aphra looked down at the stairwells, interested in the unusual sight of them. Lifts were available, too, but she did not see many that were marked as also being luminires. Music drifted to Aphra's ears from different places, as did distant laughter and the chatter of voices. She walked leisurely beside Birn, enjoying the sights and smells, her thoughts wandering to Gun.

Presently they came to a brightly lit building, sound effects and music blasting from its open doors. Above the doors, colorful images of running people were projected. Aphra paused and looked up at them as they changed and became lions and tigers running from sharp-horned deer. The display then changed again, and she saw a girl swinging from a trapeze and then tumbling gracefully through the air. Each sample game was interspersed with the words "Out of This World" spinning closer and closer, then freezing just as they seemed to be right before her face.

"Come on," Birn said, touching her arm.

They walked through the doors and into the busy foyer. A large hairy creature came up to them. Aphra could see through it, for it had been designed to be partly transparent.

"Welcome to Out of This World," it said, clasping its hands together and bowing slightly. "Do you have a specific game in mind, or do you want one made for you?"

Birn looked at Aphra.

She shrugged. "Make us one."

"Fun, fear, or fury?" it asked.

"Fun," Birn and Aphra said simultaneously, and then they smiled at each other.

"If you will step into our preparation luminire, we will devise you a game and ready your minds for projection," it said, and ambled to one of the many luminires that stood in the foyer.

Aphra stepped in after Birn, feeling excited. They sat down on the white benches inside the small room.

"Enjoy your game," said the hairy administrator. It smiled at them as the door of the luminire closed smoothly.

"Preparation beginning," came the calm voice of the computer. "Please relax. If at any time you require assistance, don't hesitate to ask. Your game will be designed specifically for your mind type. We hope you enjoy your Out of This World experience. Game will—" the voice broke off. "Malfunction," it said. "Malfunction. Unable to—"

"What's happening?" Aphra said.

"Full phase alert," said the computer. "Remain seated. You are unauthorized matter. Full phase alert."

"What's going on?" Aphra exclaimed, looking anxiously at Birn.

"I don't know," he said. "Keep calm. I'm sure it'll be all right."

"The police have been notified," said the computer. "Remain seated until they take custody of you."

"Why exactly will they take custody of us?" Birn demanded.

"Unauthorized matter," said the computer.

"Define that."

"Unable to," came the reply.

"Give me access to my sky car computer," Birn said.

"Unable to."

"OK, I can remember this," muttered Birn, and tilted his head back and looked up at the ceiling.

"What are you doing?" Aphra asked.

"*Sshh*. Let me think." In a moment he spoke in a clear firm voice. "Computer, gei gim. Seven nine three, access Gina twenty-four, five, hanowa bright eight—" he paused, and screwed his eyes shut tightly, "—gevin yol forty, three three love diamond." He stopped and opened his eyes.

There was silence in the booth, and Birn held his hand up to Aphra, warning her to keep quiet.

"Birn," said Gina's voice suddenly.

"Gina?"

"Yes," his computer replied.

"Send a message to Lev, tell her that Aphra and I are being taken into Cantabrian police custody. The only reason given is 'unauthorized matter.'"

"Understood," said Gina.

Birn sighed with relief. Then he suddenly sat up straighter. "Gina, erase your traces," he said urgently.

"I would have done that even if you had not asked me to," came the reply.

The door of the luminire opened.

Four tall faceless robots were clustered in front of the doorway. On first sight of them, Aphra drew back in dismay. There was no friendliness factored into their design, no little touch to personalize their faces, but simply three pinpricks in the center of their small, oblong heads that functioned as sensory transmission ports. But then she saw their logos marked in relief on their torsos and realized they were police units.

"Come with us," said one.

Birn stepped out of the luminire, followed closely by Aphra. The robot that had spoken to them closed one of its hands, pressing a button on its palm. Aphra saw the yellow shimmer of a force field appear around her, and another one around Birn. She could no longer hear any sound except what the police said to her. She had never been taken by the police before; it frightened her. Birn smiled encouragingly at her, appearing unruffled. She took heart at that.

They walked along with the police, each having one on either side of them. Other patrons of the games room eyed them with interest. Hovering outside the Out of This World building was a police mobile holding cell, and Aphra and Birn were made to step into it, along with two of the robot police.

The door closed on them, and all was still. The cell took off, jostling the passengers. They stood together in the small enclosed space, with nothing to look at but each other and the dark walls that held them. She saw Birn's lips move in speech as he talked to the robots, and wondered what he said.

When Aphra and Birn stepped out of the holding cell, they found themselves inside an inquiry room at the police station. The robots removed the force fields around the two of them. Then the mobile cell left via the hole in the ceiling, after which the hatch in the ceiling closed silently.

Aphra looked around the doorless room. A large flat screen was upon one wall, and before that stood a large, dark-haired android. He stood very upright, looking straight ahead, and at first Aphra was not sure he had noted their entry. But then he looked down at Aphra and Birn.

"You may address me as Sinclair," he said in a deep voice. "It has come to my attention that you are unauthorized matter. We feel it would be appropriate to isolate you until we have found that you are not posing us a breach in security. It is you, fem, who is the unauthorized matter," he said as his green eyes looked directly at Aphra, "and we feel it is prudent to bring along your companion at this time."

Aphra's blood chilled at his words. What was this thing talking about? He had not said she was *carrying* unauthorized matter but that she actually *was* unauthorized matter. What could that mean?

Birn looked at her.

"We will keep your imprint cover on," said Sinclair to Aphra, "until we have ascertained what you are."

"What do you mean, *what* I am?" sputtered Aphra, finding her voice. "I'm a fem person."

"No, you are not," answered Sinclair firmly. "It is useless for you to keep up any kind of charade with us. Our sensors have penetrated your shielding."

"What?" she exclaimed, shaking her head in disbelief. "What are you talking about?"

Sinclair's steady gaze did not shift from her face. "I don't know whether you honestly don't understand me or that your reaction is something in your defense mechanism."

Birn turned a puzzled face from the android to Aphra, then back again to the android. "What is she, then?"

"A personifid," said Sinclair simply.

"*What?*" she cried. "I'm not a personifid, you hunk of aluminum! I'm a person! A real human." She turned to Birn, and grasped his arm. "Really! I'm not what he says! I never got the Personifid Project done to me! Never! This is crazy, that games room luminire must be junk. I'm a regular person. Period."

Birn only looked at her in surprise. "What exactly is the problem with her being a personifid?" he asked Sinclair.

"But I'm not!" she exclaimed.

"The Out of This World scans detected a dangerous surge

from her," Sinclair said to Birn. "We believe this surge was intended to spike the games room computer. We are trying to ascertain its purpose."

"What?" Aphra shouted. "I'm not! I tell you, I'm not! Why aren't you listening to me? I have no idea what you're talking about. I'm a living, breathing person!"

"Your ranting and raving will not get you anywhere," Sinclair said, "so you may as well keep quiet." The android turned and beckoned to the silent police robots who stood behind them.

Aphra collapsed onto the floor, sobbing. "I'm not," she whimpered, shaking her head. "I'm me." She looked up and wiped away her tears, and then looked down at her wet hands in confusion. "Look, I'm crying. I can't be a personifid." She tasted her tears. "Salty," she said, and held her hands out, as if in proof.

"Take them out of here," said Sinclair to the robots. The ceiling hatch opened, and a circular platform slowly hovered down into the room.

"**YOU MEAN TO** say you don't remember any of the personifid process?" Birn asked as they stepped off the platform and were led away from the inquiry room by the two robots. The sound of their footsteps echoed off the steel walls, the faint smell of lemon cleanser in the narrow corridor. The lighting there was minimal; Aphra had to rely on the guidance of the robot who held her.

"No!" she exclaimed, looking over her shoulder at Birn, barely able to see his face. "Of course I don't remember it; I never got it done! This is the body I was born with!"

"You may have had a mindwipe," he said thoughtfully. "You'll have to wait here a while. I need to find Gun and talk to Lev. Hopefully, freeing you will simply be a matter of credits. We won't leave here without you; don't worry."

"Where will you take me?"

"Back to my place," he said. "Lev'll know what to do with you."

She shook her head. "Is all this because I'm supposed to have some kind of information? Gun said that. You don't want to help me, do you? You just want what you think I've got! What's happening to me? This is all so crazy!"

"I do want to help you, Aphra," he answered. "But we need to find out what's really going on before we can be of any help."

"I'm a real person," she continued without heeding what he said. "I thought we were beginning to be friends. I trusted you. Why don't you trust me?"

He said nothing, but just looked at her.

She met his gaze and tried to determine what emotion was in his eyes, but it was much too dark for her to see his eyes clearly, let alone decipher his expression. "I am a person!" she shouted angrily over her shoulder at him. "My name is Aphra Vessey! I'm twenty-three years old! I have parents and a brother and a sister!" At the thought of them, she crumpled into tears again.

"This way," said one of the robot police, directing Birn to keep walking straight ahead while Aphra and the other robot turned into the corridor to the right.

"Don't worry," Birn said, as they parted. "I'll be back soon."

Aphra was pulled down the corridor, the robot's grip on her arm tight and unyielding. It took her to a small, brightly lit cell and placed her inside.

"Let me out of here!" she screamed, and pummeled at the door. "Your stupid computers are malfunctioning! I'm an ordinary person!"

"Tranquility given," came the voice of a computer.

Aphra wiped the tears from her face and sat with a sigh on the padded shelf. The silence of the cell was overwhelming, and all she could hear was the sound of her own breathing. She looked around at the pale green walls and at the small darkened screen on the wall to her right. She turned her back to it, suddenly self-conscious.

After a moment, she looked down at her hands and the texture of her skin. With two fingers of her left hand, she pinched her right hand hard. She winced and looked down at the white mark she had made on the skin. As she watched, it slowly turned an angry red. "I can't be a personifid," she said. She smoothed her hand, trying to rub away the soreness. "I'm me."

❯   ❯   ❯

"Clever," Sevig hissed, his face dark with anger as he viewed the Cantabrian police files. He looked coldly at Craf and into the black pinpricks that were his eyes.

"Pardon me, sir, but doesn't this tell us that there is a high probability she has what we're looking for?" asked the robot.

"It does," Sevig said, his brow furrowed. "But it also means that our best option is to get hold of her physically rather than try remote access. Who knows what it will do if we try to probe her? We can't risk it. She needs to be in our possession. That way we can contain any little tricks he may have left."

He moved to the window and looked down at the street below, his strong profile illuminated by the night lights of the city. "Where's Mari?"

❯   ❯   ❯

"Aphra Vessey," said a metallic voice.

She jumped in surprise and looked at the open doorway. One of the robotic police stood outside.

"Come with me," it said.

She stood up uncertainly. "Has Birn come to take me already?"

"You have an authorized pickup," said the robot flatly.

She followed the robot as its metal feet clanked loudly on the steel floor down the corridor and out of the cell area.

It paused at the end of the corridor and turned to her. "Here is your release card."

She took the thin plastic strip from its hand, and the robot pointed to a door ahead of her. "I do not want to see you here again. Your fine will increase if you are brought back to us." Then it turned and clanked back down the corridor.

The door slid open for her, and light streamed into her eyes. She squinted a little and went out into the foyer of the police station. The walls were a brilliant, shiny blood red accented in green, startling and vivid at first sight. For a moment she stood still, wondering where to go. The air of the city and the rich aroma of foods breezed in through the wide-open exit in the far side of the foyer. In the middle of the foyer, black seats encircled a bank of angled screens set in a low round pedestal. Some people sat there talking to faces on the screens of those who were imprisoned in the cells.

Birn was nowhere in sight, and as Aphra scanned the dozen or so faces in the foyer, she did a double take. The man with long, wavy light brown hair and pale eyes was walking toward her, a lazy grin on his face. It was the man from the sky car that had been prowling around Lev and Birn's home. Had he followed her all the way from there? She began to move quickly in the direction of the wide exit that led out onto the street. A robotic police unit stood in the middle of the open doorway there, reading the cards of those leaving. "Hel—" she began to call, then almost choked as the power of speech was taken from her and her legs were invisibly bound.

The man stood before her now. She looked up with fright into his calm gray blue eyes while he smirked down at her.

"Come on, my love; let's take you home," he drawled, and took her by the hand.

When she heard his voice and looked closely at his face, realization dawned on her. She knew him! She mouthed his name, still unable to speak, but he did not see her do this. He had already turned away and was leading her to the robot standing in the exit. He passed his own thin card to it, then took Aphra's and handed it over as well.

"Authorized," said the robot, as it scanned their cards. "Free to go."

They walked briskly from the building, her hand still held firmly by him, her feet in step with his. She did not pay any heed to their surroundings; she was still in shock at the sight of him. If only he would look at her and see in her eyes what she had seen in his.

They came to the nearest luminire and entered it.

"Car bay G," the man said.

The door opened, and they got out and stood in the large parking bay. Hundreds of sky cars were packed together in tight, orderly lines.

"Now, where did they leave my vehicle?" he said as he looked out over the sky cars. "Jock McHaggis, where are you?"

In answer to his voice, a burgundy sky car with blue and white flames on the roof rose slowly from its spot twenty meters away from them and made its way over.

"Good boy, now sit," said the man.

The sky car slowly lowered to the ground in front of them, and the nearest door slid open.

"Get in," he said to Aphra, pushing her into the car.

She tumbled onto the seat and sat there hugging herself. She was still unable to speak. But it was nothing artificial that prevented her from being able to take her eyes from his face.

He got in next to her, and the door closed. "Request departure," he said lazily, bending forward to take a small container from the compartment before him.

A square on the windscreen darkened, then became clear, revealing a pleasant fem face looking at them with a smile on her cyan lips. "We hope you enjoyed your time here—" she began.

"Yeah, yeah," said the man, and began to eat small oval snacks from the container.

"We are preparing your departure now—" continued the fem.

"Well, get a move on, will you?" he said. "I don't need to listen to your yammering."

"All communications are disabled until you have left Cantabria," she said. Then she smiled again. "You have been cleared to leave. Please come again." The screen darkened.

"Take us out, Mr. Sulu," said the man.

The sky car moved slowly upward toward the opening that had just appeared in the ceiling above their heads. It increased speed as it was drawn upward into a dark vertical passage.

Aphra gripped her seat tightly. The hatch below them closed, and the lights in the sky car became the only illumination.

"Angus, I would very much like to see a movie," said the man.

"Yes, your worshipfulness," came the slightly deranged-sounding voice of the sky car's computer. "And what would you like to see, you warty old toad?"

"Something from the twenty-first century, in the sci-fi category, methinks," answered the man, leaning back into his seat. "I could do with a good laugh."

"As you wish," droned the computer in a deep voice.

The whole windscreen darkened, and the movie started. Aphra now began to relax in the warmth of the sky car. She still looked at the man, gazing at his face. He stared straight ahead, watching the movie.

Then after a moment he turned to her. "Stop gawking," he said. "I'm trying to watch this. How can I do that with you eyeballing me?"

She said nothing, as her vocal chords were still paralyzed, but she looked at him without fear.

"Stop it, or I'll make you stop," he warned, shaking his finger at her.

She turned away then and looked at the black side window. After a moment, they ceased traveling upward and began moving forward. The window cleared, and she could see the arid landscape around them. The clamped feeling about her throat eased, and she turned back to the man.

"Antha," she said.

"What?" he said lazily, then turned abruptly to look at her, surprise showing on his face. "So you've got my name, have you?" he said, and then turned back to his movie again. "Well, it doesn't matter."

"Antha, it's me: Aphra."

"Yes? Is that supposed to mean something to me?"

"Don't you recognize me?"

"Should I?"

"I'm your sister."

"Oh, hello," he said, looking at her, apparently unmoved. "Prove it."

She began to pull down the thick rubbery covering over her imprint.

"Leave that on," he said hastily, grabbing her wrist.

"Then how can I prove it if you don't read my imprint?"

"OK, just expose it quickly. Boris, read it when you see it," he said to the computer.

Aphra pulled down the covering, revealed her imprint, then quickly covered it up again.

"What have you got, Senór?" Antha asked.

The computer made a sound as though it was clearing its throat. "Announcing Aphra Vessey, twenty-three-year-old fem, who currently squats like a bloated fiend in Min City in the Tunin district—"

"Skip all that," interrupted Antha. "Tell me bloodlines. Bloodlines!"

"Yes, *kemo sabe*! Registered as father, Anthony Goodlea, registered as mother, Lanora Wainright, incubation and birth were synthetic—"

"How nice for you," Antha said, looking down at Aphra.

"Ooh, looky!" the computer said. "DNA taken from screened gene pool AG7—"

"You're top notch," Antha said. "Harold, tell me if there are any registered siblings."

"Two. One of them is you, you ugly mug—"

"Hello, sister," Antha said with mock affection.

"—and the other is Ashley Vessey."

"Did the parents only have volume 'A' from which to choose names?" Antha said derisively. "That's enough, store all her information away in your metal head for a rainy day." He looked at Aphra. "Well, what's your point? You're my sister; so what?"

Aphra's mind was spinning. Her life was playing out like a dream all of a sudden. "Let me go, if our blood ties mean anything to you."

"They don't, so I won't," replied Antha with a grin.

"Don't you remember me? We loved each other once, didn't we? At least that's what I remember."

"I've had my memory removed. You should have it done, too. It makes things so much easier."

Aphra studied his face, trying to determine if he was serious.

"I do wish you would stop staring at me," he said with a mock posh accent. "It does makes one ever so uncomfortable."

"You *are* my brother," Aphra said, desperation creeping into her voice. "I remember you. We played together when we were young!"

"What games did we play?" he asked, looking back to the movie that was still playing on the windscreen.

"I—I don't know."

"Well, I'm convinced. Sister! Come to my arms!" He began to eat snacks from his container again.

Aphra slumped back into her seat. "You're a very strange person."

"Thank you."

"Don't get your knickers in a twist," came the voice of the computer, "but we are being scanned."

"Already?" Antha said, sitting up. "Is it who I think it is?"

"Nope."

"Who then?"

"I can't get that radio station from here," replied the computer.

"Oh, well, we'll try again when we're closer to home," Antha said. He looked at Aphra's wrapped wrist, his brow furrowed in thought. "You're pretty for an android," he said, and pressed his forefinger to her lips while giving her a warning glare. "I don't usually pick your sort up." Antha then altered his voice and spoke in a soft feminine voice. "You'll be so glad you did, honey." He grinned at her and sat quietly a moment, with his finger still pressed against Aphra's lips.

"Scan finished," said the computer, and played the sound of audience applause.

Antha tickled Aphra under the chin and then sat back in

his seat again. "Police," he explained, looking sideways at her. "They're always snooping about and listening in on personal conversations."

"Won't they be able to tell that both voices were you?" Aphra asked.

"Not unless they decide to analyze their sound file and see that it has been tampered with by my computer."

"But they'll know I'm not an android."

"Will they? I wouldn't be too sure about that. Besides, I just want to give them something interesting to listen to. It must be boring being a lump of scrap metal."

❯ ❯ ❯

"She was taken by Cantabrian police but released shortly after," said Jamon.

"Released?" Sevig said. "How could they let her go so soon?"

"Her file appears to have been manipulated to obtain her release. It no longer states she is a personifid with unauthorized matter, but that she was arrested in the act of burglary. Her fine was paid, and she was released."

As the computer talked, Sevig stood from his desk and began to pace in front of the windows of his office.

"I attempted to trace the source that altered her file," said Jamon, "but was cut off. I'm sorry, sir, but whatever it was I encountered had enough power to throw me off. I was not able to realize at once that my tracing had been altered and that I was thrown into a completely different sector. I have never encountered anything like it. I thought I was the most powerful computer there was. You have always told me that."

"Lavinia," Sevig muttered, his hands clenching and unclenching.

"I did, however, obtain the name of the person Aphra was released to. It was Antha Vessey."

"Antha? Well, finally we have some control. He can't be as brainless as I thought. Perhaps his self-proclaimed bounty-hunting prowess is more than just—"

"Incoming call from an unknown source," interrupted Jamon.

Sevig was about to say "display" when a screen flickered to life in front of him and a face appeared.

"Back off, Sevig," Lev said.

Sevig paled and stood still at the sight of her.

"I know what you're doing," she said curtly, "and I will do everything in my power to see that you will *not* recover the data and use it. Drop this, Sevig, or it will ruin you."

Sevig regained his composure and smiled coldly. "It's good to see you again, Lavinia. All this time I'd been thinking you were dead. Imagine my relief when I found out it wasn't true."

"I did what I had to do," she answered. "I decided I wasn't going to be controlled by you any longer." Her brown eyes narrowed, and she looked at him intently. "Is it true that Imogen is still alive? Do you have her, Sevig?"

"Terminate the call," Sevig said.

Lev's face still illuminated the screen. "I'm warning you! If you have any iota of decency left, drop this immediately. You know it's wrong. We were wrong. *Do you have her?*"

"Why is she still there?" Sevig shouted. "Jamon, disconnect!"

Lev looked imploringly at him. "Tell me!"

"I have no idea what you are talking about," he said.

"Sevig, please. Leave it alone."

"Terminate!" shouted Sevig.

"Trying to, sir," came the voice of Jamon.

"Bury it," Lev pleaded. "Destroy it so no one can ever use it! Can't you see it won't work?"

"Terminate!"

"Very well," Lev said. "Since you refuse, I will do everything in my power to stop you from resurrecting our work. And if you have Imogen, I *will* find her. Good-bye, Sevig."

Finally, mercifully, the screen disappeared.

❯   ❯   ❯

"Where are you taking me?" Aphra asked, looking at Antha as he threw small snacks up in the air and caught them in his mouth. The sun was low on the horizon outside the sky car windows. "Why am I even with you? Why did you pay for my release?" She reached into her pocket and brought out her portable Life Enhancer.

Antha smirked as he saw it. "Feeling a bit nervous, are we?"

"Tranquility," Aphra said self-consciously into the Life Enhancer, then held it against her temple.

"Oo, straight into the brain! We must be feeling desperate!"

"Answer my questions," Aphra said, turning to look at him.

"It worked! You're more assertive already. I must get myself some of that stuff. Are you on a constant dose of it? Why take some now? You weren't anxious before. I'm not that frightening, am I?" He grinned.

"I don't know," she said, faltering. "I just suddenly remembered I had it. I don't usually carry it around with me. I don't think I was feeling very anxious; I just took a dose without thinking."

"That's the spirit. Don't think, just take!"

"Clarity," Aphra said into the Life Enhancer, and went to hold it against her temple.

"Hey, whoa, hold on there," Antha said, gripping her arm. She looked pleadingly into his eyes. "But I feel confused."

"So? I feel confused most of the time. It's pleasant once you get used to it."

She scowled at him. "Stop joking. I don't feel well."

"Lie down then. Don't just pump more of that stuff into you. Biff, recline her seat and support her legs."

Aphra found herself lying down slowly as the seat moved beneath her, and she rolled over onto her side facing away from Antha.

"Aphra is beginning to show signs of a fever!" came the gleeful voice of the sky car computer.

"Well, don't tell me; just do something about it," replied Antha. "You be the doctor and fix her. *Without* any heavy brain-altering elements. And get me a link to José while you're at it."

"Why have you trained your computer to respond to all those stupid names?" Aphra muttered.

"Go back to sleep," Antha said.

"I wasn't asleep."

"I know; I was just hoping you were."

"What is it?" This was the mild voice of a man. The communication was audio only. "You have her, don't you?"

"Of course I do, José. She's acting strange, though."

"That's no reason to contact me. Just do your job, and I'll do mine."

"She's unconscious!" crowed Antha's computer and cackled with laughter.

"What do you mean, unconscious?" José cried. "Keep her alive, you idiot!"

"It's not my fault," Antha said, shrugging. "I've told my computer to fix her. There's nothing I can do."

"You keep her alive, or there'll be no payment."

"Yes, I'm well aware of that, amigo. Like I said, there's nothing I can do. It's up to the computer, which really means it depends on you as you're the one in command, your highness. I don't speak computerese."

"Incoming call from Sevig," announced the computer.

"Cut him off," José said. "He'll know you have the fem. There's no need to speak to him right now."

"Attempted connection flushed down the drain," replied the computer. "Immediate retry in progress. He don't give up so easy, do he?"

"Don't allow him through," José said.

"And there's no need to verbalize everything," Antha said. "He can try to contact me all he likes; I don't need to hear about it. What progress on the fem? She's still breathing, isn't she?"

"Yeeahhh," replied the computer.

"Don't scan her, do you hear me?" José said. "It's strange that she's out like this. There's no reason why she should be unconscious. According to the Cantabrian information, she's supposed to be a later model personifid."

"She's a personifid? You didn't tell me that," Antha said, looking over at Aphra.

"She could be an android and it wouldn't matter to you."

"True, but apparently she's my sister."

"All the Vesseys in this galaxy and this one has to turn out to be related to you? What are the odds of that happening?"

"Approximately five hundred thou—" began the computer.

"Nobody asked you," Antha said.

"Ooh, touchy!"

"Is it a problem to carry out your part of the deal?" José asked.

"No. I don't even know her. She's my sister according to a database, not according to my own memories."

"Treat her with caution. And don't even think about double-crossing me."

"Yes, ma'am! Well, we are now coming up to the beautiful Hunly rock formations, so it won't be long before we get to the lovely city of Benton," Antha said, gazing out the window to the high craggy rocks in the distance. "Talk to you later."

"Don't mess this up," José said. "Disconnect."

"Nice talking to you, too, you big girl's blouse." He cast a look at Aphra, then checked the surrounding landscape. Sky cars flew in all directions as far as the eye could see, traveling across the rocky ground. "OK, mister computation circuit-head, I'm going to need you to do a check of everything in your range—every vehicle, stone, and petrified cow dung. Keep me notified of anything even resembling a scan—any wimpy power surge you can detect tickling your exhaust pipe, *anything*. Give me manual control of the vehicle now."

The half circle of the steering wheel rose slowly from where it had been sitting flush with the dashboard and positioned itself in front of Antha. He gripped it, pressing the accelerator sensor on the right part of the steering wheel once to maintain the speed they were traveling at.

The sky car moved at a steady speed toward the Hunly rock formations—a large belt of rocks that thrust their jagged peaks up into the twilight sky. The setting sun behind the rocks cast long shadows that reached along the ground toward them.

6

APHRA OPENED HER eyes and sat up. "You still haven't answered my question."

"She awakes!" Antha exclaimed. "What question?"

She glared at him. "I wasn't asleep. I told you that."

"Oh, yes, you were. You've been right out of it."

"No. I've been awake all the time. I felt a little unwell, but lying down helped me feel better. I never fell asleep." She looked out of the windows and was somewhat surprised by seeing the shadowy walls of rock that rose up on both sides of the sky car. The sky car was moving swiftly, not far above the ground, winding through a narrow ravine. "Where are we? Do you live out here?"

"Listen, you must be faulty goods or something. You *were* unconscious for a while. The computer monitored it. You were out, OK? Stone cold out. I've heard of personifids like you. You should have paid extra to get a better deal or at least waited for a better model."

"I'm not a personifid," Aphra said.

Antha took out a weapon. "Laser knife," he said into it,

and then swung it down on Aphra's fingers.

She screamed as three of her fingers were cut off her left hand and dropped into her lap.

"Not so loud! Are you trying to deafen me?" Antha protested, and tapped the laser knife off and slipped it back into his pocket. "What, did I get your leg as well? You don't feel anything, do you?"

"I—I don't know," she answered. She had felt a sharp sting, but that was all.

He took her hand and held it up to her. "There you go, see? Look at the ends. Doesn't look like anything a person would have, does it?"

Aphra stared down at the glistening ends of her fingers and the circuitry within, unsure of what she was seeing. It did not seem possible that this was her own hand.

"Hello? Is anybody there?" Antha said after a few moments. "Earth to Aphra, come in, Aphra."

She tried to answer him, but her lips faltered and trembled. All she could do was stare at her hand.

"Come on, now; don't freak out on me," Antha said, giving her shoulder a nudge. "You're just a personifid, that's all. You can't feel any pain in your fingers, can you? And look—what's left of them can move just fine. Don't worry, we'll glue them back on later."

It was true; she felt nothing as she slowly moved her fingers. There was no blood. No bone. She began to shiver.

"Wrap her with a bit of warmth, Billy Bob," Antha said to the sky car computer.

"OK, Barf," came the reply.

Aphra leaned back into her seat, feeling as though she had just been immersed into a hot bath. "It can't be," she said through chattering teeth.

"Yeah," Antha said. "You're a personifid. I'm pretty sure you're not an android. Let me guess, you got a C-series model? They're making headlines for being faulty."

"Yes, I know that," she said distantly, turning her hand this way and that. Maybe she really had become a personifid and had had a selective mindwipe. But mindwipes were supposed to erase the memory of the actual process, not the memory of the decision to have it done. It did not make sense, yet the mechanical innards of her fingers glared up at her as she flexed them slowly.

"Bad news for the Sevig Empire," Antha said, "all those malfunctioning personifids. But that isn't stopping people from getting it done. Now they're saying the new series is safer. We're supposed to believe them?"

"But I never got it done," Aphra said, still staring at her hand. "This isn't right."

"Maybe you just don't remember."

"No! I haven't saved enough credits yet to have it done. I was going to get the very best. I've seen the news stories on the C-series models. I work for the company that makes them! I wouldn't have gotten one of those. Sevig Empire has phased out those models anyway."

"Renamed them, you mean," Antha said.

"I was going to get the E-21."

Aphra had been intrigued by the latest personifid model as soon as she had seen it. The most easily customizable body so far, able to be reshaped as often as desired, the E-21 had withstood the trials for soul protection with the highest ratings possible. It did not come cheap, and Aphra had been saving for a deposit. The rest she would have to pay off over the next sixty years. Most people chose no deposit to pay it off over the next hundred years. What was a century when you had eternity to play with? Even though this was possible, Aphra did not feel easy with the idea of being tied to payments, with mounting interest, for a hundred years. She needed to be free to afford any upgrades. Besides, something better might come along while she saved.

"The E-21, eh?" Antha said. He whistled. "Ouch! That would hurt your credit."

"I don't remember having it done. I didn't have it done."

"You can't argue with the proof," Antha said. He picked up one of her severed fingers and wiggled it at her.

"No," she said quietly. "But can you get your computer to scan me to make certain?"

"Nope. No scans. Not here anyway." He tossed her fingers one by one into her lap. "This little piggy went to market, this little piggy had roast beef, this little piggy went wee-wee-wee all the way home!"

Aphra gathered the fingers up into her right hand and looked helplessly at them.

Antha took out his weapon again. "Laser glue," he said into it. The weapon buzzed in response. "OK, apparently that is not a fighting tool. How about…sticky chewing gum?" The weapon buzzed again.

"Stop it!" cried Aphra. "Just get your computer to reseal them! Now!"

He laughed. "Yes, fem."

❯   ❯   ❯

He sat upright, roused again by the voice. "I *am*," he said in answer to the rage in his mind. "I *will*."

"See that you do. I am most disappointed in you. There she was, almost in your grasp, and you were not fast enough. That is not good enough. Do not allow yourself to be outmaneuvered again. *Listen* to me."

He nodded.

"We have the coordinates now. Are you receiving them?"

"Yes, I have them. What would you have me do?"

In response to his question, a blast of fury filled his mind, momentarily disrupting all his thoughts.

"Follow and capture!"

He nodded again. It seemed perfectly clear now. He did not know why he had not seen it before. Follow and capture—what else could there be? That was the only way.

"Is it still clear, Brainbox?" Antha asked as the sky car slowed to a halt then sank to the ground.

"No scans detected, Fish-face," answered the computer.

"Let's go." He took Aphra by the shoulder and pointed at the end of the dark ravine. "See the rear end of that sky car sticking out over there? That's where we're going."

She looked at him, aghast. "I'm not going outside! You can't make me! I won't go; it's too dangerous."

"It's only dangerous if we're out there for too long, and we won't be."

She looked in the direction he indicated, but she could only see the varying shades and shapes of rock in the steep walls of the ravine. "I can't see anything."

"Down there," he answered, still pointing. "You can run, yes?"

"I'm not going to do it," she said. "Drive alongside that car if you want me to get into it, because I'm not setting foot outside."

Antha ignored her and swiveled his seat around. He bent to the floor of the sky car. "Open."

"Voice key recognized," came a tinny voice as a panel in the floor slid open.

"Destruct pattern three," Antha said.

"Destruct pattern three now in operation," answered the voice.

Antha grinned at Aphra, who sat gazing at him in disbelief.

"Destruct?" she whispered.

"As in *kaboom*. I'm going to run to the other sky car now. I suggest you do the same." Antha opened the door, and a rush of hot air filled the vehicle. He got out quickly and ran through the ravine.

"Computer, stop the destructing!" Aphra cried.

"Door is open," replied the sky car's computer. "Shall I close it and do a little dance?"

She pounded the console in front of her. "Don't you know what's happening? Stop that bomb in the floor from destructing!"

"I'm sorry, Fluffy," the computer replied. "I can make no sense of what you are gibbering on about. Are you still feeling unwell?"

Aphra looked desperately at Antha, who had almost reached the other sky car. She could just make it out in the fading light, a black streamlined model set against the dark rock. She opened her door and stepped out into the stifling heat. The shock of it made her stand still, momentarily holding her breath. If she breathed in, how soon would it take for her to be overcome by the atmosphere?

"Run, you idiot!" shouted Antha, as he turned and looked back at her. "Don't stand there like a gorm!"

His voice spurred her to action, and she ran toward him. Not used to such uneven ground, she tripped and fell, her hands outstretched to break her fall. It hurt her, and she lay stunned for a moment, breathing shallowly. Then she thought of the bomb behind her. She got up and made her way through the ravine, watching every footstep and trying to negotiate across the rock in the dim light.

The door of the other sky car slid upward as Antha came to it. He got in, then turned to see where Aphra was. "Faster!" he shouted. "What are you doing? Don't walk, run! Get in here now!"

Aphra heard the hum of the engine starting and tried her best to move more quickly across the rocky ground. She was almost there and about to step in when the first sky car exploded. She screamed and dived into the passenger seat. With the door still open, the sky car lifted and moved away, shuddering as the explosion rocked it.

Antha gripped her and pulled her into the vehicle as the door closed across her legs. The door clamped her lightly, and Aphra realized Antha was commanding the sky car's computer to keep the door down so as to have a hold on her instead of springing automatically open at contact. She got a better grip of the seat and pulled herself in all the way, then the door shut properly.

"Set off the second charge," Antha said, settling himself into his seat.

"Second charge activated," replied the deep masculine voice of the computer.

Aphra heard a deep boom in the distance, but she saw nothing as she twisted in her seat and looked all around. They were now traveling quickly through the rock formations and had left the burning sky car behind. The vehicle they were in was very clean, no scuffs or marks were visible inside, the black seats were firm, and new car smell filled the air.

"No scans being detected," said the computer. "One unidentified sky car just now within range of beacon four."

"Keep to the plan," Antha ordered.

"Another unidentified sky car now within range of beacon one."

Antha shifted uneasily in his seat.

"Preparing to join main route."

In a few moments they exited the largest of the rock formations and came out into traffic flying overhead. Other sky cars, all brightly lit for night travel, came out from different parts of the rock formations, and Antha and Aphra joined the thin stream of cars that were on the main route to Georgia. They flew up into the midst of the traffic.

Some sky cars flew high above the ground and others close to it, giving plenty of space to those who sped quickly and those who traveled with less haste. Those who did not like to travel the main routes between cities found their own way across the sun-beaten earth, but many preferred the comfort of having others around them while they negotiated their way. The earth's magnetic field prevented travel between cities by use of luminires, except by those who were very rich and could afford to use the few higher-powered luminires that connected neighboring cities.

Antha leaned back and relaxed into his seat, a lazy smile crossing his face.

> 〉 〉 〉

"We've lost him," Mari said, looking uninterestedly at the screen displaying Sevig's face.

"*No*," Sevig said. "They can't be far from you. Leave the

wreck where it is. There's nothing there of interest. Get into the main routes to Georgia and Benton. They'll be in one of them, trying to blend in. We have satellite views of several sky cars exiting the Hunly formations, and we will track every one of them."

Mari nodded, and the screen dimmed then disappeared. The smoldering wreck of Antha's car lay in front of him, the smoke half-enveloping the metal body of the robot that stood motionless beside it.

"You," Mari said, pointing to the robot, one of his servants, "go on to Georgia. Check all cars on your way there, and keep scanning for the fem's imprint."

"Understood," said the robot, and got into the sky car behind Mari's.

"We're going on to Benton," Mari said to the android in the car with him.

>   >   >

"What do you mean, you've lost her?" Lev cried, her dark eyes wide. "Birn, how could you?"

"Calm down, sweetie. It's not my fault Antha's tag signal disappeared."

Lev got up from the living room couch and began to pace. The hovering screen displaying Birn's face turned from side to side to follow her movements. "No, I won't calm down! Not only have you left that poor fem in goodness knows whose hands, but she is the key to all of this! Why on earth did you stop to play a game instead of coming straight home? Now she's gone, and it's your fault!"

A sheepish smile appeared on his face. "Does this mean we're getting a divorce?"

"Don't get cute with me! We have to track her down and bring her home before Sevig gets hold of her." She pursed her lips. "Stay where you are. Give me some time to see if I can pick up her imprint."

"OK."

"Birn," she said, "look at me. Listen to me. Husband, this is nothing to be casual about. This is important!"

"I'm sorry, OK!"

"And how could you think she is a personifid?"

"Lev, the comp—"

"Disconnect," Lev said. The hovering communications pane vanished.

She walked over to the couch and sat down. "Lord, help us. Please." She stroked Ramius's soft coat as he lay curled up on the end of the couch. The puppy yawned and licked her hand. "We're in a mess. I never should have let her leave," Lev said, leaning to hug Ramius. "I didn't know. Omega," she said, as she straightened up, "we're going to have to do some serious searching."

"I understand," answered the computer. "Where would you like me to begin? The cities surrounding the last recorded location within estimated range?"

"Yes, all of them. Let's hope she goes to one of them rather than a cave somewhere."

"Would you like to send out probes?"

Lev shook her head. "Not at this stage; they're still too buggy. We'll use them only if she doesn't turn up in any of the cities."

"I am now accessing the entry logs of five cities."

Lev closed her eyes and leaned back into the couch cushions. "Let me know if you find anything."

❭   ❭   ❭

"Where are you taking me?" Aphra asked, looking at her brother.

"Georgia!" Antha answered, half-singing the name.

"What are you going to do with me?

He looked back at her, one eyebrow raised. "Haven't we been through all of this before?"

"No."

"Yeah, we have."

She laid her hand on his arm, feeling a lingering numbness in her fingers. The lines across them showed the recent joins, but other than that there was no other evidence that she had any artificiality within her. "You never told me what you're going to do with me."

He glanced down at her hand and grinned. "Oh, that's right, you went to sleep just as I was trying to explain it all to you. You must not have found it very interesting."

"Please don't play games with me."

"But playing games is what I do best. Anyway, you're just cargo; I don't need to explain anything to you."

"I'm your sister."

"Don't start with that again." Antha sighed. "I don't want to go around and around and around..." He rolled his eyes theatrically.

"I just want to know what is going on!" Aphra shouted. "Why won't anyone tell me? People are dragging me around all over the place and not telling me why! Why can't I just be left alone and free to go back home!"

"Calm down," Antha said. "Your boiler is overloading. You might start spitting gears and cogs all over the place."

She glared at him. "If it's just because I overheard something I shouldn't and saw something I shouldn't, then why can't I just be left alone? I'm not going to do anything! What could I do? I'm just a receptionist. I'm nobody!"

"Don't start howling at me!"

She shoved him. "Well, why not? I'm nothing to you. I'm just your cargo! Presumably you're going to get some credits out of me somehow. So what do you care?"

"I'll shut you up if you don't stop."

She clenched her fists. "Shut me up? If I'm a personifid, I'm stronger than you! I'll shut *you* up!"

"Maybe, but a good surge of juice will fry your circuits," Antha said, reaching forward and pressing a panel open to reveal a weapon.

Aphra brought her fist swiftly down on his arm, then slugged him in the side. "Leave me alone! I'm not a personifid!"

"You sure punch like one," gasped Antha, trying to grab her by the wrists.

They wrestled, Aphra pulling Antha's hair and punching him, Antha trying to use his weight to subdue her and hold her to the floor as they rolled off their seats. The sky car wobbled with their violent movements.

"See? I'm not a personifid," Aphra gasped when Antha finally gained control and sat astride her, pinning her arms to the floor. "I should be stronger than this, stronger than you."

"You should be," he agreed, trying to catch his breath.

"Maybe you're the personifid."

"Nope. We're both worn out, aren't we? Look at you, you're sweating and panting like a Sumo wrestler trying to win the Olympic medal for ballet dancing." Antha let her arms go and got back into his seat.

Aphra sat up, rubbing her aching right arm. She looked down at her left hand, spreading her fingers wide. "But what about my fingers? Didn't I see circuits and metal in there—or is this just some long hallucination?" She brought her hands to her temples. "I don't know what to believe anymore."

He rubbed his shoulder. "This is no hallucination, I'll tell you that much. And I don't know about your hand. It's the wrong side for having your imprint removed. Any other reason you'd have a prosthesis?"

"No," she answered, getting back up onto her seat. "I've never had surgery for anything. Never."

"Roll up your sleeve."

She pushed her sweater sleeve back as high up her arm as it would go. They both stared down at her pale skin, looking for any irregularity.

"Can't see anything," Antha mused. "Maybe it's from your shoulder."

Aphra took her sweater off and pushed the short sleeve of her shirt up over her shoulder.

Antha studied her arm and shoulder closely. "Nothing."

"But I've got this stuff in me," she answered.

"Maybe we just can't see where the surgery would have been," Antha said, settling back into his seat.

"Maybe," she said, smoothing her sleeve down. "This is crazy. I never had prosthetic surgery, and I can't be a personifid."

"Well," Antha said, "maybe you really are a personifid, but just a weak one."

"Approaching the west entrance of Georgia," came the voice of the computer.

"Already?"

"I'm *not* a machine," Aphra muttered, pulling her sweater back on.

"We'll see," Antha said, casting her a sidelong look.

The sky car slowed as the traffic became thicker. The large blue dome of Georgia lay ahead, glowing a deep indigo against the night sky.

In the lights of some of the surrounding sky cars Aphra could see the occupants inside the vehicles—here a man, fem, and two children; there two robots; over there one fem; to the side one robot; behind one man. She looked at them all, wondering which were personifids and which were real people, or whether it really mattered either way. She saw them now as shells, some containing souls, some not. People changed bodies just as though they were changing the clothes they wore. She thought about her own body. How was she supposed to be able to tell what it really was, or who she really was?

"Do you want manual control?" the computer asked, stirring Aphra from her thoughts.

"No," Antha said.

"Understood. Taking you into the city."

"And buy a personality while you're at it," Antha said.

"What kind of personality would you like me to download? Shall I display your options?"

Antha sighed. "Oh, forget it."

"We are being scanned," said the computer. "My power source and shields are holding steady, but the scan is attempting to shut me down."

"Quick, get us into the city!"

"I can't go any faster. Speeding is against regulations this close to Georgia."

"Send out a spike along the scanner's frequency."

"Spike sent."

Aphra gasped. "It's illegal to spike."

Beside them two sky cars within the flow of traffic suddenly dropped down.

"Two?" Antha said as he looked out of his window.

One of the sky cars dropped down and crashed into the roof

of another car in traffic. The other sky car that dropped slipped below the traffic and simply landed on the ground.

Antha's sky car did not slow, and soon the spiked sky cars were some distance behind them and obscured by other traffic. The one on the ground recovered quickly and resumed position in the stream of cars heading toward Georgia's west entrance. The one that had crashed was motionless on the ground.

"Why didn't you tell me we were being scanned by two?"

"I did not detect that at the time," answered the computer.

"I don't like it," Antha said quietly. He looked at Aphra. "You'd better not be more trouble than you're worth."

"What am I worth?" she asked peevishly.

"Two hundred million credits."

She stared at him with wide eyes. "Two hundred million?"

He nodded. "Yeah. Enough for me to buy the robot of my dreams, settle down, and raise little robots."

She shook her head at the price someone was willing to pay for her. But why? "Must you always joke?"

"Yes."

Aphra smiled suddenly, and he grinned back at her.

They drew closer to the west gateway into Georgia. A smaller city than Min City, Georgia had made headlines for trying to become a free city, making it easier for those without imprints to live there. The city's shields were also modified differently than most—there was no crystal clarity in them. This made it more troublesome for satellites to obtain clear imaging or focus in on any particular person.

The sky car entered one of the four ingoing lanes, and as they passed through the high-powered zips Aphra winced as she felt a slight shock. As they exited the tunnels and entered Georgia she began feeling nauseated and leaned forward in her seat, clutching her stomach.

"Welcome to Georgia," their computer said. "Which parking complex would you prefer?"

"The nearest," Antha answered, looking at Aphra doubled over in her seat. "And hurry!"

They traveled to the left around the outskirts of a large park—great tall trees and small streams wound alongside the pathways where citizens walked. None of it was real, of course, but it had recently been updated to incorporate a light breeze that ruffled leaves and drifted earthy scents around the park.

"I'm going to be sick," Aphra said, rocking in her seat.

"Yes, I'm OK," Birn said with a rueful smile, "just shaken. So much for a random scan of the surrounding vehicles! That spike…I'm guessing it was them. Thank the Tri-une Soul it was only a robot beneath me—I might have hurt somebody. Can you zap me into the city?"

"I'm not prepared to do that with Georgia," Lev answered, her face bright in the screen. "We've never had any need to do it there before. I can do it, but by the time I've made all the calculations and accessed Georgia's shield specifications, you'll probably have arrived there anyway. Just go as fast as you can."

"Heard and understood," said Gina, and Birn's sky car surged up into the sky like a rocket.

Birn gripped the sides of his seat.

"Try to relax," said Gina.

"That's easy for you to say," he muttered. "You're just a computer."

"Oh, you got some on my shoes," Antha moaned.

"Sorry," Aphra said, wiping her mouth.

"What's going on with you, anyway?"

"I don't know," she said, and looked up at him anxiously.

"Well, come on. Let's get out of here. Can you move?"

She nodded. "I think so."

"Quick as you can, then. And next time you have to puke, point away from me."

Aphra got out of the sky car as the doors opened. They were on the uppermost level of a parking building, open to the sky. She glanced up. The city's shields did not seem very far away. She could see the shape of a sky car flying overhead above the city, blurred as though it was underwater.

The luminires were in a block together in the center of the parking area. Aphra and Antha moved briskly, winding their way through the rows of other parked sky cars. The door of the nearest luminire slid open as they came to it. She involuntarily drew back. For an instant, the image of Mari leaping from the luminire had come to mind. But the luminire was empty, so she stepped inside.

"Destination?" came the pleasant voice of the computer as the doors closed behind her and Antha.

"Simnel Street," Antha replied.

"Thank you," said the computer.

The doors opened onto a busy street scene. Aphra looked at all the people moving hurriedly about their business and wished she did not have to step out amongst them—she still felt ill and was sure that it showed on her face.

"Quickly now," Antha said, taking her arm.

She was glad of his touch and felt braver because of it. They moved briskly along the line of luminires and chose another at random.

"Baker Street."

Again they got out in a different part of Georgia and moved into another luminire. They repeated this process until Aphra felt dizzy. After the sixth time of jumping in and out of luminires, they crossed to a line of waiting cabs.

"Taran apartment complex," Antha said. The driverless cab rose up in the air and whisked them away. "Say nothing," he warned Aphra.

In less than a minute they were dropped outside a large apartment building. Antha tapped in a code on a small panel to open the doors, and Aphra wondered why he had to do that. She could see Antha had an imprint because he wore the same kind of wrap on his wrist as she did.

They entered the double doors and then ran quickly through the quiet foyer. Aphra wrinkled her nose at the musty smell and felt another wave of nausea come over her. One light was flickering and buzzing above them, while the others seemed too dim, lighting the empty foyer with an unwelcoming gloom. Apartment complex? Who would live in a rundown dive like this? Tucked around the corner on their left a door slid open with a jerk and then eased shut with a hiss behind them.

Robots were crowded in this room, sitting inactive in various poses in the dark. Utility and maintenance models, all of them. They had obviously not been doing a very good job if the state of the foyer was anything to judge by. Antha moved purposefully past them and to the back of the room, where he got down on his knees. "Open sesame," he said quietly. After a moment, one of the floor panels slid silently back, and Aphra looked down and saw the rectangular metal face of a robot looking up at them. It was tall and broad with two long arms and two short solid legs.

"Get down in there," Antha said to Aphra. "Climb down using Chickenwing."

Aphra looked down at the robot Antha had indicated. Chickenwing, she presumed. "You're a Melphig series robot," she said with delight. "I used to have one exactly like you."

"Used to?" Chickenwing responded as Aphra climbed down into the robot's outstretched arms.

She dropped to the ground and looked up at the robot's flat face, the two small pale circles of eyes above the larger circle of its immovable mouth. "I traded mine in when I upgraded to my next robot, then traded that in when I got my first android."

"Traded in? There's nothing wrong with the Melphig series," replied Chickenwing. "I know I may be one of very few with legs and wheels these days, but I am running as well as ever. And look at these hands," the robot spread out its fingers and manipulated them. "Very dexterous works of art, aren't they?"

"He's a proud piece of tin, my Chickenwing," Antha said as he dropped down beside Aphra.

"Pride is an emotion," answered Chickenwing. "I do not have emotional response programming."

"Which is why I love you so much," Antha said. "Now, hurry up."

Chickenwing reached up above their heads and slid the panel shut, and in the darkness Aphra could hear the clanking of metal as the robot fixed the panel in place and locked it down. Chickenwing then switched a high-beam light on at his chest, and Aphra could see the concrete tunnels that stretched to either side of them reaching off into the darkness. They stood at a T-junction, the tunnel behind them led slightly downwards, while steps led down the left and right tunnels.

"Why do you call him Chickenwing?" Aphra asked as they walked briskly down the steps through the right tunnel. "It's an awful name."

"His name was Rupert when I took ownership of him. I thought that was much worse—watch yourself!" Antha caught hold of Aphra as she tripped.

"I'm not used to stairs," she said, steadying herself.

"Note the easy way in which I traverse them," said Chickenwing, as he clanked quietly down the steps ahead of them. "See how I place my feet exactly in the center of each step?"

"I'm so proud of you," Antha said.

"He's just trying to help me," Aphra said, pinching Antha on the arm. "Chickenwing, you don't mind having such a name? You wouldn't prefer being called Rupert again?"

"No preference," answered the robot. "Having no name would not bother me. Having one just makes it easier to know when I am being spoken to. Having a name given to me by my owner gives said owner a sense of ownership."

"In other words, it means you're like a pet rodent," Antha said.

"That is appropriate, remaining as I do down here."

They came to the bottom of the steps, and there was a quiet whirring sound as the base of Chickenwing's feet opened and he rose slightly on rubber wheels that extended out. He then rolled noiselessly along the floor of the tunnel.

Aphra looked around at the concrete walls, some sections of which were covered in graffiti. "Where are we?"

"Underground," Antha said.

"I know that. I mean, what is this place?"

"You've never been in the old tunnels of a city before? This is where it all began. Before Georgia got its shields, everyone lived down here."

"You mean like Cantabria?"

"Yes."

She quickened her step to keep up with him. "Do people still live down here?"

"A few do, deeper down. We're in the upper levels, the tunnels that were built as the city reached back up to the sky again."

"Do you live down here, Antha?" Aphra asked.

"Nope," he answered. "Are you feeling better now?"

"Yes, a little." She smiled at him. "What, you don't mean to say that you actually care?"

"I have to keep you in good condition. It's as simple as that."

"I don't think it is as simple as that," she said, looking up at his face, which was unusually serious.

He looked at her then, and nodded. "I'm beginning to suspect you're not just a pick-up-and-drop-off job. The first thing we're going to do when I get you home is find out if you really are a personifid. All the signs say you aren't, yet—oh, I don't know."

"I'm your sister," she said simply, "and you're beginning to remember me."

He said nothing.

"You're really bonded by birth?" Chickenwing asked as he rolled along ahead of them.

"Bonded by birth, maybe, but not anything else," Antha answered.

"We had rotten parents," Aphra explained.

"How so?"

"They wanted to play at being parents for a while, and then when they'd had enough of doing that, they got rid of us," Antha said.

Aphra's memories of their real parents were dim, but one thing was clear: the way in which they had parted. No amount of pleading had moved her parents, and they had left without looking back. She had been seven years old. Antha had been nine, and Ashley had been four when they were parted. The parents had divvied them up, given them over to new homes and new parents, and Aphra had never seen either her siblings or her parents again. Pain twisted inside her as she thought of it. The hurt was something she thought she had erased, but here it was, rousing itself again. The memory had not been erased. She had loved Antha and Ashley too much to rid herself of her faint, childhood memories of them. Aphra looked up at Antha walking briskly beside her, anger in his eyes as he spoke of their parents, and tears began to slip down her cheeks. She wiped furtively at them in the dim light.

"How could they do such a thing?" Chickenwing asked. "It does not seem like something a human would do. People are too emotionally attached to objects."

"It's called the right to choose to live your life the way you want it," Antha said. "And that doesn't involve anyone else. Be a parent or have a different hairstyle, it's all the same thing and depends on what you feel like doing."

"No, that does not make sense," said Chickenwing. "Where does love come into it? With people, love always comes into it."

"Not this time," muttered Antha, kicking a scrap of metal so that it scudded across the concrete and clinked against the wall.

"They procured you, so they must have wanted you," replied Chickenwing.

"Yeah, but what for?"

"I think we were showpieces," Aphra said. "But when we reached a certain age, that was it. It was time to offload us."

The light beaming from Chickenwing's chest trembled a little as he rolled over rough ground. "That does not make sense. Every person who has a baby of their own can't help but love it and hold it and grow close to it. I have seen it time and time again. Why, people have even loved me!"

"Who said our parents were people?" Antha said.

"You think that, too?" Aphra said, looking up at him. "I've thought about that and wondered if that's true."

He shrugged. "What does it matter? Even if they were people, we weren't theirs. We're tailored, made to order from designer gene pools, and have no real parents anyway."

"An adopted or tailored child is still loved and treated as though it is the property of the parents," said Chickenwing.

"But we're not property, are we?" Antha said.

"No. I am," said Chickenwing, as he rolled steadily up a slight incline.

Antha strode along behind him, Aphra at his side. "Anyway, I don't want to keep on talking about this," he said. "The two individuals who decided to pick our genes and grow us also decided when we reached a certain age that they were tired of being parents and wanted to do something different. I think they were androids."

"Androids do not get tired," said Chickenwing. "Their power cells are easily charged if they do begin to run down—which is very rare—but their programming does not suddenly change unless someone has changed it. They would not change their mind about keeping you unless someone had changed their mind for them."

"Well, maybe they were real people then," Antha said. "All I know is that they certainly didn't act like they were when they got rid of us."

"I wonder where Ashley is," Aphra said.

Antha walked along silently for a moment. "Have you ever looked? Did you ever look for me?"

Aphra shook her head.

"Forget about it," he said. "I never looked for you or Ashley, either. Maybe we do have some genes from our parents—the distant, unemotional, nonattachment ones. They're good. They make us unable to feel hurt or any of those disagreeable real feelings."

"They haven't stopped you from being sarcastic," Aphra said sharply.

"Because it doesn't work!" he said, exasperated. "There may have been a movement years and years ago that said we could eliminate feeling the sorrow of this world by isolating the genes responsible for causing us to feel this way and then fiddling with them. But no matter how hard people tried, it didn't work!"

His voice raised in passion and echoed through the tunnel.

"For centuries we've been using things to try and stop ourselves feeling this unexplainable pain and emptiness—mind arts, drugs, religion, you name it, nothing worked. We use Life Enhancers now, but they only cover over our real feelings and can't make things right—our loneliness, guilt, and sorrow still affect us. And the dumb thing is that those archaic words don't get much use anymore in our drive to eliminate those feelings—we rename them, but we can't get rid of them.

"And we think because we know more about our genes and how some of them function that we can eliminate our flaws: no more hatred, no more violence. But we can never reach the perfection we try so hard to achieve, that perfect happiness where nothing can ever bother us or hurt us. Trying to eliminate our conscience doesn't work, either. In fact, it makes things worse."

"Conscience?" Aphra asked.

"The voice deep inside us that knows right from wrong," Antha said.

"I don't—" she began.

"Forget it," he said. "I didn't mean to offload on you. It's just something I feel strongly about. I guess you could say it's my latest kick, to be off Life Enhancers and really listen to life and find out why I feel the way I do."

He went on in silence for a moment. Aphra looked at his face in the dim light, moved by the strength of his emotion.

"Ridiculous for someone like me, I know," he said. "Philosophy has always made me uncomfortable. I've always been like, what's the meaning of life? I don't know and I don't care, just get on with it and forget about it. But now...I don't know. It must be old age creeping in and making me think about this stuff."

"I have never heard you speak this way before," said Chickenwing.

"Well, I'll try not to let it happen again," Antha retorted. "You prodded a nerve, talking about my parents, and made me jabber like an idiot. Just keep moving."

"I never stopped," said Chickenwing as he rolled along.

"You sound like a Follower," Aphra teased Antha. "If you don't look out, you'll become one of them next."

"At least they try to be real," he snapped. "Doesn't sound like such a bad idea to me. It's when they act like they know the truth but don't follow it that it gets up my nose. There's no life in the ones who do that."

"But what about the Tri-une Soul?"

He looked at her. "What about Him?"

"Him?" she said. "I thought it was an it. Anyway, that's the one you have to follow, know, and 'receive.' It's creepy."

He grinned. "Creepy in an interesting kind of way."

They came to a side tunnel on their right and went into it.

Aphra saw something small scurry away from Chicken-wing's light. "What was that?"

"A rat," answered Chickenwing.

"Come on," Antha said, pulling her along. "It won't bite you. There's plenty of them down here."

"They're real?"

"Very real," Antha answered. "You should have kept some of your puke for it—it's probably hungry."

She grimaced. "Yuck! It didn't look very nice."

"What, your puke or the rat?"

"The rat!"

"Chickenwing doesn't look so good either, but he still needs a bit of grease now and then. I'm sure you can spare a finger or two to feed a poor old rat."

Aphra smiled. She looked up at Antha, a sudden fondness stirring in her heart.

He looked down at her then and frowned. "You're no personified," he muttered. "Your eyes are too expressive."

Chickenwing suddenly switched his light off, and they were left in darkness.

"Sensors detect someone in the main tunnel we just left," he said very quietly. "Arms in position, I am now facing you."

"Climb onto him," Antha said, nudging Aphra's shoulder in the darkness.

"What?"

"Get on. He'll carry us."

She stepped forward, felt around in front of her until she made contact with Chickenwing's outstretched arms, then she stood on his feet and climbed up onto one of his arms. She sat there, feeling for something to grip hold of with her hands, and ended up clutching Chickenwing's head. Antha climbed onto Chickenwing and stood on the robot's feet and held onto his other arm, trying not to bump against Aphra's knees as she sat there in the darkness.

"Ready?" Chickenwing asked.

"Yes," answered Antha and Aphra.

Chickenwing turned quickly and whirred quietly away down the tunnel. The robot sped them along, taking many turns easily without unsettling their balance very much. Aphra clung to Chickenwing, her hair streaming out behind her as they whizzed along. After a while, Chickenwing's light flicked back on—at low beam so as not to dazzle his passengers. On and on they went through the maze of deserted tunnels, scurrying rats their only companions.

Finally Chickenwing slowed and came to a halt.

"If you detect anyone within range of your sensors I expect you to move on immediately," Antha said as he stepped off Chickenwing's feet.

"Follow usual procedure," Chickenwing said. "Yes, I understand."

"Get off his arm, Aphra. He needs it."

She climbed down, and Chickenwing reached up above their heads and began undoing the bolts that held an overhead panel in place.

"I'm not sure when we'll be coming back," Antha said. "If you're not here when we do come, we'll know someone has scared you off."

"Usual procedure," repeated Chickenwing as he methodically removed the bolts from the panel and then slid the panel across.

Antha climbed up the robot's body and disappeared into the hole. Moments later, he looked through the hole and down at Aphra. "Hurry up."

She climbed up Chickenwing and through the hole. The panel slid back into place, and she heard it clunk beneath her as Chickenwing fixed it into place.

She could just make out the immobile shapes of robots lurking in the shadows. Antha turned slowly around, holding a small card in the palm of his hand, the only source of light in the closeness of the room. As he turned, the light reflected off one of the robots so that its eyes almost seemed to be glinting, looking at Aphra. It unnerved her a little. She could see now that this was another utility room.

"Clear," came the quiet fem voice of a computer from the card.

"Let's go," Antha said, taking Aphra by the arm. He led her to the side of the room between two large robots, and a door slid across revealing an empty space. They stepped into it, and the panel closed behind them.

"You're using the robot lift?" Aphra asked. "Why?"

"Because I can," he answered.

The lift hummed, and they rose swiftly.

"What was that card in your hand?"

"I had my computer make a request to the apartment building's mainframe for maintenance on the seventeenth floor, but I used my card to keep the maintenance robots deactivated. The computer is expecting this lift to activate, so it won't know that we're riding it."

Antha and Aphra stood silently inside the robot lift, and in moments the door slid open. Antha walked slowly across the hall, holding Aphra tightly by the arm. His apartment door was closest to the lift, and it opened as they approached.

"**F**ANCY FOOTWORK," SEVIG muttered. "You can't have lost them."

"I have traced their movements through the luminires and located them on the street," Jamon said. "I have footage of them entering an apartment building and going to the utility room. But that is all. And before you ask, no, I do not have footage of them inside the utility room—the building does not have a security camera in this room. Not every apartment building in Georgia has cameras in place, and the older buildings are especially free of them. There was a movement some time ago to free the city from too much surveillance—"

"So much for security."

He looked critically at Craf, who stood immobile by the door that led from the spacious room. The robot's reflection was indistinctly visible in the polished pale stone floor, while the plant next to Craf was mirrored in his body, warped across his torso.

Sevig shifted uneasily in his black leather chair behind his desk. "Where's Mari?"

"He is currently heading toward Georgia," Jamon said. "I have alerted him to the fem's whereabouts. We have a unit there already, but it was not able to follow the fem. It is now waiting for your instructions."

"Send it into the utility room," Sevig said. "Have it find out if any robots were active and witnessed anything. If not, send it underground to scout around."

"Underground?" asked Craf. "What makes you so sure the fem has gone underground?"

Sevig shot a look at him. "Where else would she go? She's not showing up on any of the building security cameras, she has not gone out of the building again, so she must have gone underground. There are sure to be old tunnels in Georgia."

"Yes. It was one of the first cities to be exposed," said Craf, nodding his head as he searched his history files.

"Why have we not been contacted by José?" Sevig asked, drumming his fingers on the desk. "He may be rethinking his position and is using Antha to hide her from me. Everybody wants a piece of the action. Even Lavinia's back from the dead. My lucky day. Jamon, open a link to José."

❭   ❭   ❭

"Omega is trying to locate her," Lev said, frowning at the screen.

"Don't get upset," Birn said. "I did my best. They were just quicker hoppers than me. Gina tried to relay their positions in the luminires, but you know what it's like to trace a hopper—it takes time to uncover the trail."

"I can't believe I made such a stupid mistake!" she cried. "Why did we ever let her go? She is a part of this and must know more than she let on."

"How were you supposed to know? Things have happened too fast. And Gun didn't tell you soon enough about what Ryan said. There's just no controlling these things. You can't blame yourself."

She sighed and closed her eyes. "I should have known. The Tri-une threw her into my path, and I didn't pay close attention. I should have been more careful. How dumb can I be?"

"Calm down—we'll do what we can."

She looked at him. "And that is...?"

"Tell Gun to get here as soon as he can, and we'll use some of his old contacts to try to flush Antha out. Meanwhile, you keep trying to crack Sevig's stuff—it can't outsmart Omega for long. Let me know when you get a fix on Aphra."

"What are you going to do?"

"Pray," he said with a grin.

She blew him a kiss. "Just...let's be careful. This is getting dangerous."

"What do you mean *getting?*"

>   >   >

"Sit there," Antha ordered, pointing at a red couch taking up one corner of the room.

Aphra did as he said. Indeed, there was nowhere else for her to sit. The small room was sparsely furnished; the long, low padded couch was the only piece of furniture there. A footrest popped out as she sat, and she pushed it lightly so that it slid obligingly back into the couch. Dismantled parts of machinery lay spread out in the middle of the coffee-and-cream colored floor, alongside patches of grease stains. On two walls were massive, crisp, colorful images of flame-wreathed sky cars. One of them Aphra recognized as the burgundy sky car Antha had blown up.

"Computer, scan her," Antha said. "Now, tell me the usual story," he said, not looking at her. She opened her mouth to speak, but the computer spoke before she could.

"You have lost four beacons here—" a screen appeared before Antha and flashed four pictures at him. Aphra saw brief glimpses of rocky landscape.

"Wait, show me the second and third ones again." The light from the virtual screen shone pale amber on his face. "OK, and the reasons are?"

"In the last recordings the first beacon shows activity nearby. It was—it was—it w-wa—ceasing scan now. Systems check in progress."

The screen wavered and disappeared.

"What happened?"

"Systems check in progress," repeated the computer. "Damage found. Systems check in progress."

"Well, you've stuffed things up now," Antha said, looking at Aphra.

She looked back at him with wide eyes. "Me? What'd I do?"

"Yeah, you," he said. "Personifid or not, you're carrying something that just tried to trash my computer."

"Systems check in progress."

"Do you know what I'm going to have to do to you now?" he continued conversationally. "I'm going to have to give you a dose of radiation. Yes, that's right, you're going to make friends with my X-ray machine."

"What's that?" she asked nervously.

"It's just a clunky old thing that people used to use instead of scanners. Whatever's in you can't wreck it 'cause it's just a machine and not linked to my main computers. I find it comes in handy."

"Will it hurt?"

"I'm sure it will be very painful," he said with a grin.

She did not know whether to believe him or not.

"OK, how's that system check going?" he asked.

"Damage found," answered the computer.

"Can you fix it yourself, or do you need Number Two?"

"Unable to fix all damage; some systems are now shut down as a safety precaution."

He scratched his chin. "Hmm. We'll see to you later—do not attempt to do any more repairs right now."

"Understood."

"Number Two, I'm going to need the protective shield in place for X-raying."

"Ready," came the voice of Antha's second computer.

Antha beckoned to Aphra.

She stood up and followed him into the next room. There was a small table in the center of the room crowded around with an array of machines. She thought at first that they might be robots, but as she took a closer look, none of the machines were familiar to her.

"I picked up all this equipment for free," Antha said as they pushed past a spindly mass of tubes and wire sprouting from a crate. "It was just left lying around and unused—some of it in perfect running order. Took me a while to figure out what some of it did, though." He swept the table with his hand. "If your clothes have any metallic fibers in them, you'd better take them off."

"What?"

"I can't X-ray you very well if you have metal in your clothing," he said as he rolled a high, rectangular, boxlike machine along the floor toward the table. A triple-jointed rod, the end of which had a large flat panel attached, extended out from the machine.

"I don't," Aphra said, folding her arms across her chest. "Just plastic."

Antha positioned the machine alongside the table. "Oh, I see: environmentally healthy, are we? Get up on the table."

"What are you going to do to me?"

"Relax. I just need the machine to scan you. It will show me what you're carrying and what's really going on with your body. And if you start making things difficult for me, then I'll make things difficult for you. It's as simple as that."

"No," she said firmly. "I don't trust that machine; it looks ancient."

He looked steadily at her. "OK then, I'm going to have to punch your lights out and lift you onto the table myself. I could use my computer to make you unconscious, but as you've already had a go at wrecking one of my computers, I won't take a chance on another. I'll try not to break your nose—I'll aim for your jaw."

"You can't be serious," she said, backing away from him.

"We haven't got a lot of time, and I'm losing patience."

The look in his eye made her climb hastily onto the table.

"That's better," he said. "You want to find out what you are, don't you? The X-ray will reveal whether or not you're a personifid."

"What about this?" she asked, indicating the wrap on her right wrist.

"Leave it on. Lie down."

She did as he said, feeling vulnerable on the cool surface of the table. Antha positioned the rod of the machine up and over her and then adjusted the angle of the flat panel. He then moved out of her line of vision.

"Lie still, take a deep breath, and hold it," he said. "Don't move."

"Will it hurt?" she asked pathetically, looking up at the panel poised ominously over her.

"Of course not."

She sighed with relief.

"I said lie still. OK, hold it."

She heard a click and a deep buzzing sound.

"Take another deep breath and hold."

She did, and heard the click and buzz again.

"OK, we'll see if those are clear enough."

"Is that it?" she asked, turning her head to look at him.

"Yeah. Painful, wasn't it?"

She smiled and sat up, swinging her feet over the edge of the table.

"In a few moments, all will be revealed," he said, waving his hands dramatically. "Will she turn out to be a personifid, or is she really a robot with nice hair and bad teeth?"

"I don't have bad teeth!"

"OK, bad breath, then."

"No!"

A light on the machine snapped on, and he gazed down at an illuminated panel. "Oh, no..."

"What? What is it?"

"You're a..." he looked at her in horror, "a...a person!"

She almost collapsed in relief. "Don't do that to me!" She put a hand to her chest and sighed. "I knew it! I—"

"Wait, that's not all. You're a person all right, but your left arm is a prosthesis and it's got some freaky-looking hardware inside it. I can't tell exactly what. I can only see outlines. I can't make out what it all is."

"How can that be?" Aphra said, looking down at her left arm.

"I don't know," he said, his hand to his chin thoughtfully. "But aren't you glad I didn't cut off the fingers on your right hand?"

She did not hear him. She was staring dumbly at her arm. "I've never had problems with my arm, and I've never had to have it replaced. When did this happen to me? Do you think I was like this from birth?"

"Do I think you had an adult-sized arm grafted onto you when you were a baby? Yes, it's all coming back to me now, the sister I had with a great huge arm attached to her puny body."

"Oh, of course," she said, reddening. "But when could it have happened? I have no memory of any surgery of this kind."

"That doesn't mean anything. You know memory can be tampered with."

"But why do I have it?"

"How would I know?" He leaned over the X-ray image and studied it closer. "And if I had to guess, I'd say your arm is... well... *armed*. That part there—" he traced his finger lightly over the image, "—looks like an explosive device."

"*What?* I have a bomb in my body?"

"That's what it looks like."

Aphra stared at the image on the screen and then slowly lifted her left arm out and away from her body.

"Yeah," he said sarcastically, "I'm sure that will help."

"Can't you do something about it?"

"Like what? Your arm has already kicked up a stink while being scanned—it would probably be even more hostile if I tried to tamper with it physically. Fem, you're dangerous goods, and the sooner I offload you, the better."

"If you're not going to help me, then just let me go," she said gloomily.

"And let someone else pick up your bounty? No way." He touched the fingers on her left hand and shook his head. "That was risky," he muttered as he left the room.

Aphra followed him, carefully avoiding brushing her arm

against any of the machines. "What are you going to do with me?"

"I'm getting really sick of that question. I've got things to figure out, so just sit out of the way and shut your mouth. Don't bother trying to leave—my computers won't recognize any commands you make, so no doors or windows will open for you. Not only that, but I've disabled the safety, so you can't make a request to the police."

"You think of everything," she said moodily. "Just not me."

"Number Two, continue giving me the security rundown—start by showing me the second and third beacons again."

❯ ❯ ❯

Ramius galloped through the corridor and into the living room, then jumped onto one of the couches, forcing the air out of the cushions with a *foo*. Lev followed at a more leisurely pace. She stifled a yawn and sat beside the puppy.

"It's your bedtime," she said affectionately to him.

His tail thumped briefly, and he looked adoringly at her with soft brown eyes.

"At least one of us will get some sleep tonight." She stroked his ears. "I don't think either Birn or I will be able to."

Ramius brightened at the mention of Birn and looked hopefully at the door to the garage.

"No, he's not coming home tonight."

"I have broken through the block of high security within Jamon," came Omega's deep voice.

"Great! Download what you can. What do you have?"

"I have some data from Aphra's personal computer, and I also have some other data that originally belonged to Ryan Haldane."

"Sounds like it could be just what we want. Good work."

"Having to pull out now, my activity has been detected. I have accessed most of what was in this particular block."

"Are we safe?"

"My identity and location have not been traced," answered Omega.

"Very good. They're sure to know it was us, but as long as they don't know where we are, it doesn't matter. Now, let's take a look at what you have. Start with Aphra's computer first; that'll be easier to analyze. What did she—"

"I have a recording of a conversation between Aphra and Ryan that has been recovered from Aphra's computer's memory."

She smiled. "You don't need me, do you, Omega? One step ahead of me yet again."

"Shall I display the call?"

"Yes."

A screen appeared in front of Lev, and she watched the recording of Ryan talking to Aphra. He had changed so much from when she had last seen him four years ago. The strain of losing Imogen showed in the look of his eyes.

"I will support the project," he said, no longer looking directly at the screen as he spoke to someone in the room with him. "I don't have what he wants!"

Lev gasped in horror as he was hit by laser fire. She watched the rest of the footage in open-mouthed shock.

Ryan crumpled to the floor and turned dying eyes at her. No, not at her: at Aphra. "Go," he whispered, looking earnestly at her. "Get out of there."

Then Mari's face thrust into the picture, and Lev heard Aphra's voice shriek "Disconnect!"

For some time after watching the call, Lev hugged Ramius and wept.

Finally she looked up at the screen and wiped her tears. "What about the other data?"

"The data I have that belonged to Ryan is coded. I am unable to unlock it without a keyword. I have run through thousands of variations of words based on what we know of Ryan Haldane, but nothing has unlocked it yet."

"Keep trying," she said, and closed her eyes as she racked her brain for ideas. "Ryan, Ryan. What have you done? Why have you dragged Aphra into this?"

She sat silently for several minutes, thinking things over, her mind working feverishly. Then she sighed. "Tri-une Soul, I need some help on this. I can't think what it could be." She breathed in slowly and exhaled, the true Tranquility calming her as she reached out in thought to the Tri-une Soul.

An image came into her mind. She could see orange, flickering flames, a small wizened hand holding tightly to a white-furred paw. It made no sense. She screwed her eyes tightly shut, trying to think what it could mean. The memory of her mother's voice drifted back to her. *The monkey wanted the chestnuts from the fire but didn't want to burn his own hand.* The wizened hand, it was that of a monkey's! She began to remember now; this was something from a childhood fable. The monkey used the limb of another animal to rake the chestnuts out from the fire. Better for someone else to take the risk and get hurt, the monkey thought. What was the other animal?

She sat up straight. "A cat! He's playing cat's-paw with Aphra. Omega, try this code: cat's-paw!"

"The third attempt using a variation of these words has unlocked the data, and it contains a recording, a message for you, and a small file. Which would you like me to display first?"

"The recording."

On the screen, Ryan, Sevig, and Craf stood in a large room. Two huge potted palm trees stood on either side of a door, and the floor was pale, polished stone. Lev recognized it as the entranceway to Sevig's Min City penthouse office at the Sevig Empire building. The door was beginning to slide open for Ryan, but it stopped as he shook his head and turned back to Sevig.

"It won't work! I've shown you that it won't work. Can't you see for yourself? Mari is no different from an intelligent android. Only God knows how his thoughts must be trapped and what has happened to his sense of who he is. There is no way to improve on this! We have failed. The experiments have failed. If you continue, you will be ordering the eventual imprisonment of thousands of souls! Don't you see? It won't work! You will turn them all into little more than robots with no will of their own! And I will not allow you to be in control of them."

"There is no failure," Sevig replied. "The technology does work. You will try again, and this time you will get it right."

"Don't you see I can't? It's impossible! You are discontinuing innocents," Ryan cried, shaking his finger in Sevig's face, "and setting others up for a life of entombment. That is not what the Personifid Project is for!" He dropped his hand and turned away. "I will no longer be a part of this. I've changed the way I see things!"

"You cannot disassociate yourself from this, Haldane. It was your idea as well. Remember that." He gripped the chain that hung about his neck and held it out toward Ryan. "Do you see this chain? This is your wife, and I will not hesitate to break this capsule and let her leak out to nothingness if you do not continue to give me your work."

Ryan staggered back as though he had been dealt a blow. "No! She is lost. I was told she was lost! Give her to me! Give her back to me!" Ryan lunged for the chain.

"Step back," Sevig said calmly, as Craf moved to restrain Ryan. "If you remove this chain by force, she will be gone. You will do what I say, or I will discontinue her."

Ryan groaned. "No!" he cried, struggling against Craf's steel arms.

"Your precious Imogen in exchange for your work. That's all I ask."

> >   >   >

The screen dimmed, and Ryan's face appeared. Lev could see little of his surroundings, but she saw that his face was pale and drawn and his hazel eyes were troubled. He looked into the camera lens reluctantly, as though he was unwilling to meet the eyes of whoever would watch the message. She gazed back at him in shock.

"Lavinia," he began, "I hope you are the one receiving this message. I am playing cat's-paw with someone. Don't think me a coward—you should know what little room in which I have to maneuver. I know you're still alive. Your hints did not fall on deaf ears. I only hope my hints have met the same reception. I have thought a lot about what you said." He paused and briefly looked away, then his eyes moved back to her once again. "I finally came to the same conclusion you did about what we were working on. I didn't want to believe you, but the trials have led me toward your opinion. Unfortunately, as you have probably guessed from the footage I've attached to this message, I did go ahead and complete the device. I have hidden it from our mutual acquaintance to secure my own position. I cannot allow it to be in his possession, but I also can't allow it to be destroyed. So I have hidden it."

Lev frowned.

"I leave it for you, Lavinia. I still believe that in the right hands it could achieve great things for our world—perhaps rehabilitation, training..." his voice trailed off, and he looked hopefully at her through the screen.

"No, Ryan!" she said, exasperated.

"I trust that you will use it for the best," he said.

"I'll destroy it!"

"I have made contact with your cousin and left information for you to use if needed. If anything happens to me, your cousin will tell you. If you have not heard from your cousin by the time you get this message, then I can only tell you that I have left the device with a friend. Lev, I know we didn't always get along, but when you changed—when you, you know, met the Tri-une—you became someone I began to trust, even as your religion separated us. I trust you now to do what is best. I know you can use this the way we dreamed we could. May your God go with you." He cleared his throat and looked steadily at the screen. "Sevig, if you are viewing this message, then all I can tell you is that the device will never be yours, and neither will my wife."

The screen dimmed.

"Show me the file," Lev ordered.

"It is a small part of the programming belonging to the Personifid Project," answered Omega, displaying it for Lev.

She studied the clump of thin blue lines and numbers in silence for a while as the image rotated before her and she saw it from all angles. "It's part of the nerve centers for a shoulder, I think. And according to this," she said tapping part of it lightly, "it belongs to the A-series. Compare this with my records and see if there is any anomaly."

"It is a perfect match with part of the upper left arm and shoulder in your records," responded Omega.

"So there's no hidden message in there with any numbers changed," she mused. "Part of an A-series arm. An arm."

"I have a question to ask you," Omega said.

"Go ahead." Lev continued to study the lines of code.

"How did you know that 'cat's-paw' would unlock Ryan's message?"

"One day when he and I were working together I called him my cat's-paw," she explained. "He had never heard of the term, and when I told him what it meant, he said he would have to remember it and use it one day. I thought of it because this is what Aphra is now: Ryan's cat's-paw. It's from an old fable; you can look it up."

"Yes, I see it. Interesting," said Omega. "With this information, I suggest that a more literal application of the term 'cat's-paw' has been used by Ryan."

Omega's meaning suddenly dawned on Lev, and she closed her eyes. "No, don't tell me it's in her arm. I thought there was a chance he might have put it in her apartment, but her arm? Ryan! Why did you have to be so obscure? Why didn't you just tell me in the first place what you had done? And now you say you left it with a friend? You didn't leave it with her; you *attached* it to her! Why do you always have to make things so complicated!"

Ramius growled and whined as he wriggled around to lick Lev's face. She went over to the kitchen and stood there a moment, leaning against the counter for support. "Omega, get Birn. I need to talk to him."

Moments later, Birn's face appeared on the communications

screen before her. "Hello, love. What have you found?"

Lev bowed her head, her shoulders trembling as she tried to gain the strength to talk. "He built it, Birn. Ryan built our device," she said in a shaky voice.

Birn gasped. "No! You're serious?"

"And he experimented with it on Mari."

Birn's mouth dropped open. "He's even crazier than I thought he was."

"I just retrieved a message from him now. It confirms everything—Ryan never stopped going ahead with our work." She looked up at Birn's face and took a deep breath. "He really did complete his own Deific device. And Birn, he didn't *leave* it with Aphra as Gun said."

"I knew it," Birn said. "He wouldn't endanger someone like—"

"Listen to me, Birn. He didn't leave it with Aphra; I'm pretty sure he's hidden it *inside* her."

Birn's gape returned. "Madness. It's madness. Why would he do such a thing?"

"I don't know." She rubbed her eyes. "We can't be too hard on him, Birn. It broke him when Imogen was lost. He was ... adrift." Lev sank to the floor and leaned against the kitchen drawers. "Birn, we need to hurry. We can't let the device fall into anyone else's hands—especially Sevig's."

"I'm doing my best to find her."

"Have you heard from Gun? I can't reach him."

Birn shook his head. "He's not answering my calls."

"What is he doing?" She shook her head. "This is a worse mess than I thought it was!"

"We'll be OK," Birn said. "We'll get it back. Don't worry."

She looked intently at him. "How can you say that?"

"Because I have to. We have to trust the Tri-une Soul here,

Lev. You and I are the only ones who know what Aphra really has. That gives us an advantage. And I don't think it is any coincidence that this has come to us. Think about it, Lev: of all the people Aphra could have run into that day, she ran into me. The Tri-une Soul must have made sure of it. And now that we know what's happened to Mari, we have to help him, too. Now," he said, giving her the wise smile she loved, "how about having some dialogue with the Tri-une Soul about all of this?"

She nodded.

>   >   >

"I am inside the city," Mari said. His head ached, a dull throbbing, and he closed his eyes for a moment. As he did, he heard his thoughts whispering to him, echoing far off as though in a long tunnel.

"Information is being relayed to you now as to her last location," Sevig said over the link. "Find her. And if anyone tries to prevent you from taking her, discontinue them."

Mari nodded. Of course he would obey. What Sevig said was always the right thing to do. He needed Aphra, and if anyone tried to stop him from getting what he needed, then he would have to discontinue them. It made perfect sense, and he felt immense relief as he thought of it.

>   >   >

Ramius nudged Lev's hand as she sat beside him on the couch.

"I'm all right," she said gruffly to him, rubbing her eyes. "It's just all a mess that I'm supposed to untangle and sort out, making sure my loved ones don't get hurt in the process." She shut her eyes and sighed. "Lord!"

A sense of peace and reassurance came to her then. Her preferred brand of Tranquility. She took a deep breath and smoothed Ramius's coat. She sat there for some time with her eyes closed, stroking Ramius absentmindedly. After a while she got up and went over to the kitchen again. Ramius stayed fast asleep on the couch.

"Well, I have to eat," she said quietly. "And I can't worry—I just have to relax and trust that things will go well. Omega, I know I always say that I don't want to be lazy and that I always want to do things for myself, but please just give me some fish and chips and don't say anything about it." She got a plate out of the cupboard and sat it on the counter. "I'd like a nice, crispy battered piece of fish—terakihi—and a heap of chips. And a kumara fritter."

Omega filled the plate with her request, and she got a bottle of tomato sauce out of a chilled cupboard. Ramius woke up and sniffed the air. Lev walked back to the couch and sat next to the puppy, warning him with a signal of her hand to keep his nose away from her plate.

"Incoming call from Gun," said Omega abruptly.

A communications pane appeared before her. Gun's sober eyes regarded her. She could see nothing of his surroundings.

"Gun, where have you been?" Lev demanded. "I've been trying to get hold of you!"

He gazed stoically at her through the screen. "I've been busy."

"Too busy ignoring my attempts to contact you," she retorted. "Now, look, I need to talk to you about Ryan. Can you think back to your conversation with him? Did you tell me *everything* he told you? I feel like I'm missing something somewhere. I just saw a message from him, and it sums up what you told me. But he said he left information with you to use. What information?"

Gun shrugged.

"Well, I now know for sure that the device has been placed in Aphra—it's in her arm, Gun. And if I know Ryan, he'll have set up some safeguards in place to make it difficult to remove."

"Safeguards?"

"It could be anything. A tricky little puzzle to keep me up half the night trying to figure it out—or a minefield of explosives that I'll have to find my way through. I won't know until I get a look at the arm. My plan is to remove the arm from Aphra, take it out into the desert, and blow the cursed thing up."

"You don't want the device?"

She shook her head vehemently. "Not at all! It's a terrible thing. Capable of incredible evil. We must prevent anyone else from getting hold of it. I haven't located her imprint, so she must still be wearing her Cantabrian muffler."

"She could be dead."

"We'll just have to pray she isn't."

"I'll see you later. Disconnect."

The screen in front of Lev disappeared.

"He's always *so* talkative," she said to Ramius, scratching his tummy until the dog's hind leg pedaled air and a goofy look appeared on his face.

> > >

"Money always works," Sevig said calmly. He and Craf whizzed along the brightly lit streets in the large, ostentatious sky car. "We will have her one way or the other."

"Your patience is admirable, sir," Craf said. "However, isn't there a risk your competitors would want to acquire the information? And wouldn't they be willing to offer more for the device?"

"Don't talk to me like that. Do you think I am unable to think of that possibility myself?"

"Sorry, sir. I was simply wanting to offer helpful advice. I did not recognize that you had thought of this possible scenario already."

"Incoming call," came the smooth voice of Jamon.

"Display."

The face of Antha Vessey appeared on the screen.

"Sevig, old boy," Antha said. "I have her, but I'm going to need more compensation."

Sevig looked coldly at him. "You think I'm just going to keep upping my price? I—"

"I'm sure you won't mind. You've got plenty to spare."

"Never interrupt me when I am speaking if you wish me to be generous to you. I will increase your price by fifty million, and I warn you that this is the last increase. If you do not give her over to me now, then I will have you discontinued."

Antha's face showed no reaction to Sevig's words. "I'm glad you agree. Disconnect."

"Well?" Sevig said as soon as the screen dimmed.

"The source was in Min City," said Jamon. "It was a prerecorded message. There was no remote activation through the source."

"Retain your link with the source and monitor its connections. Whoever transmitted his message for him will also have to contact him with my reply."

"I am not reading any imprint in the vicinity of the source of the call, sir. There is nothing to trace."

"Well, where is this unmarked person?"

"The source of the call was underground in the Gafin district at the—"

"Visual!"

"Cameras were taken offline."

Sevig frowned. "I am getting very weary of this lack of control. What about Mari? Does he have anything to report yet?"

❯ ❯ ❯

"Sensors in the tunnel below this building's utility room indicate the presence of one man and one dog," the computer said. "There is no identification available for the man."

"A man and a dog," Antha said thoughtfully. "A real dog?"

"Yes."

"Chickenwing is not there?"

"No."

"What are they doing? Are they moving on?"

"No, they have stopped beneath your access panel."

"Move on," Antha said under his breath. "There's nothing there. Keep following Chickenwing. Nothing to see here."

Both he and Aphra had gotten off Chickenwing before climbing up through the access panel, so he knew there would be some of their scent present on the ground, but he hoped that the dog would not get too interested in it and would keep on following Chickenwing. You never knew what a real dog might do.

"They are moving on," said the computer after a moment.

"Let me know if they come back."

❯ ❯ ❯

Lev sat silently studying the images, tapping her forefinger against her teeth. Then she straightened up and sighed. "Again," she said. The images shifted, and the grids of networked red and blue lines were displayed once more in front of her. "There," she said, pointing at the top left-hand corner of one of the images. "Try there." The picture changed and displayed the live footage of five security cameras in Georgia overlooking a busy street scene. "I'm going to be here all day."

Ramius put a slobbery half-chewed toy onto her knee. She pushed him away absentmindedly.

"Incoming call from Birn," said Omega.

Lev brightened and flicked her hair away from her cheek. Birn's face appeared in front of her. His appearance had been altered: he had shoulder-length curly black hair, a long black moustache, and the appearance of a wide face with high cheekbones.

"Hello, sweets," he said. "How's it going? Nice to see you're eating healthy," he said with a grin as he spotted her half-eaten plate of chips.

She smiled ruefully. "I'm OK. I just wish this was all over and done with and we had her back here again. Just think what that poor fem must be going through."

"I'm doing my best. I'm not far from the location now. Are you and your computer ready?"

"Yeah, but—"

"Jamon has just prodded our worm," Omega said. "I am changing its masked location."

"Oops, we've just been prodded again," Lev told Birn.

"Fem, if this happens too many times I want you to back off completely and cease all contact with him," Birn said. "Your safety is more important to me than anyone else's. In fact, upload more power to Gina now and leave us to do this on our own."

"No, I'm all right. You need our help."

"Don't argue with me," he said firmly. "Just do it."

"No, I'm not going to leave you to do this on your own!"

"Do you think I can't do it? Cut your connection to us now."

"No, I won't."

"Yes, you will! This is not the time to get into an argument, and you know it. It's been too risky already. Drop your connection. Gina and I can do this."

Lev grimaced.

"Yes, that's the face I fell in love with."

"I can't say the same for you," she answered. "OK, you go ahead—I'll be watching when I can, in case you need me. Please be careful."

❯   ❯   ❯

Birn sauntered along the paved street, glancing up at the traffic overhead and holding a muttered conversation with Gina. He was flanked by two robots that he had hired for the task. Gina had overridden their programming, and they walked along awaiting the chance to follow their orders.

"I wish it wasn't so busy," Birn mumbled.

"Approaching now," said Gina as Birn came around the side of a building.

"I'm ready," he said. "I hope this works."

Gina initiated a countdown. "Five, four, three, two, one."

Birn and the two robots were whisked through Gina's luminire and transferred into a particular sky car that flew overhead.

"Go!" Birn shouted as soon as he materialized in the car.

They had transferred themselves into Sevig's spacious luxury sky car. Sevig and Craf looked at them in surprise.

Birn reached for Sevig and gained an immediate advantage.

The robots lunged for Craf, but one of them ceased functioning and fell to the floor of the sky car. The other grappled with Craf as Birn wrestled with Sevig.

It lasted only an instant as Birn and Sevig were then transferred to another sky car some streets away. They resumed struggling in the smaller space as the sky car moved quickly away.

Gina was left with three tasks—continuing her attack on Jamon, working on Sevig's personal shielding so that she could subdue him, and whisking the second sky car away through the city.

>   >   >

"The man and the dog are returning."

"Wake up, Aphra," Antha said, going over to the couch and shaking her.

"What is it?" she muttered.

"On your feet. I think we're gonna have to skedaddle out of here."

She sat up and looked around with bleary eyes. "Are you going to get rid of me now?"

"Oh, go on. You're too much fun to have around. I've decided what we're going to do. The arm seems to be the only thing I need for collecting my bounty, and I know someone who can remove it. Once we whack the sucker off, you'll be fine."

"You mean you're not going to give me over to anyone?"

"You're a real fast thinker, Aphra," he said and smirked.

She impulsively hugged him, a wave of relief rushing over her.

"Stop that," he said, lightly pushing her away. "There's no time for going all sappy on me. We have to get moving right now—I think someone has found us. Come on."

She followed him into the adjacent room where he had X-rayed her. He went over to the far wall and popped open a large panel, revealing an empty compartment.

"I love these old buildings," he remarked. "Get in."

She did as he said, and he got in after her. They stood hunched over, the two of them just fitting inside the space.

"The man and the dog have materialized inside the utility room," Antha's computer said.

Antha let out an oath. "So, they have some power up their sleeves."

"The dog has led the man straight to the utility lift."

"Of course it has. As soon as they're inside the lift, jam it shut."

"They are not entering; the man is examining the control panel."

Antha leaned over and pulled the door of their escape hatch shut. "Aphra, we are going to drop downwards. I need you to shut up and not scream or anything."

"The man and the dog have materialized in the—" the computer's voice broke off.

"Activate," hissed Antha.

Nothing happened.

"Crouch on the floor and hold the grips," he said quickly to Aphra, as he threw a switch on the wall behind him.

There was a creak and a groan, then it felt as though the floor beneath Aphra dropped away and left her stomach in midair. She stifled a scream as she clung to the grips on the floor. Antha held onto a grip on the wall with both hands. They dropped straight down through the shaft. Aphra closed her eyes, trying desperately to trust Antha. He must have used this before, she reasoned, as she fought back the impulse to panic. She tried to treat it as a fear game, but as she waited for the ride to end, she did not have the secure feeling of knowing that nothing was real.

The brakes kicked in when they were three floors up, and they traveled the rest of the way skidding to a halt, then hit the bottom with a thud. Antha kicked open a panel and helped Aphra out into the utility room. He flicked on a handheld light, and they ran across the room, through the maze of inactive robots and over to the hole in the floor.

"H-R-6-1," he said tersely, and one of the robots stood up and clomped over to them.

"Your orders," it said in a thin metallic voice.

"Escape."

It dropped down into the hole, making a loud clang as it hit the tunnel floor, and Antha pushed Aphra down after it. They both climbed down the robot and into the tunnel. Then the robot swiftly folded itself up and extended outwards into a horizontal oblong shape as it hovered above ground. Aphra quickly climbed onto the back and straddled it, putting her feet into the footrests as she gripped the handle that rose up in front of her from the body of the robotic Hover-Rider. Antha got on the front and did the same, and the H-R rose up and whizzed away, responding to the controls in Antha's handgrips.

They raced through the tunnels. Aphra huddled behind Antha, using his body as windbreak. Normally she would have enjoyed a ride like this, but her fear and illness had taken the fun out of it. As they made their way through the maze of tunnels, she became very disorientated and began to feel as though her body was featherlight and floating through the air. The handle she held became the only thing anchoring her.

They whizzed through tunnel after tunnel, their beam of light throwing shadows around the walls as they passed discarded junk and scurrying rats. Eventually they slowed, and the slackening speed caused Aphra to lean heavily against Antha's back. He got off the H-R and helped her to do the same, and she clutched hold of his shirt trying to steady herself, as her legs felt unwieldy and foreign, while he put his arm around her.

"Where are we?" she said. They stood in the tunnel, the light from the H-R illuminating the steel walls on either side of them.

"We're about to go up into the city," Antha said. "Are you ready?"

She shook her head slowly. "Do you have any Strength or Mobility?"

"No, you're just going to have to summon up some of your own. We can't stay here because the rider may have been tagged. H-R-6-1, bang on the roof."

The Hover-Rider noiselessly changed back to its robot appearance, raised its arm, and clanked its fist loudly on the ceiling of the tunnel. In a few moments, a hatch opened above them, and a fem's face looked down at them. She had short, scruffy blue hair and piercing violet eyes, and she did not seem at all pleased to see them.

"Hey," Antha said amiably.

〉　　　　　〉　　　　　〉

Sevig lay in the middle of the floor in the sky car, paralyzed by Gina's shields. He glared up at Birn, his face red with suppressed rage.

The neck chain had been easy enough to remove. Once Sevig's personal shielding had been deactivated, Birn had simply slipped it off over Sevig's head—none too gently. The sky car, now masked to prevent Jamon's attempts to locate them, sat hidden in a quiet parking building.

"Gina," Birn said as he held the neck chain in his hand, "scan this chain and capsule for signs of life."

"No soul life signs found," said Gina after a moment.

Birn tossed the chain onto the floor. "Gina, get me Lev."

Lev's face appeared instantly in the windscreen, and he swiveled around in his seat to look at her.

"Where are you?" she asked. "What's happening?"

"It's what we feared," Birn said. "Imogen's not in the capsule—I just had Gina scan it. Sevig must've said what he did to make Ryan suffer and have some leverage in making Ryan work for him. Still, we had to find out if he really did have Imogen, didn't we?"

Lev bit her lip.

"So, what now?"

"Just do what we planned," she said.

He frowned over his shoulder at Sevig. "I'd rather put him into frozen storage."

"I can't do that to anyone, not even my worst enemy."

Birn looked back at her. "Yeah, I know. I was just hoping you might change your mind."

"You wouldn't be able to do it, either!"

"Maybe," he said, and shrugged.

"Let him go, Birn."

"What? Oh, do I have to?"

"We can't hide him forever. Jamon will find his imprint sooner or later, if he hasn't found it already. We have to find Aphra. She's our main priority now. Make sure you get safely away from Sevig and then release him."

"I don't like to dump Sevig while we have him in our hands. Who knows what he'll do when we let him go? We could remove his imprint, and then—"

"Didn't I tell you before? He has two imprints—one in his skull as well as his wrist."

"No, you didn't tell me that." Birn looked mournfully at Sevig. There was something wonderful about seeing the mighty ruler of Sevig Empire lying on a dirty floorboard. But he supposed the fun would have to end. "In that case, I'll get rid of him as soon as I can."

"Call me as soon as you're safely away."

"OK. Sorry we didn't retrieve her."

"Me, too."

"I love you."

"I love you, too," Lev said. "Disconnect."

Lev's face dimmed and the screen cleared.

"Disconnected," said Gina. "Birn, Jamon is coming. We have to let Sevig go."

"Sedate him and dump him on the street."

Sevig disappeared from the sky car.

FIRST, APHRA HAD been given a dose of pain suppressant and had some of her shirt lasered off. Then she had been probed in her shoulder with another laser—which had caused a small explosive to detonate. It shot out of her upper arm, bursting through the skin and exploding in the face of the man bent over her. It did no damage to him, for he was shielded.

She stared openmouthed at the neat hole in her arm—a black mark that would have looked like a sunken beauty spot if only the skin around it had not been peeled back and glistening. Her heart beat rapidly. To see more visible proof of the explosives within her, this time in such a menacing manner, took her breath away.

"I need to be able to see what I'm dealing with," said the man. He straightened up and looked narrowly at Antha through his small, round, dark glasses. He had short bleached hair and a face almost as pale.

Antha had led Aphra through a crowded building full of people, androids, and personifids—dimly lit areas revealing groups testing the latest Life Enhancers. Manic laughter had come from some of them, eyes wide open and staring as they laughed as though they could not stop, and tears streamed down the faces of others as they moaned and wailed in heart-wrenching agony. Some groups stood or sat silently, their eyes half-closed, and as Aphra looked, she had the sudden impression that they were empty personifid bodies. Androids milled around, distributing the Life Enhancers and observing those who used them. They would record the results for the Life Enhancement laboratories—officially, this building and those in it were not part of the Life Enhancement projects; nobody wanted to know how error-ridden the Life Enhancers had been while prepared and perfected for public release. A lot of fine-tuning went on that the general public was not aware of, and a lot of people were discontinued in the process. As Aphra looked at those around her, she had no idea what was really going on, but she felt too ill to care.

She and Antha had gone to an upper level, along a walkway into the adjoining building. They had pushed past the crowds and entered through a door that admitted them only when the person inside had seen that it was Antha—and only then when Antha had given him some credits owed. Aphra had not been told the name of the man, and he had lowered his glasses and looked at her as though she was something he would like to examine more closely.

"It's obvious that I can't scan the arm," he said, "so if I can't see into the arm, I can't see what I'm doing. If there're more explosives in here, I'm not going to go in blind. What do you think I am, a fool?"

"What, you've never come across a challenge like this before?" Antha replied.

The man sat on the edge of the high seat next to Aphra.

She could not see his eyes behind his glasses, but she felt them on her.

"This 'challenge,' as you call it, just blew out one of my computers when I tried to scan it. I haven't had anyone successfully spike me before."

Antha's disinterested expression did not change. "You're not going to take this job?"

"I have so many jobs on at the moment that I can't just stop everything to do this. You're lucky I've been very accommodating and taken time out right now to look at it. And now you owe me for a new computer. If you're prepared to leave her here and wait a few weeks for me to do the job, then fine."

Aphra shot an appealing look at Antha, hoping he would not do that. Surely he was in too much of a hurry to take whatever it was inside her arm and get his bounty. It had been a relief to know that this was what he planned to do now—that he had decided against handing her over to anybody else. He could have all the credits; she did not care. Just so long as he protected her.

"Two hundred thousand," Antha answered.

"Two hundred? Are you crazy? I wouldn't—"

Suddenly someone was standing beside Aphra, lunging for her, and a siren began to blare. It all happened so quickly that she did not realize what was happening until it was too late. A man materialized into the room—setting off the alarm systems as he did so—grabbed Aphra by the arm, and dematerialized with her.

Mari ripped the arm off the body in front of him. He threw it against the wall, where it sparked and fell to the ground with a clank. No cry of pain came in response to his action, and for a brief moment he considered that. "Where is she?" he said again, quite calmly.

"I don't know. I don't have any information on their whereabouts," answered Chickenwing.

Mari reached for the other arm and began to wrench it off.

"I don't see what you are trying to achieve by doing this," said Chickenwing, who was backed up against the wall in the underground tunnel and made no more attempts to evade Mari's grip. "I am not a person, so I have no pain response programming. If you are trying to coerce me into telling you where they are, this is not the way to go about it."

Mari stood still and looked at the robot. It was right: it was not a person. Just a Melphig series robot. Why had he not seen this before? This would not help at all. He had thought it would be the best thing to do, but now he saw the logic. This robot could not feel anything and would not help him find the fem. He stared at it and felt as though he had failed. He needed to hear from Sevig now, needed to know the right way to act.

Aphra found herself in a sky car hovering outside the city, with a strange man and a large furry dog. The stars were silver pinpricks in a charcoal sky, and the headlights of the sky car showed the contours and shadows of the arid rock below. Georgia lay to their left, an iridescent filmy globe that was crazily lit by the night lights of the city, a hive of activity as blurs of movement whizzed around inside.

The man let go of her arm, and the dog jumped into the front of the sky car. It stood with its paws up on her knees, growling and barking in her face. It was so loud in the small car that it hurt her ears. Aphra hunched back into her seat, looking at the unfriendly black eyes of the shaggy brown, gray, and black dog, the large pointed muzzle close to her own face. She could tell by the flecks of spit striking her face and the bad breath that this dog was a real one.

"Get off," the man said. The dog backed off so that it sat at Aphra's feet and stared at her while making a low growl in its throat. The man fingered the torn fabric of her shirt. "Did they try to remove your arm?"

Aphra glanced at the man. He was strongly built—but then again in an age of affordable physical manipulation, *every* man appeared strongly built. It meant nothing. This one had dark brown hair and light brown skin. Completely average. His face had no character, no warmth to it. It was possible he was a per-sonifid, but she could not tell; she was not able to look into his eyes for very long. He had turned from her and stared straight ahead, his keen eyes fixed on the horizon.

"Yes," she said, and looked back at the dog.

The man glanced down and touched the small neat hole in her arm. "Explosives?"

She nodded.

"Don't stare at the dog. She'll take it as a challenge."

Aphra averted her eyes immediately and looked up at the ceiling of the sky car.

"Incoming call from Antha," came the fem voice of the sky car's computer.

"Tell him to leave a message."

"Complying."

"Who are you?" Aphra asked.

The man said nothing.

She looked critically at his face. "Look, I'm getting pretty sick of being abducted and dragged around! I'm not a piece of baggage!"

The dog gave another low growl.

"You shut up and leave me alone!" Aphra said, losing patience with it.

The dog jumped up and barked in her face, forcing her to squash back into her seat with a squeal.

"Get in the back," the man said curtly.

The dog immediately stopped barking and climbed up on one of the rear seats. That puzzled Aphra: it did what it was told, yet she was sure it was real.

The sky car picked up speed, and they flew swiftly away from Georgia and into the quiet emptiness of the night. Aphra turned away from her companion and looked out the window.

What was going on? She was still trying to absorb what had happened back with Antha. Explosives embedded in her arm? What was she, a secret military weapon? She sighed. Her life no longer felt like the one she remembered. With Antha she felt she had come so close to having everything resolved. Remove the arm, remove the problem. Give her a prosthesis and be done with it. But now this guy had appeared, and she was back to where she had started. In the hands of a stranger. No closer to understanding what everybody wanted from her.

It infuriated her that whatever it was that was so important had been implanted inside her purposely. That Ryan, her friend—or so she had thought—had put her in this danger. He had even rigged her to blow up! What if she had triggered it accidentally? This was no *information* that Ryan had supposedly given her: this was discontinuation waiting to happen.

She tried to think of how and when he might have had the chance to do this to her. And almost instantly she stopped with a shock. A few days ago he had insisted on them having time alone together in the games room. Surely he had not done something to her then? She could see images in her mind of the fun game they had played together.

They had raced each other, both riding enormous tawny cheetahs. The sight of them was sharply defined in her memory. She could see the pattern of his cheetah's coat, the black-rimmed amber eyes of it looking intently at her, the black tear marks framing its golden muzzle. She remembered the soft warmth of her own cheetah's fur beneath her hands as she bent low over its back, urging it to speed ahead. Had that really happened?

And now here she was—in another sky car with another stranger trying to scoop the credits that, for some unknown reason, Sevig had offered to Antha or anyone else who might bring her in. It boggled the mind.

Perhaps if she could contact Sevig himself she could tell him she would be willing to give him whatever she had for less credits than others were demanding. Perhaps afterward he would let her go free.

After a few minutes of silence her companion turned on some loud music. It was the chance she had been waiting for.

"Computer," she said quietly. "Give me a communication link with Sevig of Sevig Empire. I want to—"

"I'm sorry, but you do not have access to any communications services," interrupted the computer, its voice close to Aphra's ear.

"Of course I don't," Aphra said, and her brow furrowed as she pouted. Then her eye caught sight of the wrap that was over her right wrist. She considered removing it. Her location would instantly be known. Perhaps Birn was out there right now, scanning for her imprint. Or perhaps Gun would see it and come to her rescue. She dismissed such a foolish thought immediately. If she did expose her imprint, she would have no way of knowing whom it might bring to her next—Mari might see it before anyone else. There was nothing she could do but wait and hope that when she reached her destination she would have a chance to escape and find her way back to Antha.

She sat back in her seat as the sky car sped across the barren landscape, and she began thinking about Antha. It had been an interesting experience to be with him. She had begun to feel a real sense of camaraderie. Being together and interacting with him brought up distant memories of when she had last been with him.

They had been playing together in the family holo-room, digging in the sand by the sea. Ashley had sat watching them, chattering away to them as they had built sandbuildings. The brightness of the sky, the grainy texture of the sand, the beautiful multicolored sea—all were indelible images in Aphra's mind. So too were the feelings of frustration on completing a sand sculpture and then having Antha ruin it. No matter how many times she asked the computer to build it again, Antha would flatten it, either by pretending to trip and fall or just by outright stomping on it.

She smiled to herself and sighed. Things had changed so unexpectedly for the three siblings. Aphra's new home had been nice, her new parents had been nice, and the things they had given her were nice, but she had found it impossible to grow attached to them. She was alone, and the new parents did not make more of an effort to gain her trust. It had been natural to grow more attached to the computers and robots in that home—they were less unpredictable and would never abandon her. Even now, her contact with her adoptive parents was minimal. They were probably fine. They were always fine.

Aphra felt angry as she thought about it. Was there really anyone she could count on to help her now? Had there ever been? Her computer Marlena was gone, and her wonderful Michael had been discontinued.

"Computer, some Tranquility please," she said, surfacing from her thoughts.

"I'm sorry, I'm not equipped with that," replied the computer.

"Just like everybody I've met lately," Aphra answered grumpily, cursing the fact that she had left her portable Life Enhancer back at Antha's apartment.

> > >

"So, you found me, José," Antha said languidly. He spoke into the screen's camera lens. "Don't take this the wrong way, but you weren't asking for enough credits. Your bargaining skills are lacking, so I thought I'd better do something about it. I was gonna give you your share. Honest! So there was really no reason to rush off with the fem." He paused and looked at the screen while trying to think of what to say next, then reluctantly said, "She's my sister, OK? Take her arm if you have to, but give the rest of her back to me." He paused. "End message."

"Your message has been saved," said José's computer. "Thank you,"

Antha sighed and ran his hands through his hair. "I don't have the computer capability to match him, you useless heap of junk. I can't track her imprint, have no idea how to get her signal—"

"She has a signal?" the man with the short bleached hair asked, swiveling around in his chair and looking intently at Antha.

"José gave me the configuration of a signal to use to track her when I first picked her up," Antha replied, "but he also told me that every serious attempt to scan her—not just from passing through a zip, but a dedicated scan—would alter the signal. This happened when I was in Cantabria. José had seen where she had gone, and so I knew where to pick her up, otherwise we both would have lost her."

"You're sure José didn't know what frequency the signal would have been altered to?"

"No, I'm not sure. He said he was only given one signal's configuration, but…" Antha shrugged.

"It is possible we can discover the signal she had when she left. N-4, have you been listening to this?"

"Yes," came the voice of a computer.

"Then you know I need you to find out what the fem's signal was when she was here and what new signal arose when N-3 was spiked."

"Searching," said N-4.

❯   ❯   ❯

"I'm not sure how much of her arm should be removed," José said.

He and Aphra were now in Benton. It had taken them less than an hour to get to the city, and José had not spoken to her at all in that time. Aphra had sat quietly, ready for action the moment the sky car door opened, but she had found it was the same again—personal shielding kept her trapped and only able to move with her captor. José's computer had altered Aphra's appearance, so they had been able to walk unhurriedly through the city streets and use the luminires without any need of hopping through them or hiding.

José took her to an apartment, and she now lay on a table with two robots standing over her. Aphra saw that one was a Medical Assistant model, and the other was just a standard Companion Multipurpose model. The M-A robot had three "arms" extended—thin quadruple-jointed metal shafts—two of them holding Aphra's left arm steady with soft pincers, and the third poised with a laser and ready to work. It had at least three other arms ready to unfold and extend from its triangular-shaped body if needed. Its "head" was angled out and over Aphra's arm, moving slowly as it examined her with magnified vision. The other robot, which was more of a humanoid shape, stood on the other side of the table and held Aphra down with one heavy hand on her upper chest, near her neck, and the other hand on her knees.

"I see the join between prosthesis and flesh," said the M-A in a precise, measured voice. "I also see sensors threaded in the join."

"There's no need to remove the arm at the join," José said. "Can you separate the arm from the body further up?"

"What?" Aphra said, struggling against the robot's hold. "How much farther up?"

José said nothing, but continued looking expectantly at the M-A.

"The join is so high up I would have to cut through the shoulder itself," the M-A said, "which would be more problematic. Also, I cannot see how far the sensors extend. I would have to scan the interior of the shoulder to know that."

"Well," José said, "you're an M-A-5-C; what do you recommend?"

"Quantity of explosives, unknown," answered the M-A. "Quality of explosives, unknown. Quality of sensors, unknown. Location of all sensors, unknown. Termination point of sensors, unknown. It is my recommendation that you take subject to an M-A-M-9-U."

José frowned. "Military M-As aren't just lying around ready for anybody to use. What can *you* do?"

"If I attempt to remove the arm, the chances of success are unknown and the danger involved is unknown. I am not equipped for such risks. I recommend that you take subject to an M-A-M-9-U."

"Why did I bother renting you?" José sighed. "All right, let her get up."

The robots retracted their arms, and Aphra sat up and turned to face José.

"You'd better take me to Lev," she said.

His face registered surprise, then was masked again by his impassive expression.

"Don't bother trying to fool me any longer," she said, scowling at him. "Take me to Lev's house right now—*Gun*."

He looked at her critically. "How did you know?"

"What, you mean apart from the fact that you don't like to talk to me, you use loud music to prevent any attempts at conversation, and you have the same, very rare, computer abilities? Duh! I have learned that no matter how changed a person might be in appearance, their personality and their soul come through their eyes. I recognized my brother this way, and now I've recognized you. You can't mask what's in the eyes. You should have at least worn dark glasses."

The corners of his mouth turned up ever so slightly.

"So what are you going to do with me now?" she asked, looking him squarely in the eye. "And are you going to start treating me like a person, do you think? This is my body, but I don't know how this prosthetic arm or what's inside it got attached to me. Are you going to tell me what you know?

I'd like the arm removed, thank you. I'm not too happy about carrying around explosives and being in possession of something that so many people seem to want! I'd rather be left alone and allowed to go back to my life if that's at all possible!"

"Calm down," he said, "there's no sense getting mad at me."

She got up off the table and shoved the M-A aside. "Tell me who I'm supposed to get mad at! If you knew everything all along, why didn't you tell me?"

He stood still, looking at her.

"Tell me! How long have you known about my arm? Since we first met?"

"M-A-5-C, give her some Tranquility," Gun said.

"I don't want any!" Aphra shouted.

"Tranquility given," said the M-A.

"Blast you," Aphra said, leaning against the table and drawing in a deep breath. "I want to stay angry at you," she said in a low voice. "You've ruined my life."

"Me? I have nothing to do with it."

"Sure." She tried to glare at him, but the anger to do it escaped her.

"I didn't know 'all along,'" he said, looking steadily back at her. "I have been piecing together a puzzle of my own. Ryan only recently told me he'd left a device of great importance with you. It wasn't until I was in your apartment and traced its signal that I realized it was actually *on* you."

"*In* me!" she shouted, the Tranquility not being able to withstand the force of her emotion. "So why didn't you tell me about it then?"

"I couldn't."

"Why not?"

"I had too much to think about." He moved away from

Aphra and picked up the sweater that was slung over a chair. He tossed it to her. "Put this on."

She threw his sweater to the floor. "Too much to think about? What kind of stupid answer is that? Give me an android any day. At least they tell you what you need to know!"

"Calm down."

"Well, you'd just better pump me full of Tranquility, because I'm not going to calm down!"

"I won't do that again. I'll have to keep you restrained until we get back to the sky car, though."

"Yes, you'd better hand me over to your buyer now," she snapped. "Do your job, get your credits! Do you know I was actually starting to like you? That's how big of an idiot I am."

He walked over to the door to the next room. It slid open as he approached it. "M-A-5-C, C-M-P-2-1, deactivate," he said over his shoulder. The robots' lights flickered out. "Come on, Zellie." The dog got up from where she had been lying in the adjoining room and trotted after him out of the apartment.

Aphra stood her ground.

A moment later he stuck his head back inside. "Are you coming?"

"No."

He shrugged. "OK, then I'll just fly back to Lev's without you." He left and the door slid shut.

She groaned and ran after him.

❯   ❯   ❯

"You can come home," Lev said to Birn's face on the screen. "Gun's found Aphra and is bringing her in."

"Great!" Birn answered. "How did he manage that?"

"I don't know, actually. He hasn't said yet."

"Is she OK?"

Lev smiled ruefully. "She's pretty upset—yelled at me really loudly—but she's eager to come here so I can work on her arm. I told her I will do my best to remove it and make sure she's OK. How are you doing?"

"Tired," Birn said, and closed his eyes. "I think I'll get some sleep now."

"Good idea."

> > >

The relief of being back at Lev and Birn's home was overwhelming. Aphra stepped out of the sky car and leaned wearily against it, her knees sagging. She and Gun were in the garage and the door in the rock had slid shut, blocking out the sunrise. The sky car's engine whined down, and Lev hastened into the garage. Aphra found herself easily returning the hug that Lev gave her.

Ramius seemed to remember Aphra from the last time she had been there, which surprised Aphra. He rushed up and mouthed her hand. Then, as soon as Zellie jumped out of the vehicle, Ramius ran around excitedly. The two dogs growled and barked at each other in play, jumping and biting at each other's ruffs. Zellie had more ruff for Ramius to grab hold of, and he took a big mouthful, so that the side of Zellie's mouth was pulled back into a silly-looking grimace. Their tails wagged furiously, and they ran out of the garage together, crashing into one of Lev's potted plants on the way.

"Birn's not home yet," Lev said to Gun as they moved toward the door to the house. "He shouldn't be much longer."

Gun nodded. "You think you can remove Aphra's arm OK?"

"I'm sure I'll find a way. Ryan wanted me to have the device, so he must have set things up in such a way as to enable me to remove it. How are you feeling, Aphra? Are you hungry, tired? What can I do for you?"

"I need some Tranquility," Aphra muttered.

"Poor thing," Lev said, looking up at Aphra. "I can't give you any Tranquility. I can only give you a quiet room and a bed to sleep in. If you're not tired enough to sleep, you can take a walk in the garden."

"Bed," she answered.

Aphra followed Lev out of the garage and on through the living room. As before, upon entering Birn and Lev's home she felt the tangible Tranquility settle around her. It brought tears to her eyes this time, and she quickened her steps to get to the bedroom so she would not burst into sobs in front of Gun.

"You have some rest," Lev said gently. "I'll fix your arm when you're ready; don't worry."

Aphra nodded and went into the room without looking at Lev.

It was the same room she had slept in before, and she sank down onto the bed and lay there quietly, the tears slipping down her cheeks as she rested in the supernatural Tranquility.

"Crazy animals!" Lev grinned as she went back into the living room and saw Ramius lying on his back with his legs in the air, pawing at Zellie as she stood over him and chomped him around the neck and face.

Gun was sitting on one of the couches with his feet up on the coffee table, watching the dogs play. Lev sat opposite him and studied his face. He had returned to his normal appearance once he and Aphra had left Benton.

"We're thinking of getting a cat," Lev said.

Gun looked at her. "What for?"

"They're nice. Don't you like them? Julian has kittens at the moment."

He grimaced. "Dogs are better. Get another dog."

"Two dogs are enough."

"You don't have two dogs."

"You and Zellie are here a lot!"

"We might come around less if you get a cat."

Lev poked her tongue out at him. The dogs jumped up and started chasing each other around the couches.

"Hey, you two!" Lev said firmly. "Go play in the garden! Go to the garden! Go on!"

The dogs looked at Lev and then raced off down the corridor.

"Omega, open the doors to the garden and leave them open," Lev said, then turned to Gun. "Can I get you anything to eat?"

Gun shook his head and stood up and stretched his long, lean frame. He walked through the living room and on into the corridor. Lev curled up on the couch to wait for Birn.

Time must have passed, because the next thing she knew, Birn was kissing her on the forehead.

"Hello, sweets," he said. "Sleeping during the day yet again, I see."

"How do you know I wasn't praying?" she said, looking up at him and stifling a yawn.

He mimicked the sound of soft snores.

She giggled. "Well, it's still very early in the morning, and I didn't get much sleep last night."

"Where are Gun and Aphra?" he said, sitting next to her and pulling his shoes off. He sniffed one and made a face. "I don't know about this natural way of living. My feet smell so natural it's almost obscene."

"Aphra's sleeping, I hope, and Gun has probably gone into the garden with the dogs." She leaned against Birn and wrapped her arms around him.

"Have you had a look at Aphra's arm?" he asked, kissing her hair.

"Not yet. She looked so exhausted I thought I'd let her get some rest first."

"Did Gun say where or how he found her?"

"Nope. I was just starting to talk to him, and, as usual, he left the room."

Birn leaned back into the couch with a sigh, his arm around Lev's shoulders. "I'd like to know how he did it. He's good. I lost her trail totally once she and Antha left the luminires. Maybe it was his Cherokee genes making him a good tracker or something."

"Don't you say that to him," Lev said, slapping Birn's stomach.

"*Oof.* I've said it to him already. He's not that sensitive about it."

"He used to hate jokes like that when we were little."

"It's not his fault his parents tailored him that way," Birn said.

"It's easy for you to say: you're untailored and natural born."

He smiled at her. "Ah, but my parents weren't, so doesn't that make me just as much a freak as you are?"

"Birn!" she said indignantly and buried her face in his chest and bit him.

"Ow! You've got a biting gene, oh, no!"

They wrestled playfully, Lev squealing and giggling, while Birn whooped and chuckled.

"No more, no more!" protested Lev after a while, trying to get up.

"Are you sure? Because I can sit on you and squish you flat."

She grinned and shoved him off, then smoothed her clothing and tidied her hair.

"I'm starving," he said, and got up and went over to the kitchen area.

Ramius and Zellie came trotting into the living room, tongues lolling as they panted. Both of them had patches of slobber on their heads and bodies where they had been biting each other. They brightened as they realized Birn was there and rushed over to see him.

"Hello, goobs," he said to them, briskly rumpling their coats with his hands, causing Zellie to lean against his legs. "Oh, Tubby's been digging again," he called to Lev, as he saw Ramius's dirty front paws. "We're going to have to get Omega to spray him with water or something whenever he does it."

"If that'll work," Lev said as she got up. "He loves water so much he might not care or even notice. He might even do it *so* Omega will squirt him."

"Still," he said, "it's worth a try."

"I'll go and find where he's been digging," Lev said as she headed toward the corridor.

"Probably in the veggies," Birn said. "That's where he dug a hole last time. I'll join you in a moment."

Lev walked down the corridor and through an open doorway to her left. She went down a flight of well-lit steps, then along the passageway that led to the right. Another flight of steps off to the right of the passage led down into a huge cavern that was planted out in lush greenery with spots of flowering color here and there. The sweet perfume of rose and honeysuckle mingled in the moist air, and she looked out over the vast expanse of the gardens and breathed in, a smile on her face. She and Birn had worked hard here in the depths of the rock, creating different sections of garden for different purposes throughout the large cavern. Flowers were a luxury, but fruit, vegetables, and grains—these were vital.

The early morning light—which was simulated here by large, overhanging globes that lit the jagged ceiling eerily—danced off the stream that wound its way through the garden. The stream gurgled and bubbled its way across from one side of the cavern to the other before disappearing underground.

Lev and Birn had made good use of the naturally occurring water. Discovering it had made them certain that this was the right place to live. Then they had bought and traded for the precious seeds and plants to build their garden.

Many years ago when the outside climate had become too harsh for plant life, people had preserved and collected as many seeds and plants as they could, and they had grown them underground. It had not been easy, and it could not be done without the help of computer-controlled climates. Certain kinds of insects and worms were also highly prized. Some people were even fortunate enough to acquire and keep beehives. Lev and Birn had made some mistakes along the way, but they had finally got their garden growing well, with Omega's help, and were able to grow a lot of their own food. Whatever else they needed, they traded for with their neighbors.

Lev grabbed a trowel from a container of tools to the side of the steps and walked across a square of lawn, taking the hard-packed dirt path that would lead her through a small rose garden and over to the vegetable garden.

"Gun!" she shouted. "You in here?"

"Yeah," came the reply from somewhere across the other side of the cavern.

"I'll be over by the veggies!" she called.

Lev crossed a small stone bridge and went over to the vegetable garden. Sure enough, there were paw prints in the soft earth, and some of the plants were disturbed. "Ramius," she sighed as she bent down to tidy things up.

She started as a wet nose nudged her arm.

"Ramius! There, look," she said sternly to the puppy. "You're not allowed to dig here." She held one of his front paws and made a digging motion in the dirt, then gently slapped it. "No digging! You shouldn't even be wandering around on this part!"

Ramius licked her hand apologetically.

"Go on! Get off the veggies. Go find Gun. Where's Gun?"

The puppy's eyes widened and his ears twitched, and he ran away with his nose to the ground.

Presently Birn came wandering over eating a plateful of hash browns and two fried eggs. He sat on the stone bridge and watched Lev. "Oh, I forgot to tell you: I brought Imogen's capsule home with me."

Lev laid her trowel down and turned to stare at him. "I don't know if that was such a good idea."

"I thought Omega would be able to check it better than Gina."

"But Omega gave Gina the capability to check for soul life signs. If there had been any, Gina would have found it."

Birn shrugged.

"Where is it now?"

"I left it in the sky car."

"Omega," Lev said, "I want you to check the capsule in Birn's car for any trace of a locator signal or homing beacon."

"No..." Birn said. "You don't think—"

"I'm hoping not." Lev stood up to wait for Omega to report.

>   >   >

"Sorry to disturb your meeting, sir," said Jamon, "but the tracer on the sky car slowed and then disappeared. Last position is southwest of the Pacific Sea—the satellite view showed the sky car going under some rock formations there. Mari is on his way."

"Good," Sevig said, turning away from the screen displaying a grid of faces of those who had linked-in for a conference. "This must be where she hides. In the meantime, keep trying to locate Antha and the fem. He should have contacted me by now to arrange delivery of her. I don't appreciate his tardiness."

>   >   >

"I don't get it," Birn said. "If our masks can cover an imprint, why wouldn't it do the same to a signal?"

He took another bite of hash browns as he sat there on the bridge looking at Lev, his hair shining in the simulated morning sunlight.

"Theoretically, it should," Lev answered as she sat next to him. "But if he knows we're using masks, then hypothetically he could find a way to break through. He seems to have done that already. Otherwise how could he have known about it when Gun took Aphra back to her apartment? I've altered our mask since then, so hopefully we're safe, but there's no knowing what Sevig's computer learned from your contact with him."

"It's too complicated," Birn said, kicking a stone into the garden.

"It's too irritating, you mean," Lev said. "I just want to be left alone. I don't want the past to be dug up again."

"We could move and go live somewhere else."

She looked sidelong at him as they sat together on the stone wall of the bridge. "No, I'm not going to. Why should we?"

"Because he wants to discontinue you, Lavinia! And I'm not going to let that happen."

She stared moodily out at the stream beneath the bridge. "You don't know that. Perhaps I should talk to him again. Do you think I should talk to him again?"

"And say what?"

"I don't know—ask him to forgive me, tell him to get over the past and leave me alone? Tell him we have Aphra and are going to destroy the device, so there's no reason for him to come out here?"

He frowned. "It can't be that simple. This is Sevig we're talking about. Besides, after what I just did to him to get hold of that capsule around his neck…well, I can't see him being in a forgiving frame of mind."

"Which does Sevig want more, the device or Lev?"

It was Gun's voice. He was standing behind them beside the bridge.

"Oh, Gun," Lev said. "I didn't hear you."

Gun walked onto the bridge, the dogs trotting at his side. "Which would Sevig want more?"

"The device, I hope," Birn said. "But I'm sure he wants Lev, too."

"No," Lev said. "I don't believe that. It's been four years since I disappeared from Sevig's labs and faked my death. You'd think if he really hadn't believed I was discontinued, we would have seen more evidence of that before now." She sighed and leaned against Birn. "I can hardly believe he used to have such a hold over me. It seems like ancient history." She smiled up at him. "If it hadn't been for you, I don't know what would have happened."

Birn wrapped his arm around her. "Yeah, but I think I caused more resentment and bitterness to come spewing out at you from Sevig."

"I don't know why he was so jealous—his attention had already turned to Imogen by the time I met you. Do you really think he had something to do with her accident?" Lev closed her eyes as pain rose up at the thought of her best friend. "Maybe I should've stayed at Sevig Empire... tried to investigate some more, but I..."

"You weren't able to," Birn said gently. "Don't start feeling guilty about it again. You did the best thing by leaving. Maybe it's time we packed up and got ourselves a nice little spaceship of our own and cruised the galaxy."

"I prefer being a hermit here on Earth. Besides, look at all this," she said, indicating the garden with a sweep of her hand. "We've worked so hard on it, and it would be a shame to leave just when we've got it growing well."

Gun leaned against the other side of the bridge, facing them. "You two really aren't serious about leaving, are you?"

"No," Birn said. "We just don't know what to expect from Sevig, that's all. Whether he has used a signal and penetrated our mask, we don't know. We can either stay here and wait for someone to show up, or we can leave now."

"Omega's security won't let anyone through, though," Gun said hesitantly.

"Theoretically, yes," Lev said. "We've never had to test it before."

"And Sevig is only seeking you out now that you have Aphra—he hasn't come after you before," continued Gun.

Lev nodded.

"Give him what he wants, then, and maybe he'll leave you alone."

"No! The device must be destroyed!"

Gun looked at her thoughtfully. "Is it really that bad?"

"Yes!"

"What is it exactly?"

Lev sighed. "OK, look, here's the short version. A long time ago, back when we worked for Sevig, Ryan and I began to work on an idea. We wanted to create a special program for the personifids that would effectively prevent them from being able to do evil."

"Evil?"

"Back then we used the phrase 'wrong decisions that lead to harmful effects.' Basically, we wanted to be able to stop people from doing rotten things. No more wars, no more bombing, no more intentional discontinuing of others, no more rape, and so on. As you know, the attempts to weed out that kind of behavior through the selection of genes did not work because, at the time, the presence of the soul was not factored in. When it was, then there were some who thought that once the soul was transferred into the artificial body it would no longer be affected by the genetic inheritance of the human body—that the soul is pure and it is the body that is corrupt and produces corruption. Now that we have thousands of personifids, we have seen that this has not been the case—there has been no reduction of bad behavior.

"Now, you can't manipulate a soul the way you can DNA. Ryan and I thought we should alter the personifid brain so that it would not permit any evil action. We began our task with the best of intentions, only desiring that we could somehow prevent the horror of the evil things we saw happening every day in this world. But as we learned more about what enabling this program would require, we began to see that the solution was something that should not be inflicted upon anybody."

Gun looked from her to Birn and back. "And that would be?"

"Maybe I should show you." Lev buried her face in her hands. "I don't know," she said, her voice muffled. "Why did I do this? How could I have done this?"

Birn laid his hand on her shoulder. "You didn't know," he said gently. "Like you say, you did it with the best of intentions."

She rubbed her eyes and took a deep breath. "So many evil things are done with the best of intentions." She looked over at Gun. "See, in order to make this work, someone in the design process has to define the qualities of good or bad, right or wrong, to equip the personifid brain to make the correct judgment. And by the time we got fully into trying to make a clear definition of this, we found ourselves in over our heads—it's just endless. Then of course, we found that for a person good and bad is often subjective, so what gave us the right to make that decision for them? We turned to a study of religions to find commonalities of what is referred to as good or bad, but even then we found variations. And that was only one of our problems. Look at this. Omega, go back to our old records of the Deific device and display footage of the modification of our last trial subjects."

A screen appeared, hovering alongside them on the bridge in their garden chamber. They watched as it showed the interior of a brightly lit room. Two personifids, a man and a fem, stood motionless in the center of the room, while Lev and Ryan walked slowly around them, examining them with handheld brain activity meters.

"These personifids had recently been convicted of serious crimes," Lev explained, "and correctional authorities in Min City had authorized their status as eligible for behavior modification trials at Sevig Empire. Precisely what kind of trials were going to take place...well...we didn't make that known."

"Shielding in place," came the voice of Omega on the recording.

Ryan checked his meter. "We're ready; go ahead."

"Device implants activated."

The personifids swayed a little on their feet and looked around the room.

"Tell me who you are," Lev said to them.

"I don't know," said the fem slowly, while the man stated his name.

"You are free to go," Lev said. "What would you like to do?"

The fem opened her mouth slightly but said nothing.

"We've lost her," Ryan said as he watched his brain activity meter. "Is she comatose?"

"Yes," answered Omega.

"I would like to..." began the man. "I would like to sit."

Lev indicated a chair against the wall behind him.

He turned and looked at it. "I would like to sit."

"You may," Lev said.

He sat carefully and looked straight ahead, his arms hanging stiffly by his sides.

"Don't tell him what to do," Ryan said to Lev. He smiled encouragingly at the man. "Listen, friend, what would you like to do? Can you feel any desire at all?"

The man stared at them. "I feel..."

"At least he is speaking," Ryan said in an aside to Lev. "That's an improvement."

"I think he speaks only because we question him," she

answered. "He seems to be functioning all right otherwise. We can leave him now."

"Friend, you are free to go," said Ryan. "You may do whatever you wish to do."

Lev and Ryan left the room, and the door closed behind them.

The screen in front of Birn, Gun, and Lev dimmed. Then the date display shifted, indicating that much time had passed. The screen cleared again, showing the same room. The man still sat in the chair, staring straight ahead. The fem now lay on the floor, rolling from side to side and uttering strangled sounds.

"She's fighting it," Lev said to Gun as they watched. "This was all she was physically capable of doing. She gave up eventually. He remained a drone, unable to do anything at all unless we told him to do it. All emotive-based choices were impossible for him to act on. Because we were tampering with the decision-making algorithms, we were not only taking away the ability to choose to do the wrong thing, but we were also taking away the ability to choose to do the right thing!

"For instance, when you dissect the decision to kill, you're led back to what is supposedly simple. Hate, envy, and greed are just some of the possible foundations of that decision. So if you inhibit passioned emotions, not only do you affect the ability to feel an emotion such as hatred, you are doing just the same for the ability to feel love. Our attempt to work this out was an absolute failure. In eliminating the decision for bad, we naturally eliminated the decision for good."

"Couldn't you separate the negative emotions from the positive?" Gun asked.

"Omega, close the file," Lev said, waving her hand at the screen, causing it to disappear. "Ryan believed so. I didn't.

What you're asking is to prevent people from thinking. We're talking about free will here. Thought and emotion are often interwoven; one will precede the other and lead to action. You can't suppress one without affecting the other. It reduces the personifids to little more than drones, unable to make decisions for themselves. The soul can no longer 'drive' the personifid body freely, so in effect it becomes trapped.

"That's what I realized we were about to inflict on free souls, whoever paid for the newest and greatest personifids. I had helped create the device that would eliminate free will and turn people into puppets. And all the time I kept thinking about something I'd found in my study of those world religions—well, just one of them, actually. As I'd studied the religion of the Tri-une Soul, I'd seen the One, the Son, weeping in a garden, wrestling with a choice. All of mankind held suspended by His ability to freely choose His path."

She leaned against Birn and closed her eyes. "That's when I knew...well, that's when I knew a few things. The first thing was that here I was, living my life as a liar. Not only lying to myself, but also to other people. And living my life as a hater and a user of other people."

"You weren't that bad," Birn said. "Don't be so hard on yourself."

She looked at him, seeming almost indignant. "Yeah, that's what I thought at the time! I thought I was a good person. I tried my best, did what I thought was right. Then the Tri-une Soul came along and told me different. It was a huge shock! All of a sudden I found I was looking at myself through a whole other filter, and I could see all the rot in my life, all the lies I told, all the sneering criticisms, deliberate cruelty to other people—especially Sevig. Our relationship was so twisted that what we thought was love was neediness, desperation, manipulation."

She pressed the heels of her hands against her eyes and shook her head. "*Bleh.* In that moment I saw myself clearly then. All it took for me to see it was meeting the Tri-une Soul and listening to what He had to say about my life and my work. Talk about shame! What felt even worse—because I felt I didn't deserve it—was that He offered to forgive me and make things right in my life, clear out all the lies, the hatred, everything. It was like being stripped bare in front of someone who could see everything, everything you'd ever done, yet loved you anyway.

"It changed everything for me. I began to see the personifids in a new light. For almost fourteen years I had worked on the project, my goal being to extend life for all people indefinitely. It was what I dreamed of—life on our own terms. It's what mankind has been desiring for centuries! I pushed myself to create better and stronger models, capable of holding onto a soul for longer.

"No one on the outside has been allowed to learn just how faulty the personifids actually are. They're better now, but back then it was still really early on in the project. You know, I couldn't even become one myself after seeing all the accidents that occurred in the first trials we did. But the commercials have everyone believing they're infallible.

"Yet death comes to everyone eventually. The personifid technology doesn't defeat it; it just pushes it back, where people hope it is swept aside and ignored. Humans have showed they're the biggest ignorers of death on the planet while simultaneously being the biggest fearers of it—all throughout history there have been attempts to prolong life and stave off death. Yet it wasn't until the personifids were created that we were able to talk about death more openly. Or should I say 'discontinuation.'" She smiled ruefully. "We use that word as though we believe that now, yes, we have finally won the battle, we have finally won over death.

"Yet when I read about the Tri-une, I saw that He's already done that. I could hardly believe my eyes when I saw that's what He offered to me—freedom from spiritual death. Personifids can't offer that. All they can offer is to become even greater shielders of our own soul, even greater ignorers of death, and all the while we become more narrow and twisted in our fear.

"So amazing that He could forgive me for what I had been trying to do. He died so that I might live. And He came to life again so that I . . ." She paused for breath, tears welling up in her eyes. "I knew then I had to stop working on the Deific device. I had to destroy all my work. I had to disappear." She swept a tear from her cheek. "It all seems like it happened such a long time ago," she said. "I thought I had destroyed all our work when I left and took Omega."

"Maybe you should have given Ryan a mindwipe while you were at it," Birn said.

"I guess I underestimated his capabilities."

"You aren't responsible for Ryan's decisions," he said, and kissed her. "All we can do now is try and clean up the mess he left."

"You never told me this before," Gun said morosely.

"Lev didn't want to talk about it when she left the labs," Birn replied. "You know how she was then. She'd been through a lot."

Lev stood and brushed the dirt from her trousers and picked up her trowel. "Birn's right, Gun. Once I met the Tri-une, all my work suddenly seemed ridiculous and presumptuous. I suddenly saw that the only aim of creating the Deific device was to replace the Tri-une Soul's voice—as though a human-made device was somehow more capable of defining what was right and wrong. Ryan could never see it. I'd had a complete change of heart about our work, but he wouldn't even listen to my objections."

"Nobody else is working on a Deific device?" Gun asked.

"I can't be sure," Lev said glumly. "It's a universal idea, after all. I do know that Ryan and I kept our work secret because we were going to release it and surprise the world and revel in the accolades." She gave a wry smile. "Now look at us—he's dead and I'm in hiding, having faked my death."

"You made the right decision," Birn said.

She was silent for a moment, considering his words. "Ironic, isn't it?"

Gun picked up a stone and threw it into the stream. Ramius and Zellie bounded off after it. "How much did Sevig know about all of this?"

"He knew all of it," Lev admitted. "I wish he hadn't known, but I was still entangled with him at the time, and he was funding the work I did with Ryan. What a fool I was!"

"You can't keep kicking yourself," Birn said. "You've left Sevig behind."

Misery crossed Lev's face as she watched the dogs splashing about in the water. "I thought I had, but he's caught up with me again," she said. "I can't allow him to make use of the device. I can't! Who knows what he would do with it? Nobody should have it, least of all him!" She threw her trowel onto the path. "I won't allow it!"

She placed both hands on the bridge railing and leaned against it, gazing out at the distant side of the cavern, tears gathering in her eyes. "I don't know what he wants with it. I was beginning to think he had some twisted idea about using it on Imogen, but I just don't know if she is really still alive, as Ryan believed. I wish I did know."

Gun got up and walked away. He wound his way through

the gardens and up the steps out of the cavern.

"What are we going to do about Mari?" Birn asked. "If it's true what you say, that Ryan altered Mari with a prototype of the device, we can't just leave him under its effect."

"It's complicated," she said. "I'd have to get into his brain and see what can be done. In our other trials, the coding within the brain and throughout the personifid body became so fouled up that the easiest thing to do was to discard the personifid and give the soul a new body. But you're right; we can't leave Mari like that. I'll have to help him."

"Aphra is showing signs of illness," came Omega's voice. "I am attempting to bring her body back to normality."

"Don't touch her left arm yet," Lev said hastily. "Is she awake?"

"No."

"What's wrong with her?" Birn asked. "She's been sick before. Why?"

Lev turned to him. "I suspect Ryan did a hatchet job on her. When he removed her arm and gave her the prosthetic, he must also have done a selective mindwipe and replacement memory of that time. It's not generally known, but many people end up brain-damaged or just plain mad from mindwipes and memory reintegrations. Aphra's fortunate she has only experienced physical illness. This was not Ryan's field—he should never have overseen this at all."

Birn frowned. "He never should have done this to Aphra at all, you mean. The guy was insane."

Lev shook her head. "Stop saying that about him. He was only doing what he thought was best. Her symptoms make me think he did this very recently to her. With some rest and care she should recover. Omega, is Aphra well enough to begin the removal of the arm?"

"Yes."

"Right then. I'd better wake her up and get this over and done with."

Birn caught hold of her arm. "We've forgotten someone."

"Who?"

"Julian! If Sevig has been able to penetrate my sky car's mask and keep in contact with his blasted tracer, then we need to lock up tight. And that goes for our neighbor as well, just in case."

"True," Lev said. "We'd better be prepared." She headed for the steps.

❭   ❭   ❭

The old fem whistled to herself as she cleaned underneath the chickens' roosting perch, the tangy aroma of the chicken coop surrounding her. Straggly mousy-brown hair escaped the knot at the nape of her neck as she bent over, scrubbing with a rag, her thin arms moving vigorously. She looked over at the green plastic nesting box, soft shredded plastic spilling over its sides, and disappointment showed on her careworn face.

"Only one egg this morning," she said to the five hens and rooster that were milling around hopefully behind her in the coop, waiting for her to give them some feed. "You'll have to do better than that, fems."

"Julian," came Omega's voice.

"Yes?"

"Birn advises you to lock yourself in, as dangerous company may be expected in this area."

She straightened up slowly, with one hand to her hip. "You tell them I want some more greens for my birds."

"Do you wish me to lock up for you?"

"No, I can do it. Now go on home." Julian left the chicken coop, tossing her cleaning rags down on the stone floor and reaching for the chicken feed. She threw a scoopful into the coop, and the chickens dashed over to it.

"Not for you," she said, pushing away a ginger cat that was trying to get its head into the feed bin. A gray kitten tried to creep into the chicken coop but was gently zapped by the force field that kept the cats out and the chickens in. Julian picked the kitten up, rubbed its head, and gave it a kiss. "There," she said, "I told you, didn't I?"

She walked from the small, cubbyhole cave of a room that served as home for her chickens and down a short dark hallway, the sound of her soft shoes patting the uneven rock floor. An amber glow came from the lamps in her living room, spreading into a block of light on the hallway floor and wall, illuminating her face kindly. Eight more cats were in this room; two kittens wrestled with each other on the wine-colored rugs on the floor, three older cats were asleep on the battered old brown couch, and the others were on their own blanket-draped chairs and looked up at Julian's approach.

"Lock up," she muttered, as she shuffled along. "I should just do away with the door altogether. I don't need it."

> > >

"Aphra, wake up," Lev said.

Aphra moaned and rolled over.

"I'm sorry for not letting you sleep, but I think it's important that we deal with your arm now."

Aphra sat up and swung her legs over the edge of the bed. Then she leaned forward, her head in her hands. "What's happening to me?" she asked thickly. "I feel awful."

"I don't think Ryan really knew what he was doing. He should never have worked on a real person. I'm so sorry he used you like this."

"He was my friend," Aphra answered simply. "The only person I really knew. And look what he did to me."

"I'm sorry."

Aphra looked up at Lev, her face clouded with a frown, for those words did not make her feel any better about her situation.

"I will remove your arm and see about getting you a replacement—"

"He took my arm! It was my arm, and he didn't ask me before he took it! He just took it! What kind of a friend does something like that?"

"But I thought you wanted to become a personifid. Birn said you told him you did."

"What does that have to do with anything?"

"Just that Ryan wouldn't have given your body the respect it deserved if he knew you were planning to throw it away anyway."

Aphra muttered wordlessly.

"Hey," Lev said, "I'm the one who used to advocate doing just that! I was developing the Personifid Project along with Ryan."

Aphra looked at Lev appraisingly, surprised by this new piece of information. "I don't recognize you," she said slowly. "I thought I knew what all the important developers looked like."

"A few years have gone by since I was working within the Personifid Project," answered Lev, as she sat down on the end of the bed. "I was there in the beginning when we made exciting breakthroughs in personifid soul transfers. If it hadn't been for Bob Lumin—the inventor of the luminire—and his comprehensive work on the soul's attachment to the physical body, then perhaps we would still be struggling to make the project work."

"Why did you leave Sevig Empire?" Aphra asked.

Lev's dark brown eyes filled with sadness. Aphra saw the change of emotion in her and felt a surge of sympathetic feeling in response. She wanted to sit nearer to Lev, to put her arm about her as Marlena had done so many times to comfort, but she felt too awkward to do so.

"A number of reasons," Lev said. "One was that I worked too hard, reached burnout, ignored it and pushed onward with Life Enhancements and did not allow myself to stop. I finally collapsed, and after that my brain simply refused to work properly for me."

Aphra listened silently, shocked that anyone could talk so calmly about this sort of subject. She looked at Lev and wondered if she was right to trust her.

"It was the best thing that could have happened to me," Lev continued. She smiled as she saw Aphra's eyes widen at that revelation. "Once I stopped and allowed myself to feel, allowed myself to do nothing, I began to learn more about myself and others than I ever had done before. So I left the project behind and came out here with Birn."

"You're still burned out?" Aphra asked tentatively.

Lev shook her head. "It took me a long time to come right and be able to think analytically again for any length of time. I began by doing physical work, gardening, planning the interior of our home, nothing too demanding. I like to think I am as mentally sharp as I used to be, and perhaps even more so, but I certainly don't work long hours in programming as I did while on the Personifid Project—I find I get tired more quickly. So my whole way of life has changed."

"But you are able to help me?"

"Yes, of course. Perhaps I shouldn't have told you about my mental collapse right before I work on your arm." Lev grinned mischievously and gave Aphra a sisterly squeeze. "I just want you to feel at ease here and know that I will do my best to help you. I feel partly responsible for what has happened to you, and I want to help fix things."

"I do trust you," Aphra said thoughtfully. Lev's hugging her had taken her by surprise, and she looked at the floor, uncertain how to feel about having received an affectionate touch from a real person. She did not know whether she really did trust Lev, but she had said it because she wanted to believe it. Lev was unlike anybody she had ever met—she exuded an air of confidence and ease that Aphra wished to have for herself. To be surrounded by real people, with the tangible sense of a life force within each of them, contrasted starkly with her relationships with robot and computer companions of the past. Yet if people could be like Lev, maybe it would not be so bad.

"Good. Come on then," Lev said, getting up and going over to the door.

Aphra slowly got to her feet and followed Lev, pausing at the door to place a hand against the wall to steady herself.

9

"WHERE ARE THE others?" Aphra asked as they entered the lab.

"They're keeping watch on the vultures gathering outside," Lev answered. "Mari, a couple of androids, and Antha are all in the area."

"Antha is here?" Aphra asked.

"Not far from here, yes."

Aphra said nothing, briefly wondering if she should reveal that she and Antha were related. It would be awkward trying to explain to Lev about her family history. It never made for agreeable conversation, and she certainly did not want to talk about it while she was feeling so ill.

"Sit on this chair," Lev said, indicating a low seat, which Aphra gladly took. Lev then pushed another chair over to Aphra's left side and sat down. "Omega, give me a little height. Put an armrest extending out here." Lev pointed at the side of Aphra's chair as her own chair rose slightly. She took Aphra's left arm and laid it out on the clear armrest. "Higher," Lev said, and Omega moved the armrest upward. "Stop. Put safeguards for explosives, spikes, and worms in place. Give me magnification." Lev bent over the arm and peered at it through the magnification field that Omega provided. "OK, give me an internal view as well."

Aphra shut her eyes, hoping nothing would explode.

"Hmm, tricky."

Aphra opened her eyes and looked sidelong at Lev. "Can you do it?"

"Ryan has rigged the explosives with sensors—tiny threads, probably a few thousand or so," Lev said without looking up. "I can work my way through, bypassing them all, but it may take some time."

Lev held out her right hand. "Laser finger, smallest beam, please." Omega attached a minute laser beam to Lev's forefinger. Aphra saw nothing; it was too small for her to see without magnification. Lev moved her finger so that the beam shone on one of the sensor threads. "Isolate this one. Show me what it's made of. Detach it if you can do so safely."

❯   ❯   ❯

"I have found signs of dwellings in this area," said Mari as he sat in his sky car looking at the screen. "Last position from the satellite leads to a rock face. Scans show it is solid rock."

"Ignore the scans," Sevig said. "Blast it."

Mari nodded. He moved his hand over the sights in front of him, and the weapons from his sky car discharged. "No effect," he announced as he looked at the untouched rock face. Something inside him felt strange, out of place. He looked at his console, checking his weapon banks to see if the problem was there.

"Again," Sevig said.

Mari moved immediately to obey, his hand moving heavily over the laser missile release. He watched as the red laser fire appeared to be absorbed by the rock, again causing no effect. It made no sense to him. There should be fragments of rock exploding off the rock face, not this strange absorption. But he did not pause to consider it. He merely fired again. The rock face stayed immovable—a gray craggy mass looming in front of him, shadowed by his sky car.

It began to hurt to see the wall there. It was torture knowing what he had to do, yet not being able to follow through. He tried again, his head aching from the effort of will.

"Blast it," he repeated to himself. "Blast it again."

❯   ❯   ❯

"Well, that tells us someone is in there and protecting their little fortress," Sevig said to Craf as he watched the screen in front of him that displayed the point of view from within Mari's sky car.

"Sir, incoming call from Lavinia Michelson," said Jamon.

"Display."

"Hello, Sevig."

Sevig looked coldly at the lovely dark face superimposed on his screen. "Lavinia. What do you want now? Do you miss me?"

"I have Aphra, and Omega is now removing the Deific device from her," Lev replied.

Sevig drew in a sharp breath, but that was the only visible reaction he gave to hearing that information. "I have to admire your nerve, reappearing as you have and keeping up the act that nothing ever happened between us."

"Call off Mari and his friends," Lev said. "I'm going to

destroy the device. You'll never get your stinking hands on it."

"You're still as pleasant as always—being dead hasn't affected you in the slightest."

"You never had Imogen at all, did you? It was just a ploy to draw me out. It worked on Ryan, and now it's worked on me. You knew it would."

"It brought your hired thug after me."

"Birn is my husband. If you don't call off Mari, I will cause irreparable damage to your mainframe systems—"

"Oh, Lavinia, I'm surprised at you. I thought you were above threats of violence and revenge and that sort of thing. It's not very Christian of you, you know."

"Don't talk to me about what's Christian and what isn't! You told Ryan you had his wife captive and then ordered his discontinuation! How could you do such a thing! I—"

"Before your temper flares out of control—much as I always enjoyed it when that happened—think about what you're saying. You would have Imogen be my Bathsheba, when she is nothing of the sort. You know you're the only one I ever loved," he said sarcastically, "so why would I keep someone else's wife captive?"

"Don't sneer at me. You never loved me."

He laid his hand on his heart. "You wound me."

"Shut up. Look, I don't know whether you have kept Imogen alive, but if you have, I'll find out and I'll—"

"You'll what?"

"She was my best friend, Sevig! She never wanted you. She loved Ryan! I don't know what you've done with her, but if you do have her and you're hoping to use this device on her to make her love you, it won't work."

Sevig stared at her, tight-lipped.

"It won't work," Lev repeated. "It can't work. Give her a

personifid body if you haven't already, and let her go free. If you use the device on her, you would cause Imogen to be little more than an emotionless android. She would no longer be the Imogen you know. You would destroy her!"

"Disconnect!" shouted Sevig, slamming his fist down on the desk.

The screen in front of him disappeared.

"Blast it all!" he shouted, leaping up. "Now!"

"Sir," said Jamon, "Mari's weapons are having no effect."

Sevig kicked his desk and threw his chair at the wall.

"Rage," said Craf, watching with interest. "Yet another emotion I do not have."

>   >   >

Lev sat with her head bowed for a moment, wiping away the tears that had gathered. Aphra, who still sat in the chair next to her, reached over with her right hand and touched Lev gently on the arm.

"Are you all right?" she asked hesitantly.

"I will be." Lev looked at Aphra and smiled feebly.

"Can we come in?" came Birn's voice through Omega's com channel.

"Sure," answered Lev. "Just don't let the dogs through."

Birn and Gun entered the lab. Aphra met Birn's friendly smile, glad to see him again. He brought with him a sense of security, and she was interested in that, for he was merely a person. She looked briefly at Gun, unsure whether she was glad to see him or not. He always seemed so calm and under control, and it intrigued her that he could be like that while shunning Life Enhancers.

"Omega's shields are holding," Birn said. "Good thing, too,

because Mari is doing his best to get through them. How's that arm coming along? Are you almost done?"

"Omega doesn't need my help to remove it," Lev said. "We looked at the sensors Ryan has used and recognized the coding. Ryan made it pretty easy for me."

"You've been crying; what's wrong?"

"Sevig," she said simply.

"Don't let him get to you," Birn said, as he put his arms around Lev and held her. "It's all in the past. You're with me now."

Lev buried her face against his chest. Her shoulders shook as she cried silently. Aphra watched uncomfortably out of the corner of her eye, careful not to appear bothered by seeing Lev's emotional behavior, yet also wondering if she should try to offer more comfort. No ideas occurred to her about how to do that, so she sat quietly.

"All sensors in the prosthetic arm have now been deactivated," said Omega.

Lev took a deep breath and turned to look at Aphra's arm. "Is it safe to remove the arm? How does Aphra's shoulder look?"

"Aphra's shoulder is healthy, but because it is a fully integrated prosthesis, removal does have a small amount of risk."

"This is not my area of expertise," Lev said. "I'm used to dealing with robots." She bit her lip. "Omega, can you do it on your own?"

"I have all the required medical and physiological programming. I will seal the shoulder, but it will be possible to fit it with another prosthesis at a later date."

"I don't want to see any of this," Aphra said, pulling a face at the thought of seeing her arm being removed.

"Omega, visual and audio environment for Aphra," Lev said. "Play her a movie."

Aphra was immediately enveloped in her own virtual reality and could see only a small empty room around her as she heard Omega say, "Please select a movie." The wall in front of her lit up in a grid of many different movie trailers, and she looked at them all. "None of these," she said, and the wall changed and displayed another group of trailers. "*Desert World*," she said, as she saw a trailer for one of her favorite movies. The grid of trailers disappeared, and her chosen movie was then displayed on the wall. Aphra looked down at her left arm, saw nothing unusual about it, grimaced, and sat back to watch the movie.

Outside of her isolated environment, Birn, Gun, and Lev saw the relaxed expression on Aphra's face as she gazed past them, and knew Omega could begin to remove the prosthetic arm.

〉　　　　　〉　　　　　〉

"This is near where I left a beacon," Antha said as his sky car scudded across the barren landscape. "So, José really does live around here. I knew it!"

"Still unable to pick up the fem's signal again," came the voice of the sky car's computer.

"Well, keep your ears open."

"Incoming call."

"Go ahead."

"Identify yourself," said Mari as his face appeared on Antha's screen.

"You first," Antha said.

"Identify yourself, or you will face the consequences."

"Oh no, I wouldn't want to do that," drawled Antha. "I don't like consequences—or any kind of quinces, really.

Oranges are much more to my taste."

Mari looked blankly at Antha.

〉 〉 〉

"Mari and Antha have begun attacking each other," said Omega. "Also, Antha has destroyed the android that was investigating the outer sky car entrance."

"How long until the arm is removed?" Birn asked. "If they're busy walloping each other, it should give us the chance we need. We can slip out and detonate the arm before they know what's happened."

"Ninety-six seconds until complete separation," said Omega.

"How will you get out? They're right outside the garage," Lev said.

"If we use the H-Rs, we can get into the narrow gullies around here—sky cars won't be able to follow us through them," Birn replied.

"I'll go and ready the H-Rs," Gun said as he ran from the lab.

"I'll meet you at the porch," Birn called after him.

"But the sky cars are faster and safer!" Lev protested. "Gun! They might drop explosive charges down into the gullies onto you!"

Gun ignored her and disappeared through the door.

"The shields will hold," Birn said, catching hold of Lev as she started to go after Gun. "We'll be all right."

"But the H-Rs' backup power cells are unreliable. If you lose power, you'll be an easy target!"

"Gun fixed them." He held her steady and looked down into her eyes. "Lev, this is the best way. Gun and I have already made our plans, and we're ready to do this. We got the H-Rs out and gave them a test run, and they're fine; all systems are fully functional."

"I don't like it."

"Would you rather we stayed here and let Mari blast his way into our home and take the arm? Lev, we have to do something; we can't just stay here. This is the best way—we can sneak out through the porch, get a safe distance away from here, and detonate the arm. As soon as Mari and the others are drawn away from the garage, you and Aphra must get into one of the sky cars and get out of here."

"But what about you? How will you get away from them?"

"Send the other sky car to pick us up."

"I don't know," Lev said, looking anxiously at Birn. "Can this work?"

"It's our best option right now." He kissed her forehead lightly.

"Be careful," she pleaded, hugging him.

"Of course we will. Our lives are in the Tri-une Soul's hands, though. Always. Don't forget that."

"How could I, after everything He's done for me? You just make sure you're not anywhere near the device when you explode it."

He smiled at her. "Of course."

"Removal of prosthesis complete," said Omega. "Protective seal and shielding of Aphra's shoulder now in place."

"Are Mari and Antha and the other android still outside the garage door?" Birn asked.

"Yes."

"I hope they stay there a little while longer." Birn gingerly picked up the prosthetic arm, leaned over and kissed Lev firmly on the lips, then left the lab.

❯   ❯   ❯

Birn walked briskly along the passageway that led to the right, careful not to run while he held the arm. He soon came to where Gun and the two Hover-Riders were waiting—beyond the open doorway that led to the jagged hole in the rock over-looking the sea. Gun sat on his H-R, looking out over the edge, scanning the horizon for any movement. Birn quickly went up the steps and through the doorway, got on the other H-R, and secured the prosthetic arm in front of him.

"Ready?"

"Ready," answered Gun, and they moved off swiftly.

❭   ❭   ❭

Aphra's movie suddenly stopped. She looked down at her left arm. A holo-replacement arm was there, a strong and vivid image that no shadow was able to rest upon. The ends of her shoulder-length hair dangled down into it and disappeared, giving the impression of growing down into the arm. She tried to move it, shrugging her left shoulder, but the arm simply shifted curiously at her side in response as it matched the movement of her shoulder.

Her mind felt oddly detached. Omega must have dosed her up on pain suppressants and emotion absorbers. She looked at her arm, but it seemed as though she looked on someone else's body.

"Aphra," Lev said, drawing her attention. "Try not to look at it. We haven't got time to do anything more right now. We have to leave; we're in danger here. Are you ready to move? Do you feel OK?"

"I think so," she answered, and got up out of her chair slowly, feeling oddly off-balance. She looked at Lev and told herself that this must be real now. She tried to make her brain accept what she was seeing, that she must no longer be in virtual reality watching a movie that Omega was playing for her. "I feel...funny."

"It's the pain suppressors," Lev said. "Don't worry about it."

"Antha and Mari have now changed course and are following Gun and Birn," said Omega.

"Display that," Lev said, taking Aphra by her right arm and helping support her as they walked across the lab.

Two small screens hovered before them. In one, Lev and Aphra could see Antha's sky car racing away ahead of Mari's. Both sky cars were blackened and scarred, but intact. Aphra mutely watched, hoping her brother was all right. The other screen showed Birn and Gun speeding across rocky ground on the H-Rs.

"Keep trying to disable their sky cars," Lev said. "Are you able to get a fix on Mari or Antha yet?"

"Unable," said Omega. "No luminire lock possible."

"That's strange."

The screens merged as Gun and Birn went down into a gully and disappeared from view, while Antha and Mari flew overhead. The criss-crossing of laser fire went from Antha to Mari and down into the gully.

Suddenly a huge explosion came from the gully. An orange and black fireball surged up into the sky. Mari's sky car swerved to avoid it, and he crashed into a rock formation. His sky car went down into the gully and was lost to sight.

"Was that my arm blowing up?" Aphra asked.

They stopped short of the lab door. "I hope so," Lev said. "But what a place to do it! Birn, Gun, what happened?"

"Connection failure," said Omega. "Unable to reach either of them."

"Try again."

"Unable to connect."

"How can you be unable to connect? You've been tracking the H-Rs, haven't you? What is their position?"

"Unable to connect to either of the H-Rs."

"You don't think they crashed, do you?" Aphra asked.

"I don't know," Lev said, watching the screen anxiously. "What about movement? Can you detect any movement down there? Can you hook up to a satellite and show me where they are?"

"External scanners are offline."

"What are you talking about? How can they be offline?"

"Internal scanners are now offline," Omega said. "I suspect there is a spider in my system, but I am unable to search for it. I recommend I shut down all unnecessary functions. Now commencing protection and detachment of data files in specified order of importance."

"Oh, no!" Lev wailed.

"You do not wish for me to proceed?"

"Yes, proceed!"

>   >   >

Birn lay dazed on the ground some distance from the smoldering wreck of his H-R.

"Get up," said the voice again, and a hand tugged at his sleeve.

He opened his eyes and saw Julian standing over him.

"You can't stay out here," she said curtly.

He got up slowly and rubbed his head. He felt a warm stickiness and drew his hand away, looking bleary-eyed at his red-smeared fingers.

"You're not hurt too bad." Julian walked away through one of the narrow gaps in the gully. She led the way through the winding rocky pathways, walking briskly over the uneven ground. Birn stumbled after her, hardly knowing what he was doing. Julian ducked into the hole that was the entranceway to her cave.

Once through the shields and into the tunnel that led to her front door, Birn sucked in the refined air and breathed easier. The dark rock walls were cool, and he placed his hand against them, the rough texture jolting his senses.

The front door slid across as Julian came to it, and they went inside.

"I've lost power from your computer," she said, not looking at Birn, "but my little old computer is working fine." Two of her cats hissed and one growled as they saw him, and they hopped off the couch and ran behind it. One of the kittens slunk from the room, its ears flattened back against its head. The other cats and kittens in the room looked warily at Birn.

"Lost power?" Birn repeated dully. Then he looked at his companion and realized where he was. It was Julian. And Julian was not good with people. Sometimes she found Birn's size and appearance intimidating. "Thanks, Julian," he said gently. "I'll not bother you or stay long. Do you mind if I use your computer?"

She waved her hand dismissively at him as she left the room. "Go ahead."

Birn sat heavily on a chair, and one of the friendlier cats came up to him and rubbed against his legs. "Computer," he said, clearing his throat. "Let me speak to Lev."

"I do not understand," came the subdued voice of the computer.

"Lev," he said, his head in his hands. "Put a call through to Lev."

"Unable to place calls. I do not have that function."

"No way of getting a message out?" he asked, raising his head.

"No."

"Distress signal?"

"No."

He sighed and rubbed his head. "Do you have any robots here?"

"Yes, one."

"Ask Julian if I can borrow it, and if so, send it here."

"The robot is in disrepair and no longer functions."

"Show me where it is."

›　　　　›　　　　›

"What do we do now?" Aphra asked as she and Lev hurried to the lab door.

"We need to—"

Suddenly Aphra's holo-arm flickered and disappeared, and she shrieked. She looked at the stump in shock. More of her shoulder was gone than she had expected.

"Look at me," Lev said firmly, reaching up and waving her hand in front of Aphra's face. "You're OK. We've just lost power to keep the holo-arm there, that's all. Don't look at it, do you hear me?"

Aphra looked down into Lev's dark eyes and gulped as she fought back the rising panic. She felt no pain, only light-headedness, and she told herself it was nothing. It was just a fear game unlike any she had ever been in. Lev's steady gaze, the kindness and concern in her eyes, imbued her with a sense of reassurance.

"Calm down," Lev said. "You're OK. You know I don't

have any Tranquility to give you, don't you?"

Aphra smiled weakly.

"That's better," Lev said. "Now, let's go. We have to get to the sky cars and go after the boys. We can't rely on Omega to protect us anymore."

They approached the door to the lab, but the wall in front of them refused to disappear and reveal the opening beyond. "Blast! The door won't open," she said. "Omega, open the lab door. Can you hear me, Omega? Are you able to open the door?"

The light dimmed for an instant, and the door disappeared. They were met by a warm rush of air from the corridor. Unfiltered, unmodified air.

"The outer shield must be down!" Lev exclaimed. "Come on!"

They ran through the corridor, Lev supporting Aphra, into the living area before stopping at the door that led to the garage. It was closed, and repeated commands to Omega had no effect—the door remained shut.

"What do we do now?" Aphra cried.

"We send robots out," Lev said tersely. She pulled Aphra along with her and back out of the living room.

They went back through the corridor and down the flight of stairs that connected to the lower passageway. Lev ran lightly down the stairs, but Aphra clutched the rail with her right hand and went at a slower pace. She willed herself not to look at her left side but instead to get into a gaming state of mind.

There was an old-style nonautomated door opposite the foot of the stairs. Lev turned the handle to open it and went into a small dark storage room. "If only all the doors were like this," Lev muttered. The light from the corridor gleamed and reflected off the half-dozen robots that stood or sat inactively.

"C-M-P-5-1, C-M-P-5-2, V-R-1-1, V-R-1-2, activate," she commanded.

The lights of the four robots came on, and they swung to their feet. They were sturdily built figures, having no outer casings of the sort that would modify them either into androids or personalized robots. "Awaiting orders," they said simultaneously, in flat metallic voices.

As Aphra joined Lev, she recognized all of the models and felt relieved that they were good, reliable machines. Just the sort she would want in a fear game. A rush of excitement went through her, mingling with a disturbing sense of irrationality.

Lev went quickly to a shelf and picked up two thin, hand-held screens—the remote controls for the Virtua-Robots. Then she looked at Aphra. "Do you think you can do this?"

"I don't know. I'll try," Aphra replied, holding out her hand for a screen.

"All right. You four, take your weapons and get outside. Go through the porch opening, get down to the ground together, then head northwest to the gullies. Be alert for any movement; expect to be attacked. Defend yourselves. Search for human life signs, as I want you to look for Birn and Gun. Accept orders only from myself, Aphra here—"

"This is my voice pattern," Aphra said to the robots.

"—Birn, and Gun," continued Lev. "OK? Now, go."

"Understood," replied the robots. They clanked off along the corridor and up the steps.

"I think I'll activate the others in case we need them," Lev said, as she looked in at the remaining two robots in the storage room. "We may need a Hover-Rider to get out of here, but we need to see the positions of those outside first. H-R-6-1, V-R-1-3, activate."

"Awaiting orders," responded the robots as they stood.

"V-R-1-3, patrol the corridors swiftly; alert me to any intruder. Go."

"Understood," said V-R-1-3, and dashed past them with dizzying speed, headed for the upper level.

Lev pointed at the remaining robot. "H-R-6-1, come with me."

"Understood."

"You've not personalized these robots?" Aphra asked, as she and Lev walked swiftly along the corridor to the open doorway that led down into the garden, the H-R robot following behind them. The fact that the robots talked with metallic voices, had no proper names, and had answered in textbook fashion had not escaped her notice.

"They're machines," Lev answered. "We don't use them for companionship. I used to have robots that I loved and cared for, but when I became a Follower, I learned the Tri-une Soul didn't want me to waste my love on them."

That idea struck Aphra like a solid wall. Waste her love? How was that possible? Love could not be wasted, could it? She thought of Michael, Marlena, Carmel, and the artificial friends she had made in games rooms. Her love for them had been real, genuine. How could loving a friend be wrong and wasteful? Even if the friend was not entirely alive. Yet as she thought of them now, the loss of Michael did not make her feel empty inside. She felt that way only when thinking of Ryan. Ryan was irreplaceable, and she hurt in that place in her heart where he had been. Why was it so different?

She did not finish the thought. She stood at the top of stone steps staring in astonishment at the huge, lush cavern. "Tendous! Amazing! I can't believe you've got all this down here."

"We have to have it to be able to survive out here," Lev

said. "Sit here on the steps; you'll be able to handle the controls better."

Aphra sat and settled the handheld screen on her knee. She tapped the power on, and then saw the visual coming from one of the V-Rs. It was flying down the cliff, looking side to side at the rocky landscape. The two C-M-P robots did not have hover capabilities, so they had connected to the V-Rs and were being carried down. Now and then the other two connected robots came into view on Aphra's screen, and she could see them turning their heads and scanning their surroundings as well.

❭   ❭   ❭

"Are you able to turn life support off?" Sevig asked.

"Not yet, sir," answered Jamon. "Not only have I not been able to access their life support systems, but I find I am having difficulties within my own ethical programming complying with your request."

"Override it. Do as I say."

"I will try to, sir. Outer shields are down, and I am sending one unit inside—it is beginning to cut a hole through the rock as I am still unable to unlock and open the door."

"Only one? Where are the others?"

"One android has been destroyed. Mari is down but still functioning. His sky car is in need of repair—"

"Yes, yes, but how far away is he?"

"Mari is approximately two kilometers away."

❭   ❭   ❭

"I see it!" exclaimed Aphra, as she watched her screen. The visual from her V-R's point of view showed the intruding android standing in the gully outside the entrance to Lev and Birn's home. Laser in hand, it was busily cutting a hole in the outer garage door. "V-R-1-2, blast it!"

"No, wait," Lev said. "It might be a personifid! V-R-1-1, check target for soul life signs."

But it was too late, Aphra's V-R had already fired its weapon, causing the android to spasm and turn from its work. As the V-R fired, one of the C-M-P robots automatically followed suit.

"Blast it, blast it!" cried Aphra, and giggled as the screen showed the android leveling its weapon directly at her.

"No soul life signs shown," came the crackly voice from Lev's screen.

"Discontinue the target," ordered Lev.

The android had no chance against the four robots. It was quickly blasted into a tangled lump of steaming metal and plastic.

"Give me a visual of the garage door," Lev said. She watched as her V-R walked across the rocky ground to the remains of the android and showed the gaping hole in the garage door and a limited view of the sky cars inside. "I think we should split up," Lev said to Aphra. "One of us needs to go after Birn and Gun, while the other guards our home. I'll take one of the sky cars and go after the boys. You patrol the outside."

"OK," Aphra said eagerly.

"V-R-1-1 and C-M-P-5-1, get into a sky car and search for Birn and Gun," Lev ordered. "C-M-P-5-2, remain with V-R-1-2. Omega, can you open the garage door?"

Aphra and Lev sat silently and watched their screens, but the garage door did not move.

"Omega," Lev said, "open the garage door."

"Unable to enter garage," said the V-R-1-1. "Do you wish us

to proceed back up into the porch and through the house to the garage?"

"No, I want you and the C-M-Ps to continue blasting a hole in the garage door large enough to get a sky car out. Make sure you don't damage the sky cars!"

"V-R-1-2," Aphra said, "turn around and keep watch."

The robots got to work, three of them using their laser fire to widen the hole the android had begun. Through Lev's screen a cloud of dust and the bright surge of lasers was visible, while Aphra's screen showed the surrounding rock formations and views of the sky. No enemy sky cars were in sight.

"I don't know if we should stay here," Lev said abruptly to Aphra. "Maybe we should blast the living room door open and get into the garage and use the other sky car. The outer shields are obviously down. I don't think Omega can protect us anymore."

> > >

"This robot's not the only one who isn't functioning properly," Birn said wearily to the smoky gray cat that weaved in and around his ankles. "I can't think straight." He dropped the robot's arm, and it fell with a clatter to the floor, causing the cat to dart away.

"You don't need that arm, anyway," Birn said to the robot.

"I—don't—neeeeed—arm," repeated the robot haltingly.

"No. Now, stand up."

"Staaaand—up," said the robot, but it did not move. It was a fairly small, older model in roughly humanoid form. Humanoid in that it had two arms, two legs, and a body in correct proportion to its head. The metal it was made from was old and tarnished, as the robot had not been used or cleaned in a long time. The robot had been sitting in a small alcove off Julian's main hallway, with its arms and legs detached and placed beside it. Lev had given the robot to Julian, and Julian had removed the arms and legs from it, not liking the idea of having a robot able to wander around her home at will.

Birn had reattached the legs, but when it came to the arms, he had become tired and was unable to see which wires should be connected. It was just a blur to him now, so he gave up and sat on the floor and leaned against the wall. His head wound stung, and there was a ringing in his ears.

"Stand up," he said again to the robot.

"Staaand—up." This time it began to move; it drew its feet closer to its body and tried to stand. After a few attempts, it stood upright. It stood there silently and did nothing, as Birn had briefly dozed off. The gray cat rubbed against Birn's hands and climbed up his chest and butted its head against his chin.

Finally he stirred and looked around. "Robot," he said. "I need you to go outside and go north. No, south. No." He paused as he tried to think.

From somewhere in the house, Julian screamed.

Mari stared at her, a dull sense of relief spreading through his mind. This was a fem—surely he must be in the right place now. He stood in the doorway, the periphery of his vision hazy, the fem the only clear figure. Small blurs scurried away from his feet and out of the room. She screamed again, and he walked to her. He must make her stop that noise. It hurt his head to hear it.

"Don't discontinue her" had been the last words he had been told. "Take all fems alive. Discontinue everyone else."

He reached down to the fem, not heeding her feeble attempts to strike him, and gathered her up in his arms. He was about to turn and walk out of the cave when a strange voice spoke. The words made no sense to him at first since it was not a voice he was authorized to listen to. Then he heard his name.

"Mari, stop. Don't do this."

He turned and saw a blond muscular man standing there, sagging against the doorframe on the far side of the room. He had dried blood on his face and neck from a wound on his head. He put the fem down on the floor, and she lay in a heap at his feet. He must protect the fem. This man must be discontinued. It was only right.

"Mari, can you hear me?" said the man.

His weapon had come easily to his hand, and he clutched it gratefully.

"Mari, no!"

He knew the words, words of command. But this was the wrong voice to tell him such a thing. He pulled the trigger and smiled to see the man fall. It was so easy to do the right thing. Sevig would be pleased. He took hold of the fem by the arm, the most precious part of her, and began to drag her from the home.

❭　　　❭　　　❭

"O Tri-une Soul, help us," breathed Lev. She and Aphra were sitting on the steps, staring in disbelief at their screens. "Gina, can you get a fix on them?"

"V-R-1-2, take evasive action," Aphra said urgently. "Blast them when you can."

"Understood."

Aphra's C-M-P robot was down and no longer functioning,

and the V-R flew swiftly around the rock face and in behind the outcroppings. The sky car that hovered overhead fired again, but missed—rock exploded into dust, but the V-R had seen the incoming strike and had moved in a flash. The other two robots had made it into the garage and got into one of the sky cars, then scraped their way out through the hole. Through her V-R, Lev was now able to communicate with the sky car's computer and make use of its scanning capabilities.

"Yes, I have both Julian and Birn," came Gina's voice, transmitted from the sky car. "Whom should I retrieve first?"

"Can't you get both of them at the same time?"

"Unable to at this time, I—"

"Get whoever is in the most danger," Lev ordered.

"Retrieving Julian now."

"I have an idea," Aphra said to her screen. "Get up underneath the sky car, attach yourself to it, then do what you can to disable their weapons and blast through at them."

"Understood."

V-R-1-3 whizzed down the steps toward them. "Intruder!" it trumpeted to Lev and Aphra.

Lev looked up at it. "Omega!" she cried. "Are you able to deal with the intruder?"

No answer came.

"That's it. We'd better get out of here. Aphra! Come on! V-R-1-3, go and fend off the intruder."

"Understood," it said, and left immediately.

"You," Lev said to the H-R who stood silently beside her, "change into a rider now."

It swiftly folded and extended, snapping into Hover Rider form as it hovered in front of them. Lev got on quickly, but Aphra struggled to climb on behind her. The screen slipped in her grasp as she tried to hold onto both it and the H-R with one hand. The dogs, who were lying at the bottom of the steps on the grass, raised their heads and looked up at them. Ramius got up as soon as he saw what Lev was doing.

"What should I do with this?" Aphra cried, looking for a place to stash the screen.

"Retrieving Birn now," came Gina's voice from Lev's screen.

Lev looked over her shoulder at Aphra. "Just put it in the H-R; there's space in front of you by the handle. Gina, get over here right now!"

Aphra jammed her screen into the compartment that slid open, then took a firm grasp of the H-R's handle. "I'm ready, go!"

"I am under attack," said Gina, her voice partially obscured with static. "I will come as soon as I am able to."

"Can you retrieve us from where you are?"

"Not recommended at this time. It is too dangerous."

"Do it as soon as you can! What about Gun's sky car computer: Casey? Can you activate her?"

"There is no response."

"We'll have to try to get through to the garage ourselves," Lev said. "Ramius, up!"

The puppy leapt up onto the H-R and Lev grabbed hold of him and settled him in front of her, then reached around him to take hold of the H-R's controls. Aphra felt the coolness of the H-R's shields settle around her.

"Zellie, no," Lev said desperately to the other dog, as Zellie got up on her hind legs and put her front paws on the H-R. "I can't hold you as well! Stay in here! Stay!"

Lev accelerated the H-R up the steps and out of the cavern.

As they zoomed along the corridor heading for the flight of steps that would take them back up to the living room levels, a loud explosion shook the walls around them. A fine mist of dust sprayed down before the next flight of steps and Lev braked hard.

"What was that?" she cried.

"Scans show the sky car in the garage has been destroyed," said the H-R. "Intruders have gained access and are detected in the upper level. Recommended path of escape is now through the lower exit."

Lev turned the H-R around, and they sped back along through the corridor.

"Can you open the lower exit door?"

"I am unable to access the parent computer to obtain the controls for the door."

"Omega!" Lev shouted. "If you can hear me, it's vital you open the basement door!"

"Can't we blast through it?" Aphra asked.

"We may have to."

"Intruders now entering this level," said the H-R.

"Shut up!" shouted Lev.

"Do you not wish to be notified further?"

Lev answered by accelerating down the length of the corridor.

> > >

"They are in our sights now, sir," said Jamon.

Sevig smiled. "Show me."

On the screen before him, he saw the point of view of his V-R as it rushed through a house. It was racing down an interior corridor behind Lev and Aphra, laser blasts spewing from its weapon. The weapon blasted holes through the walls, causing chips of stone to scatter in all directions. Surges of electricity crackled around the fems with every laser hit on them, and Sevig could just make out their untouched forms behind it.

"We are unable to penetrate their shields yet, sir."

"I can see that," retorted Sevig.

"I am searching the Omega computer for shield data, but still meeting resistance."

"Have you tried spiking the H-R?"

"Yes, sir, but the shields are still in place."

"You can do better than this," Sevig said grimly. "You have already disabled Omega. You should be able to take care of a simple H-R."

"It is an independently modified H-R, sir."

"You cannot evade me, Lavinia!" shouted Sevig, as he watched Lev circle back and dodge as she and Aphra turned and flew straight toward the V-R to try to get past it.

"Do you wish me to transmit this message?" Jamon asked.

"No."

"I am through the shields now."

"Take them!"

Lev and Aphra disappeared, leaving a dog sprawled on the H-R as it slowed and came to a stop. Then to Sevig's surprise, the dog disappeared as well.

"What happened? Do we have them? Why did you take the dog?"

>   >   >

"We're away clear," Antha said, accelerating. "There are two more sky cars heading this way in a hurry, but we'll stay ahead of them easily."

"Good," Gun said.

Antha looked down at the arm that lay at Gun's feet.

"You're sure this thing isn't going to explode?"

"Shouldn't."

"Is my sister safe?"

"Should be. You got attached to her?"

Antha nodded, a wry smile on his face. "The fond stirrings of family and all that."

Gun stared straight ahead, watching the craggy rocks speed by.

Antha felt himself relaxing. After the intensity of the gun battle, the smoothed-out ride and cool air was a Tranquility of its own. "Don't you have family?"

"They mean nothing to me," Gun said briskly.

"I see I've struck your favorite topic of conversation," Antha said and grinned. "You know, this Indian look suits you—an impassive, dark, and brooding appearance. It's you!"

Gun said nothing.

"My fem will activate the message to Sevig shortly," Antha said, "unless you'd rather we contacted him ourselves."

"It makes no difference."

"What is it, anyway?" Antha asked.

"What?"

"In the arm. What is it? Seems like there's a lot of frenzied grasping for it."

"It's a modification device for personifids."

"That does what?"

Gun shrugged.

"How am I supposed to start a bidding war for it if I don't know what it is and can't describe it to the other bidders? 'Er, it's a modification device. I dunno whatfur. And that's why y'all should want it.' Yeah, that'll work. But here's what I think—I'm thinking we should make duplicates of whatever it is and sell them to all bidders."

"I made a deal with Sevig," Gun said firmly.

"And a more trustworthy fellow you would never meet," Antha said brightly.

"Incoming call from Sevig," said Antha's sky car computer.

"Don't allow it through," Gun said. "Just tell him yes, we have the device, yes, we are going to sell it to him, and yes, we're on our way."

"Relaying message," said the computer, then after a long pause it spoke again. "You have received a message in return. Shall I play it?"

"No."

"Yes," Antha said.

"No!"

"Why not?"

"We don't need to hear from him. Just get to the drop-off point and make the exchange. Nothing needs to change."

Antha looked at Gun skeptically.

"Head over to that rock formation," Gun said, pointing to a small grouping of craggy rocks in the distance. "I need to take a leak."

"What, now? Can't you hold it?"

"No."

"Well, be quick about it."

Antha flew the sky car down behind the rocks and landed. Gun got out of the vehicle and started to walk away. Then he looked at Antha and took the prosthetic arm with him.

As soon as Gun turned his back, Antha reached into his pocket and brought out a weapon. "Zapper," he said quietly into it as he watched Gun walk over to the rocks.

It came as no surprise to him to see the previously hidden sky car come out from under a rock formation and rise into view. It was gray and sleek, built for speed, and it hovered silently across the rocks and then down to Gun. The door opened to let him inside.

"I knew it!" Antha shouted. He got out of his sky car quickly, the rush of hot air hitting him as soon as he left the safety of the shields.

Gun turned and saw the weapon aimed at him, and then kept walking to the waiting sky car.

"You're not taking all the credits!" Antha said, running over to the sky car.

"Leave your weapon then, and come with me," Gun answered, as he bent and stepped inside.

Antha shrugged, put his weapon on the ground, and got in next to him.

"Meg-2, give my companion a security scan," Gun said as the door closed behind Antha.

"Companion is human," answered the feminine voice of the computer. "No communication links found. Emitting no signals. Unable to locate imprint. All clear."

"I love my family very much," Gun said firmly, looking at Antha, "and I take no chances."

"You don't trust me?" Antha said in wounded tones as he grinned.

"Meg-2, take us to Min City, masked."

"Masked," answered the computer as the sky car rose up into the air and began to fly swiftly.

Gun swiveled in his seat to face Antha. "Of course I don't trust you. And that's why you're coming with me, so I can keep an eye on you."

"Just as long as I get my half."

"Don't worry about it. I'm not the double-crosser here."

"No, you're just the one with a sky car stashed out of view that I knew nothing about," Antha said.

"I couldn't talk freely in your sky car—I had no way of knowing who else might be listening."

"Suspicious type, aren't you?"

"Meg-2, music," Gun said as an end to conversation.

❯   ❯   ❯

"Antha and José have disappeared from satellite view," said Jamon. "They exchanged vehicles, and their new vehicle was then masked and I cannot pick it up."

"We have their assurance they are bringing the device here," said Craf, speaking in a reassuring tone. "No need to begin worrying."

"I'm not capable of worry," answered Jamon.

"I was not directing that comment toward you. I was selecting my response according to Sir's facial expression and behavioral habits. Note how Sir is tapping his finger on the arm of the chair and also the slight furrowing of Sir's eyebrows. It indicates—"

"Silence!" Sevig snapped.

❯   ❯   ❯

Julian grappled with the yelping Ramius and tried to keep him from clambering onto Birn, who lay unconscious on the extended seat beside her, his head lolling to one side.

They were in Birn's sky car. Gina had luminired in Julian and Birn—and Ramius—and now they were speeding away from a laser-firing pursuer.

"Shielding now in place for Ramius," said Gina. "I will hold him still for you."

"Yes, yes, but what about him?" Julian said, letting go of the puppy and pointing with a trembling hand at Birn's bloodied head and side. "What can you do to make the bleeding stop?"

The sky car ducked and weaved suddenly, avoiding another barrage of laser fire from their pursuer as they flew through the maze of gullies.

"I have placed a pressure shield on the wounds; the blood should cease flowing soon. I am currently monitoring his condition."

"Is that man after us?" Julian asked, looking anxiously through the rear windows at the sky car that sped after them.

"I can't say who is inside that vehicle, as I am unable to scan the interior."

They dove downwards, deeper and deeper into the shadows of the rocks.

"What do we do now? I don't know what to do!" Julian exclaimed.

"I am not receiving any more commands from Lev. I will continue evading our attackers."

The sky car tilted violently to the left as it flew through a small gap, but the passenger shields held them in their seats.

"I want to go home," said Julian as she closed her eyes and hugged herself, rocking back and forth in her seat.

"I don't recommend that at this time. I am unable to protect you if you remain there."

Julian nodded dolefully.

Birn groaned and opened his eyes. "What happened?"

"Hello, Birn," said Gina.

Birn sat up slowly and felt his side. "Lev?"

"I could not get to Lev and Aphra in time," answered Gina. "By the time I tried to lock onto them for luminiring, Ramius was the only one left in position."

"Easy, Tubby," Birn said, sluggishly trying to calm the puppy who was straining against Gina's shielding. "Where are we?"

"You are with me," said Gina. "Lev and Aphra have been taken, and as soon as I can evade this sky car, I will follow them."

Birn looked out the rear window, bursts of laser fire briefly lighting the walls of the gullies. "Taken? You mean, Sevig—?"

"It appears so. They disappeared, and one of the sky cars that had been attacking your home then left immediately."

"You're sure Gun doesn't have them?"

"There is a possibility he is with them. I have been unable to penetrate the sky cars' shields to see."

"See if you can contact Gun. Tell him to contact me if he can." Birn looked at the little figure of Julian huddling in her seat, seeing her for the first time. "Julian," he said.

She looked up at him and shook her head, tears coming to her eyes.

"I'm so sorry," he said gently.

"Another attempt to spike us has just been made," said Gina. "The shields have not been penetrated, though."

"Can't you outrun them?"

"I can't reach maximum speed down here; I need to be clear of the rock formations."

"Clear of the rock formations and become an easier target," muttered Birn. "Can you blast them? Are there any soul life signs?"

"Still working on penetrating their shields," answered Gina. "I need Omega."

"Well, get him to work on it then!"

"My link to Omega has gone."

"*What?*"

"Home systems were under attack. I don't know what happened to Omega, but Lev had to use the robots to communicate with me."

"Gina, you're just going to have to get out of these rocks, use a mask, and then accelerate to maximum speed to get us away," Birn said. "If Lev or Aphra or Gun aren't around here, there's no need for us to stay. Get us to Min City."

❱   ❱   ❱

"We just have to hope Birn will come after us," Lev said.

"You don't look very hopeful," Aphra said nervously. She had not wanted to speak at first, with Mari sitting opposite them, watching. But that was all he did. He said nothing to either of them as the sky car carried them across the desert.

Lev had finally explained to Aphra what the Deific device was, and Aphra had listened, interested in the sense of shame and despair Lev had imparted as she had spoken. To know that this was what Ryan had hidden in her arm, that this was to usher in the next phase of personifid capabilities, left her cold. She could not work up any enthusiasm at all for the idea of having her decisions made for her.

"Well, we need Omega," Lev answered. "I don't know if he'll come back online and be able to help us. It's useless without him, really. I hope Birn has managed to find Gun—I hate the thought of him being out in the open somewhere."

"Can't you do anything?"

Lev shrugged and looked at Mari. "Will you not talk to us?" she asked him. "I know what has happened to you, and I know that you must be able to hear me on some level."

"He's a personifid, isn't he?" Aphra ventured quietly. She was growing tired in the warmth of the sky car, and the excitement of the game had begun to wear thin. Lev's jacket was now slung across Aphra's left shoulder to hide from sight what had happened to her. She could not bear to think of it.

"Yes," Lev said. "And he's had the device used on him, I think. Mari, do you recognize me?"

He looked blankly at Lev as though she was not there.

"You worked with Birn Addison once, do you remember? At least if you can't respond to me, try to respond to the Triune Soul's voice. I know you're not lost to Him. His voice is greater than all others', even Sevig's. Please. I don't believe it's possible that the device could block Him. Try to hear Him!"

"It's no good, my dear," came Sevig's voice over the sky car's com channel.

"Let him go, Sevig," Lev said. "It's not right what you're doing to him."

"Yes, it is. Mari owes me, and it's only fair I get some recompense."

"Not like this!"

"I will speak to you soon. I do look forward to seeing you, Lavinia."

〉　　　　　〉　　　　　〉

Sevig watched the screen in front of his desk, a self-satisfied smirk on his face. "All speed," he said. "And as soon as they're within luminire range, bring them here."

"Yes, sir," said Jamon.

Craf entered the room. "The preparations are complete."

"Good, good," Sevig said.

〉　　　　　〉　　　　　〉

"Gun, there is an urgent request for you to contact Birn," came Meg-2's voice. "Will you respond?"

"No. Is he all right?"

They traveled swiftly, high above ground, and the blue dome of the shields of Min City grew larger on the horizon. Daylight was beginning to fade and cast a dark orange glow far below them on the rocky ground.

"The injury report from Gina shows he is stable."

"Good."

Antha looked at him sideways. "Stable? You got his H-R to malfunction and crash, and this is the best you could do? You should have eliminated the threat."

"Birn's no threat. He's family."

Antha's eyes widened. "Family? You made someone from your own family crash? I thought you were getting rid of someone who would take the arm from us by force!"

Gun said nothing.

"So . . . you blow up your own family? Wait a second, you're confusing me. You say you love your family, then you tell me that the guy you just caused to crash is family? Man alive! I'd hate to see what you'd do if you only *liked* someone!"

"It's not like that. It's better this way."

"Yeah, sure."

Gun shot a look at him. "My family needs to stay right out of this."

"Your family—"

"Gun," interrupted Meg-2. "You have another urgent message from Birn. Shall I play it?"

"No."

"It is urgent."

"No."

Antha stretched and yawned. "Oh, go on, Bomb, or whatever your name is. Play the message. Sounds important; it could be that your daily subscription to *Girly Hairdo* needs renewing."

"It is urgent," repeated Meg-2.

"Play the message," Gun said, reluctantly.

A small square appeared on the windscreen in front of Gun, Birn's face inside it. "Gun, are you there?" Birn said, looking anxiously at them. There was caked blood on his forehead. "Contact me as soon as you can. I've lost Lev and Aphra. I'm assuming Sevig has got hold of them—I can't find them anywhere, and I'm currently tracking a sky car that has left the area. It seems they're heading direct for Min City. Talk to me."

"End of message," said Meg-2.

"Call him back right now," demanded Antha, and then turned to Gun. "I thought you said my sister would be safe!"

Gun was staring at the screen, his usually stoic expression troubled. "I thought she would be. I really thought she would be, once we had taken the device away. Meg-2, get Birn *now*."

"Gun, thank goodness," Birn said, as his face reappeared on screen. "Where are you? What on earth are you doing?"

"Where's Lev?" Gun returned.

"I told you: I don't know! They're both gone, and the only lead I have is to follow one of the sky cars that left right after I lost track of Lev and Aphra."

"Can't Omega scan it?"

"Omega is down," answered Birn. "I'm in Gina right now, and we can't scan the sky car. We're following its power traces— but we're so far behind I can't even see it in view."

"Send me the coordinates of the car you're tracking. And don't worry, I'm taking care of things."

"I'll have Gina send them right now. I'll join you as soon as I can."

"Disconnect," Gun said.

Birn's face disappeared.

"Coordinates received," said Meg-2. "Sky car located seventy-seven point five kilometers behind us. Do you wish me to display a satellite view of their exact position?"

"Not yet," Gun said. "Scan for imprints."

"Searching. Sky car's shields diffusing my scans. However, it is a shield specification I know. This is Jamon's work. I can get through easily. Imprint found for Mari Van Lierde, personifid. Two unimprinted persons also detected."

"Scan for a Cantabrian wrap."

"One found."

Antha sat upright. "That has to be Aphra. Turn this sky car around!"

Gun hesitated for a moment, his eyes on the steadily growing blue dome of Min City.

"Turn around!" Antha shouted. "My sister's back there!"

"Meg-2," Gun said. "Can you get a luminire lock on the unimprinted persons?"

"I need to be closer," the computer answered.

Gun nodded. "Go back. Lock on when you can."

The sky car swooped around in a wide circle and began to jet off in the direction from which it had come.

Antha turned to Gun. "Who's Lev? How many others are involved in this?"

Gun turned and looked straight at Antha, his eyes dark and intense. "Lev is my cousin."

"Oh, I see, more family. What next, a long-lost twin brother?"

Gun faced the windscreen and said nothing.

"What are you not telling me?" Antha asked. "Why is my sister not safe despite us having her arm? What's going on here?"

"I don't understand. Both she and Lev should be safe. Sevig can't want either of them. He only wants Imo—" Gun stopped himself.

"Imo? Who's Imo?" Antha studied his face narrowly. "I've hit on something, haven't I? Your long-lost twin brother, Imo." He paused and waited for any kind of reaction, but Gun remained stoic. "Imo, better known as Ammo, twin brother of Gun. An explosive pair, known to blow up family members. Ammo, the great—"

"Her name is Imogen," Gun snapped.

Antha smiled. "So...your twin *sister?*"

Gun gazed straight ahead, watching the horizon. "She's not family."

"I see," Antha said. "Right, right. Imogen's your..." He raised one eyebrow and grinned. "She's your hot femmie? How does she come into all of this?"

"It's not any of your business. And she's not mine."

"Easy, tiger, you look a little riled up. I can tell this because your nostrils are flaring."

"Meg-2, music!"

Instantly, music began blaring through the sky car.

"Oh, no, you're not going to shut me up that easily!" Antha shouted, gripping hold of Gun by the shoulder and forcing him to turn and face him again. "Be fair and tell me exactly what is going on! I'm a part of this too, now! If my sister is involved in something more that I don't know about, then, well, I need to know about it!"

"Music off," Gun said, his voice barely heard.

Antha let go of him and settled back into his seat, his face set with determination. They faced each other squarely for a while as the sky car flew on.

Gun finally turned back and faced the windscreen. "Meg-2,

Antha has permission to question you about Imogen. Music."

Pounding music filled the sky car once again.

Antha covered his ears with his hands and stared disbelievingly for a moment at Gun. Then he sighed and leaned back into his seat, his hands still firmly clamped over his ears. "Meg-2," he said. "You call this caterwauling music? Can't you restrict the sound to his side of the sky car? At the very least, put a shield around me so I don't have to hear it!"

The music was instantly blocked.

"That's better," he said, lowering his hands. "A cone of silence. Now, tell me. Who is Imogen?"

"Imogen Takarangi is a twenty-eight-year-old fem," replied Meg-2. "She is registered as discontinued, but that registry is false."

"OK, but what has she got to do with everything?"

"Please be more specific."

"Tell me why she is tangled up in this bounty-hunting job."

"We have strong proof that she is still alive and that Sevig has her."

"So?"

"She is being held against her will, and her soul is without a body."

"How do you know that?"

"Some time after Imogen's registered discontinuation, Ryan discovered she may still be alive and shared his suspicions with Gun."

"Wait a minute; who's Ryan?"

"Imogen's husband."

"Where is he?"

"Recently discontinued."

Antha chewed his cheek thoughtfully. "OK. Go on."

"Previous to his discontinuation, Ryan had been unable to

obtain more information pertaining to Imogen's whereabouts. Gun took matters into his own hands. I have been gaining access to Sevig's computer systems to locate Imogen. I have found her. It only remains now that I free her. I was finalizing my preparations to do so when Ryan contacted Gun again just one day before his registered discontinuation.

"Ryan had a message for Gun to pass on to Lev: Imogen was still alive; Sevig held her imprisoned; he had hidden a newly created device that was greatly desired by Sevig. Ryan had rigged this device with a signal to make it easier for Lev to find. However, Gun did not pass that piece of information on to Lev."

Antha nodded. "He kept his family in the dark to protect them."

"Yes. Gun said he did not want her to be put in harm's way. The importance of that was then confirmed by the unexpected discontinuation of Ryan."

"The device—this is what I was hired to help him get hold of in Cantabria?"

"Yes. Gun was given the device's coded signal. He did not activate the search for the signal until he was in Aphra's apartment in Min City, as this was where he expected to find it. It was then that Gun discovered where the device was hidden."

Antha looked over his shoulder at the fem arm lying on the back seat of the sky car. "In my sister's arm."

"Yes."

"Are you going to tell me what the device is?"

"No, your permissions extend only to knowing the events concerning Imogen."

"This device is connected with her somehow?"

"We suspect so."

"So...now Gun has the device, and Sevig has Imogen."

"Yes."

Antha leaned comfortably back in his seat and looked over at Gun. "Right. I think I've heard enough. I still don't understand what more my sister has to do with it, though."

"That information is unavailable to me, also," Meg-2 replied.

"OK. Tell Gun I understand now—he's got the hots for Imogen and is going all out to rescue her. So romantic of him. Who would have guessed that he had such depth of emotion going on under his dull façade?"

The sky car suddenly swooped around and coursed back in the direction of Min City again, powering through the sky at great speed.

"What's happening?" Antha demanded.

"I was almost within luminire range of the sky car, but all three occupants have just disappeared," said Meg-2.

"*What?*"

〉 〉 〉

Lev, Aphra, and Mari materialized in Sevig's penthouse offices. Aphra found herself standing in front of Sevig himself. He sat behind a gleaming desk, his fingertips pressed lightly together, a brooding look on his face.

Here she was in the office where the whole thing had begun. She glanced at the door to the hallway, the door she had been standing beside when she had overheard Sevig's argument with Ryan.

Aphra had never been this close to Sevig before. She was surprised to see faint lines on his forehead, indicating an imprint there. This had never been visible before when she had seen him on screen. She was conscious of how she must appear, the jacket slung around her shoulders in an attempt to hide her disfigurement. But he did not look at her.

"We don't have the device," Lev said, "so you've brought us all this way for nothing."

Sevig looked her up and down appraisingly.

She returned his gaze evenly. "Go ahead, search us," she said, with a brisk sweep of her hand. "It was in Aphra's arm, but we removed it and have blown it up."

"You removed it, yes," answered Sevig. "But it has not been destroyed. I will have it shortly."

Lev shook her head. "I don't believe you."

"Antha is on his way to me now with it. You didn't see him outside your little hovel?"

Aphra glanced at Lev. If Antha had it, he would soon be there to collect his credits. She could rely on him for that. She did not know whether to feel embarrassed about him or relieved that her ordeal would soon be over.

"What do you want with it, Sevig?" Lev demanded. "At least answer me that! And why have you brought us here? If you have the arm, why do you want Aphra now? Surely you don't care that she overheard your brutal conversation with Ryan? You know it is of no consequence to you, so let her go!"

Lev slammed her fist down on his desk, and Sevig gave an almost imperceptible nod to Mari. Mari moved immediately to restrain Lev.

Sevig smiled and leaned back in his chair. "I need a test subject. She will do nicely. Having you here is . . . just a bonus."

"What do you mean? A test subject for what?"

"Don't be absurd, Lavinia. I shouldn't have to explain myself to you, of all people."

"How can you even think of using the device?" Lev cried. "I

thought you were smarter than this! You're not a bad person, Sevig, not really. Don't do this!"

He looked at her through narrowed eyes. "You once told me I was—let's see, what were your words? Ah, yes—an evil, twisted deviant. Your opinion of me has not been altered, I would venture to guess. You think you can placate me with lies now? You think you can manipulate me the way you always did?"

"I'm sorry for what I did back then! I'm sorry!"

He got up from his chair and walked over to the window. "You're sorry," he said under his breath, then turned to look at her. "Is this where you tell me that you've changed and you're no longer the harpy you once were? Moan, moan, whine, whine, I'm so sorry, I'm not like that anymore... I never meant to try to kill you... It was all an accident and it wasn't me..."

"Don't put words in my mouth!" Lev said, glaring at him, her fists clenched as she strained against Mari's arms. "I admit everything I did to you was wrong, and I'm sorry! I wish I had never done anything to hurt you, but I did, and I'm sorry for that. But I can't change the past! I could have had a memory erasure and started new, but I chose to face the wrong things I had done."

He gave a snort of derision. "Chose to face them by running away!"

"How could I stay with you? How? You were destroying me!"

"Enough!" he shouted. "Silence them, Jamon! Mari, take them to the transference chambers!"

Mari led the struggling fems away.

Lev and Aphra did their best to strain against the hard grip of Mari's hands, trying to twist away from his cold grasp. But it was useless. He walked them into Sevig's personal lift, and the door slid shut behind them.

"Mari, let us go," pleaded Lev as they descended. "You don't know what you're doing. Let us go!"

"I know perfectly well what I am doing," he answered. "I am taking you to the transference chambers. It is the right thing to do."

It suddenly struck Aphra what that meant. "No!" she screamed. "I'm not ready. I don't want to!" She tried to wrench free of his grasp, but she could not. She began kicking and kneeing him with all her strength.

He looked down at her, his eyes clear and beautiful in their lack of emotion. So like an android, so less a person. Aphra quickly became bruised and weary, and she ran out of the strength to keep on trying to free herself. Mari's tight grip held her upright, and she bowed her head, trying to tell herself it could not be true, this could not be happening to her.

"Mari, please," Lev said. "What are *your* thoughts? Can you hear anything beyond Sevig's commands?"

The lift door slid open, and the underground personifid transference facility lay before them.

It was a vast rectangular hall, dotted with small, round, windowless personifid chambers that seemed like bubbles emerging from the smooth synthetic floor. Aphra had never been down into any of the transference laboratories before, and this one struck her as cold, gloomy, and impersonal, nothing like the bright welcoming colors she had seen in the adverts. Sandalwood, the cleansing scent of choice for Sevig Empire, stung her with its overwhelming stench.

No real people were there in the laboratory, but a handful of robotic carriers sat on the ground inactive next to each chamber. She recognized the models and shivered. These were robots assigned for the gruesome task of the removal of dead bodies—squat, crablike machines with large pincer hands capable of wrapping all the way around a human body. Once the body was in their grasp, it was placed on the robot's back and closed in behind a screen, kept from view while they journeyed to a morgue or matter destroyer.

Mari took Lev and Aphra past personifid chambers one and two. When they came to chamber three, Mari pushed Aphra inside. She saw him take Lev further along to chamber four.

Once inside the doorway of the small chamber, Aphra was transfixed by the sight of the personifid body there. It sat reclined in the middle of the room—steel rods reaching up like tentacles from a small hub beneath the body, holding it in place. Milky, unseeing eyes gazed upward in the pale mold of its face.

She knew now that this was to be her body and looked at it with loathing. It was a blank, not designated as a fem or a male, unclothed as though it had no need for such trivial attentions to detail. The face was equally without character—a standard mask of pallid lips, eyes, and skin waiting to be personalized by a creator's touch.

A sudden hum behind her made her jump. The door behind her began to fuse shut, locking her inside.

"No!"

She screamed and pounded her fist against the door. Now that she was faced with becoming a personifid, she knew she did not want to become one at all. She realized something in that moment: the excuses she had made to herself about saving for a large enough credit deposit before choosing to become a personifid—those were lies she had told herself. Nobody saved for deposits. She had never really wanted to have it done.

She sagged against the door, lacking the strength to fight. She would die now. The physical body she had been born with, the original housing of her mind and soul, would be discontinued to free her consciousness to pass into the mechanical body before her. How she would die she did not know. The method of discontinuation of the human body was not something that was spoken of in the Sevig Empire promotional materials. She turned and looked at the personifid. Would she die by poisonous gas, or would it be by laser?

Aphra pressed back up against the door, hoping for some way of escape.

"Brain scan now in progress," came the chamber computer's pleasant fem voice.

"Tri-une Soul, I know You can hear me!" Aphra shouted. "Get me out of here!"

> > >

In his top floor office, Sevig was pacing back and forth.

"Take this from me by force," Gun said in an onscreen message that Sevig was listening to for the third time, "and I will blow it up. I say again—release Imogen, Lavinia, and Aphra to me…unharmed…by the timestamp at the bottom of your screen. If you do, the device is yours."

"How much longer do we have before he acts?" Sevig said abruptly.

"Two minutes," replied Jamon.

"Is there nothing you can do? Haven't you found him yet?"

"He is too well protected, sir. I need more time. I recommend that you give him the fems and take the device. Then we can form a plan of getting the fems back at our leisure."

"I won't give her up!" Sevig shouted. "He won't destroy the device. He can't. It's his only bargaining tool!"

"Another incoming call from José," said Jamon. "Again, I am unable to track the source."

"Display!"

"One minute left before I destroy the device," Gun said. The screen dimmed again.

"I will have Lavinia create another device!" Sevig said, shaking his fist. "I have her now. She will simply have to re-create her work. I don't need anything else. José can do what he likes. No one can manipulate me!"

❭   ❭   ❭

"Send the arm to Sevig," Gun said.

Antha turned and looked at him, as the arm disappeared from view. "What are you doing? Are you crazy?"

"Look," Gun said, "he's not going to give Imogen over to me. He would've done so by now. He's thinking he can keep Lev and Aphra captive as well, which he can. So this is what I've got to do."

❭   ❭   ❭

The arm appeared on the floor in front of Sevig.

He stared at it. It was a fem's graceful arm. The hand was curled limply as it lay there, the slim white fingers almost touching his shoes.

What it contained was something he had been wanting for so long that he felt almost giddy as he looked at it. This was the key to all his dreams, the point to which his entire life had been hurtling.

He began to reach down, to take the hand in his.

"Sir!" cried Jamon.

A white-hot flash burned into Sevig's eyes.

❭   ❭   ❭

Gun and Antha saw the top part of the Sevig Empire building blown apart. A massive fireball burst up into the sky, and plumes of smoke rolled upward like an atomic blast.

"Whoa!" Antha said. "Aphra! Was she in there? Aphra!"

Gun's sky car flew quickly over to the building. "Calm down," he said. "She wasn't in there. Last tracked position is sub-floor one, remember?" He took a weapon from the holder that rose up in the middle of the sky car. "We're going to have to go down there and find them."

"You're kidding, right?" Antha said. "The building will be swarming with security and emergency responders, and you expect me to go down there?"

"Meg-2," Gun said, "have all security measures in place."

"Security activated."

Gun held a wrist clamp out to Antha. "Put this on. It'll keep you connected to Meg-2."

"No way."

"Look, we have to go down there. They're not showing up on the scans, so I can't get them out by luminire. Meg-2 can take care of most of the security. She is overriding their computer as we speak. At the most all we'll have to deal with are a few robots and androids."

"A few robots and androids," mimicked Antha as he slipped the wrist clamp on, then took a weapon from the holder.

"Just pretend this is a fear game," Gun said.

"I'd better not," Antha said, looking at the weapon and adjusting it. "I always lose those."

"Well, at least you've had practice at it. Meg-2, we're ready to go. Put us down in the last positions you have for Lev and Aphra."

〉   〉   〉

Sevig Empire was in an uproar. All people were evacuating, causing a rush on the luminires, along with urgent calls for cabs from the upper floor windows. Not many sky cars were willing to venture near the flaming building in response to the calls, so people turned back to the lifts and luminires.

The robots and androids of Sevig Empire coordinated the evacuation, making sure humans had priority, while the others stood aside. Once all persons were gone, most of the robots and androids would then begin to leave the building and await further instruction.

Security in the personifid laboratories underground had been stepped up, and robots were now patrolling the areas. Life support systems had been shut down as soon as all persons had been evacuated. It was the standard security setting for the labs to prevent any theft or fire from occurring.

Enormous robotic fire extinguishers from Min City and smaller ones from Sevig Empire rushed to the scene of the explosion and were hovering around the flames. Pollution controllers came alongside them and began to siphon all the smoke from the area.

Gun and Antha materialized in the personifid laboratory. The lights had been turned off and chambers powered down, but they were both shielded and able to see and breathe due to the wrist clamps they wore that kept them connected to Meg-2.

Meg-2 had shut down Jamon's security field so that the two of them could move freely. Now she was battling with Jamon for access to all systems.

〉　　　　　〉　　　　　〉

Mari saw the glow of Gun's and Antha's lights. It was a shock to his senses in the darkness as he stood by the lift door. There were not supposed to be any people here. If anyone was going to enter the lab, they should only have been able to come through the lift, not by any other means. For a moment, he did not know what to do. Then he remembered that protecting the fems was his job. No one should get to them.

"No," he called, his own voice sounding distant. He readied his weapon. "Do not approach."

He could hear them talking urgently to each other, and their lights moved rapidly. Laser fire began to flicker across the laboratory, and he heard the clangs of steel as robots ran to apprehend the men.

His personifid eyes adjusted to the light, and he saw the men duck and weave behind the chambers, androids and robots swarming in on them. The exchange of laser fire was dizzying. He felt his brain riddled with activity as he stood there.

He then saw that the men remained untouched. Lasers spread tendrils of electricity around them as their personal shieldings were hit, but they themselves kept moving freely. This would not do. They were too close to the chambers the fems had been placed in. They were dangerous and needed to be discontinued. He began to run.

He came upon them as they rounded chamber six. He raised his weapon to fire, just as the men also raised weapons.

The burning hot pain struck him full-force in the chest, and he found himself falling.

The floor was hard.

He lay on his side, trying to move. He must get up. He must.

〉   〉   〉

It was exacting work, for most of the robots were able to move more swiftly than Antha or Gun could. But it was not until the robots had discovered that their lasers could not penetrate the shields that the real trouble began.

The security robots began trying to run right into Gun and Antha, attempting to physically break through. No trace of programming in their brains that told them to preserve human life existed—these robots had been altered by Sevig himself.

Antha found it difficult to just stand there as the robots threw themselves at him. The natural impulse was to dodge and back away or raise his arms protectively. But it was a mistake to raise one's arms. The dead weight of a robot flinging itself at an arm, no matter how the shielding protected it, forced the limb back as the shielding scorched and crackled over the robot. An arm could break if Antha was not careful and levelheaded enough about how he reacted.

The robots' own protective shielding had been deactivated by Meg-2, so Gun and Antha's weapons were able to make short work of them. Speed was required, and a steady hand, to radiate laser fire in all directions and yet not rupture any of the chambers. But it was not long before the men had discontinued all of the robots and androids. Meg-2 secured the doors and now had further control over Jamon's systems.

Antha stood gasping for breath, leaning with one hand against the nearest personifid chamber. "Not a bad fear game after all," he said. "Just like dodgeball."

"In their last known positions, they were each standing outside one of these," Gun said as he walked back to one of the chambers. "They must be in there still."

"Unless Sevig luminired them out," Antha said, wiping his forehead.

"He didn't have time, plus Meg-2 would have seen them."

"How do you open these things?"

"I don't know. Meg-2, power up the personifid laboratories."

The lights came back on, and a pleasant computer voice said, "Now reactivated. Personifid transference in progress."

"*Stop!*" Gun shouted.

10

THEY STOOD WAITING, tense with anticipation.

"Process complete," said the computer after a few moments. "Now ascertaining security of placement. Placement confirmed. Personifid secure."

The thin yellow outline of a door began to appear in the smooth shell of the round chamber. Once the internal laser had finished cutting through, shielding lifted the door and moved it out from the chamber and to one side.

Lev was the first to go inside, leaving the others outside to wait.

The personifid in the chamber swung its legs off the side of the chair and stood slowly, the long, thin limbs moving easily.

"Who are you?" Lev asked.

The personifid turned its head slightly to look directly at Lev.

"Do you know who you are?" Lev asked firmly. "Do you know your name?"

"I am..." began the personifid. Its fem voice came out smoothly and clearly, but she stopped as if searching for what to say next. "God's child," she said. "I am God's child. I will not— I will not belong to Sevig."

"Imogen?"

"Imogen," repeated the personifid.

Lev threw her arms around Imogen, who stood quietly and looked at Lev's dark head against her shoulder. No emotion showed in Imogen's large doe eyes, but she hesitantly raised one hand and placed it against Lev's back.

"And I was worried it might be Sevig," remarked Antha, as he stood there by the doorway with his arm around Aphra.

Aphra was leaning heavily against him, drained from the sobbing that had burst from her as soon as he had rescued her from the other transference chamber.

"I will not belong to Sevig," Imogen said, looking over at them both. Her creamy heart-shaped face was stunningly pretty beneath her long, shimmering chestnut hair. The personifid was a fem that looked like Imogen, but was more refined, more beautiful. Sevig had obviously spent time perfecting the appearance.

"That's right. You won't," Lev said, drawing back and wiping the tears from her eyes. "Imogen, how do you feel?"

"I feel—I see—color..." She paused and said nothing more.

"Has she got a loose circuit?" Antha asked.

Aphra nudged him in the side with her elbow.

"No, she's doing well," Lev said. "Her motor skills are excellent already, and her soul-body connections are working well. Imogen, don't be afraid. You're fine. It will begin to make sense to you soon, but slowly. We're taking you out of here."

"Ryan?"

Lev stopped. She appeared about to speak, then shut her mouth and pursed her lips. Finally she said, "Ryan's not here."

"Lev?" Imogen said.

"Yes. I'm right here with you."

Gun interrupted. "We need to get out of here. Our security may not last for much longer. Meg-2," he said in a low voice, "we're ready to go."

"Omega 2?" Lev said incredulously, then disappeared, along with Imogen.

Aphra and Antha were next to be luminired into the sky car.

>   >   >

Aphra closed her eyes as everything went gray around her, and she fell limply back onto the cushioned seat of the sky car. The relief was overwhelming, and she buried her face against her brother's shoulder, not wanting to cry again. "I need some Tranquility," she whispered, and giggled as the thought of it suddenly struck her as being funny.

"Don't we all," Antha said.

Lev and Imogen were beside them in the car. "Did he call this computer what I think he did?" Lev said.

"Omega-2," Gun confirmed as he appeared in the sky car.

Their seats were all facing each other as the sky car flew along with the streams of traffic through Min City. The sky car was already well away from the Sevig Empire building.

"High-falutin' name for a computer," Antha said. "It always has to be a Greek letter to sound impressive. Does nobody ever get tired of that? I prefer a good solid name like Bill."

Aphra grinned at him.

"Omega-2?" Lev said again.

"You gave me full access to your computer, so what did you expect?" Gun said and swiveled around in his seat to face the front windscreen. "I just made my own adjustments."

"Where am I?" Imogen said suddenly, and she began to get

up, her head bowed as she tried to stand in the sky car.

Lev touched her arm, causing Imogen to flinch and look down at her. "Rest easy. It's all over now. You're safe."

"Safe," repeated Imogen, as she sat down again. "Sevig?"

Gun moved his hand lightly across the console in the sky car's dashboard.

"Checking Sevig Empire for all imprints assigned to humans," Meg-2 responded. "One found in the lab you just came from. The imprint belongs to Mari—"

"Mari!" Lev exclaimed. "He's still there? We can't leave him."

"What do you want me to do with him?" Gun asked.

"Bring him with us," she said urgently. "I owe him his life. But make sure he can't move."

"Meg-2, you heard her," Gun said.

Mari appeared instantly on the floor of the sky car. His eyes were half closed and a shallow hole was burnt into his chest, revealing wires and circuitry beneath the charred edges of his clothing. Aphra stared down at him as he lay at her feet. This was the personifid who had seemed so threatening? Now he seemed little more than an inactive android, damaged and unable to hurt her.

"Do you have his soul life signs?" Lev asked in a hushed voice.

"Soul life signs present," Meg-2 responded.

Lev let out a sigh of relief.

"Incoming call from Birn," said Meg-2.

Gun gave a nod. "Go ahead."

"Is everyone safe? Are you secure?" came Birn's voice as he appeared onscreen. He looked anxiously around at everyone crowded inside the sky car, then his expression visibly relaxed.

"Yes," Gun said. "We're on our way out."

"Glad to hear it. *Very* glad to hear it."

"What happened to you?" Lev exclaimed as she turned and looked at the screen and saw his bloodied head.

"I'm all right, don't worry. I probably look worse than I am. Your cousin has got some answering to do."

Lev shoved Gun's shoulder. "Gun, what did you do?"

"Give me an inquisition later."

"I certainly will," Lev said.

"I'm sorry you and Birn were dragged into this," he said.

"I think Aphra is the one who was dragged into it all," Lev said, looking sympathetically back at Aphra, who was nestled against Antha.

"I didn't mean for anyone to be dragged into it," Gun said quietly.

"Except me," Antha said in his drawl. "Bounty-hunter for hire—always expendable, aren't we?"

The corners of Gun's lips twitched.

Birn's gaze moved to Antha. "You're the guy who was after Aphra. Antha, right? What are you doing here?"

"I've got my bounty, and I'm taking her in. I'm going to see how much I can get for one of her legs."

They all broke into laughter, except Imogen, who sat quietly.

"Ignore him, Birn," Gun said. "I'll fill you in on everything when we get back."

"Yeah, sure you will," Antha said wryly.

Imogen turned and looked at the image of Birn on the screen.

He looked back at her, and his mouth dropped open. "Imogen?"

Her ruby lips curved carefully into a smile.

"Yeah, it is you," he said, and broke into a broad grin.

"Different, but still you. Good to see you safe and well." His eyes moved to Lev's face. "Where did you find her? Was she with Sevig after all?"

Lev nodded. "Yes, he had her. We discovered her in the personifid labs. When Gun powered up the labs, he found that three of the transference chambers were occupied. He knew that Aphra and I were in two of the chambers and realized that Imogen must be in the third. All the lab computer could tell us was that it was an unidentified detached soul recently placed there along with a personifid body. I think we can guess why Sevig had put her in there and what he was going to do with the Deific device."

"You were in the *what?*" Birn exclaimed.

"It's OK, love," Lev said. "We're safe now."

Antha looked down at Aphra. "Well, I don't know... I think we should put Aphra back in there. She came out looking half-baked."

Aphra sniffled and giggled as she sat there limply.

"What about you, Aphra?" Lev asked. "Do you want to come and stay with us until you feel better? Or would you rather go home or stay with Antha?"

Aphra sat up and looked blearily out at the other sky cars whizzing past her window. They were far from Sevig Empire now, and she longed for the comfort of home. No more traveling, just uninterrupted peace and quiet. "I think I just want to go home now and crawl into bed and sleep."

"Good idea," came Birn's voice. "I'm looking forward to doing that myself."

Lev leaned forward and caught hold of Aphra's hand. She removed the firm wrap from her imprinted wrist. "Can't leave you alone in Min City with that on; you won't be able to go anywhere. Meg-2, check Aphra's police records and imprint information. Is it safe for her to return to her home? Also, make her an appointment to receive a new prosthesis. I'll pay for your new arm," she said. "After all you've been through, it's the least I can do."

"There is no warrant for her arrest," replied Meg-2. "There is nothing untoward. She can resume her life in Min City with no problems."

Aphra sat back against the seat cushion and gazed out of the window at the passing skyscrapers. Resume her old life? How long had she been away from it? It seemed like a lifetime. How could she go back to normality? Boring, lifeless normality. Her mind drifted to thoughts of the Tri-une Soul. Was it coincidence that her cry had been answered in the transference chamber and she had been rescued? She was curious to know. She had felt that strange Tranquility come to her, there in that chamber, and wrap around her. "What about my job at Sevig Empire. Have I been let go?" she asked.

"Records show that there is a request for you to be personal assistant to Sevig," answered Meg-2.

"What?"

Lev looked thoughtful. "He probably made that request the day he started looking for you. This way, if you happened to show up to work, you would have been sent directly to him." She leaned over and patted Aphra's knee. "You're sure you want to be dropped off home to your apartment? You're welcome to stay with us if you don't want to be alone right now."

"I want to visit you some time," Aphra answered, feeling strange at the thought of doing something like that with real people.

"Aphra's apartment currently has no personal computer assigned," said Meg-2. "Would you like to have one installed? It will be in place by the time we get there. I can install the same model as you had previously and make the personal adjustments for you."

"Just put a standard in there," Aphra said, waving her hand dismissively. "I'll customize it later—it'll give me something to do."

"Records also show a male android companion used to reside with you. Would you like a replacement model sent to your home?"

Aphra blushed, and Antha guffawed loudly. "No," she said firmly. "I think I would like to know more real people. Make sure that I have Antha's code so I can call him anytime I want."

He groaned.

"And give Aphra our codes as well," Lev said.

The sky car soon came to the fourteenth-floor entrance to Aphra's apartment building, and Antha helped her get out. She stood in the doorway to the building, looking in at the people in the hovering sky car. Real friends, people she trusted.

"I hope we'll see you soon, Aphra," Lev said. "Let me know if you have any problems with your replacement arm. And don't let it be too long before you visit. Not more than two weeks! I promise we won't do anything other than the most boring thing you can think of. Never again will we do something like this together!"

Aphra grinned. "I'd like that." She waved to them as the sky car flew away.

Then she turned slowly, took a deep breath, and went into the entrance hall. Her apartment door slid open as she came to it, and she stepped inside. Her first impulse was to call out to Marlena and tell her she was home, but she stopped as the words were about to leave her lips. The room was quiet, and her android companion, Michael, lay deactivated and damaged on the floor. She smiled faintly at the sight, feeling as though it was a toy from her childhood lying there.

"Computer," she said as the door slid shut behind her.

"Yes, Aphra?" said a plain fem voice. "Hello and welcome. Would you like to begin my setup sequence?"

She trudged across the room to her bedroom door. "Later. I need something to eat."

〉　　　　　〉　　　　　〉

Mari opened his eyes. He found himself looking up into a pair of brown, almond-shaped pearls set in a black oval. Black strands fell down around the ovals, and he stared, trying to make sense of what he was looking at. He became acutely aware that life seemed to come from the brown pearls.

After a moment his focus sharpened, and he realized that it was the face of a fem looking at him, and a familiar one at that. She seemed to be saying something, but he could not hear her.

His body was heavy and did not feel as though it belonged to him, for at first it would not move. He had no commands in his mind, and he felt strangely empty.

"…will work after a while," Brown Pearls said. "Just relax, Mari. Very soon you are going to feel a rush of emotion. When it happens, don't be afraid; your body will handle it OK."

He sat up and bent forward, his head oddly light and pain free.

"Are you able to speak?" she asked, putting her hand lightly on his shoulder.

Her touch was strange; the connection shocked him and jolted him upright.

"That's fine. You're OK," she said soothingly. "You felt it. Good."

His memory felt fragmented, and he sat there silently, waiting. But the forceful commands did not come. As he listened, he discovered that something or someone else was in its place. He could tentatively feel it inside his mind. It was a still, small voice.

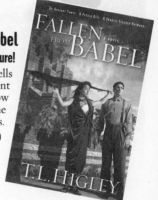

Strang Communications, the publisher of both Charisma House and *Charisma* magazine, wants to give you 3 FREE ISSUES of our award-winning magazine.

Since its inception in 1975, *Charisma* magazine has helped thousands of Christians stay connected with what God is doing worldwide.

Within its pages you will discover in-depth reports and the latest news from a Christian perspective, biblical health tips, global events in the body of Christ, personality profiles, and so much more. Join the family of *Charisma* readers who enjoy feeding their spirit each month with miracle-filled testimonies and inspiring articles that bring clarity, provoke prayer, and demand answers.

To claim your **3 free issues** of *Charisma,* send your name and address to: Charisma 3 Free Issue Offer, 600 Rinehart Road, Lake Mary, FL 32746. Or you may call 1-800-829-3346 and ask for Offer # 93FREE. This offer is only valid in the USA.

---

www.charismamag.com